Praise for *Shoot Your Shot*

"One of the best debut novels I've ever read—I ate this book up! *Shoot Your Shot* is fun, sexy, and brimming with heartfelt emotion."

—Lauren Blakely, #1 *New York Times* bestselling author of *The Girlfriend Zone*

"A hilarious, sexy debut from an author who truly knows her hockey."

—Rachel Reid, *New York Times* bestselling author of *Heated Rivalry*

"[Lexi LaFleur Brown] debuts with a heartwarming, slightly steamy hockey romance about embracing vulnerability, taking risks in love, and allowing oneself to be happy."

—*Library Journal*

"An entertaining tale right from the beginning, you won't want to miss picking up *Shoot Your Shot*."

—*Romance Reviews Today*

"LaFleur Brown's voice is evident throughout the book, which is funny, sweet and full of joyful queer characters and vibrant inclusivity."

—*ELLE*

Also by Lexi LaFleur Brown

Shoot Your Shot

Visit the author at lexilafleurbrown.com!

Evening the Score

LEXI LAFLEUR BROWN

MIRA

MIRA™

ISBN-13: 978-1-335-01695-9

Recycling programs for this product may not exist in your area.

Evening the Score

Copyright © 2026 by Lexi LaFleur Brown

All rights reserved. No part of this book may be used or reproduced in any manner whatsoever without written permission.

Without limiting the exclusive rights of any author, contributor or the publisher of this publication, any unauthorized use of this publication to train generative artificial intelligence (AI) technologies is expressly prohibited. Harlequin also exercises their rights under Article 4(3) of the Digital Single Market Directive 2019/790 and expressly reserves this publication from the text and data mining exception.

This is a work of fiction. Names, characters, places and incidents are either the product of the author's imagination or are used fictitiously. Any resemblance to actual persons, living or dead, businesses, companies, events or locales is entirely coincidental.

For questions and comments about the quality of this book, please contact us at CustomerService@Harlequin.com.

TM is a trademark of Harlequin Enterprises ULC.

MIRA
22 Adelaide St. West, 41st Floor
Toronto, Ontario M5H 4E3, Canada
MIRABooks.com

HarperCollins Publishers
Macken House, 39/40 Mayor Street Upper,
Dublin 1, D01 C9W8, Ireland
www.HarperCollins.com

Printed in U.S.A.

26 27 28 29 30 LBC 5 4 3 2 1

For anyone who's never let a single thing go in their entire life.
Revenge is cheaper than therapy anyway.

ONE

Olivia

I'll hold on to a grudge until it burns my palms. I am my father's daughter, after all. At least I'm gripping a grudge and not a hockey stick like he did; holding on to something until it kills you is hardly healthy, but it's the Hinckley way.

It only took two trips from the car to the eleventh floor to move my entire life into my sister Tori's spare bedroom. A temporary stay while I figure out a more permanent living situation. My mom didn't give me much notice when she decided to sell our childhood home and buy a condo in Arizona. She said she couldn't take one more Minnesota winter.

When my mom turned over the keys, I didn't know where to go. The housing market is more brutal than any harsh snowstorm and I'm still paying off student loans. Imposing on Tori isn't ideal, but it's my best option. I can't show my face at Nookomis's—my grandmother's—house. Too many memories haunt that place, and I'd rather not disturb the dead.

"Let's get you settled and then we can watch the Freeze preseason game." Tori picks up my second stack of boxes with ease.

She's always trying to get me to watch the Minnesota Freeze

game or play pickup hockey with her beer-league team, but my passion for the game died along with our dad. "I'm really tired from the move. I think I'll get some sleep."

As Tori opens the door, it dawns on me that I've never actually seen her spare bedroom. The space formerly belonged to Ivy, Tori's roommate-turned-girlfriend. My mom mentioned Ivy had some online craft hobby, but I've been so focused on my own freelance business that I haven't been the most engaged sister. It's a small room and every inch of space is decorated with some creepy craft. Dozens of beady eyes stare back at me. The room is filled from ceiling to floor with varying taxidermized animals. From four legs to two wings and even just heads, it's like walking into Noah's ark if things had taken a dark turn on the boat.

"On second thought, I think I'll watch the game." I drop my stuff at my feet.

"I'd say you'll get used to it, but you don't. I'm two walls away and don't dare sleep with a foot untucked." Tori dips out as quickly as she entered.

On my bedside sits a trio of mice figure-skating. The formaldehyde and wet-dog stench are already giving me a headache, but at least the room comes with a desk. Not only is this my temporary bedroom, but it's also my office.

I love my job, but freelancing is a grind. It was supposed to be a temporary fix while I tried to break into the competitive data science market. The increased use of AI means fewer jobs, and almost a year later, it's still my main source of income. I get by, but I couldn't get out of my mom's house.

"Food's here!" Ivy shouts from the kitchen.

Whatever regret I'm feeling over my choice to move into Ivy's room dissipates when I see they've ordered my favorite pepperoni and olive pizza. I take a plate to the kitchen table and dig in. I'm about two slices deep when I overhear the Freeze game go into its first intermission report.

Camille Duval, decorated women's hockey legend, sits on the panel teasing viewers with breaking Brody Parker news. His name gets my attention but isn't enough to pull me away from another slice of pizza and my Nintendo Switch combo meal. Tori, who watches attentively from the living room couch, turns the volume up. Even from the corner of my eye, Brody's highlight reel looks more like a shampoo commercial. His black silky flow peeks out under the back of his helmet, flapping in the wind like a dog with its head out the car window. His flashy smile is brighter than fresh ice and so wide I swear he's had a few extra teeth put in. Everything about Brody is arrogant and showy, but that's what happens when you're raised by Erik Parker.

Brody is the NHL's hottest free agent, and all anyone could talk about all summer long. When free agency frenzy came and went, Brody remained unsigned. Everyone thought he was being selective, waiting for a winning team to make some moves and free up cap space for him on their roster. Fans theorized that his dad's alma mater, the Tampa Storm, was a shoo-in to land the centerman. As weeks passed without a deal, it became clear to everyone that Brody was trying to secure himself the biggest NHL contract in history. He loves the attention—just like his dad.

As the Brody fancam wraps up, Camille announces that Mr. Indecisive has made his choice—the ink is dry and the deal is done. Tori gasps; how anyone can still care after months and months of Brody's edge play is beyond me.

The Minnesota Freeze logo flashes on the screen, floating beside Camille's shoulder, then an action shot of Brody photoshopped into the team colors of forest green and gold pops up. I choke my bite of pizza down in one hard gulp and drop my handheld game. There are seven Anishinaabe Grandfather Teachings, but none of them could have prepared me for this. There is no breath deep enough, no drink strong enough, and no thought happy enough to regulate the rush of rage pulsating through my body.

Tori lunges off the couch and jumps in front of the TV. Despite her best attempt at a screen, I can still see his headshot as Sports News Network says they will be joined by Brody and his family live via video call momentarily.

"Move!" I barrel through the apartment toward the TV.

Tori bends her knees and stands like a defenseman ready to protect her new flat-screen. "I'll move, but promise me you won't freak out."

"Move or I *will* freak out."

Tori sidesteps out of the way, but the image of each Parker family member holding up a Minnesota Freeze jersey is my final straw. I let out a guttural scream, one so primal all the hairs on my body stand up.

Ivy is back from the bathroom, probably to taxidermize me. "Did the Freeze score?" she asks in earnest.

My sister pulls her fingers out of her ears. She shakes her head and cringes, but any attempt to divert Ivy goes over her thick head of coppery hair. My chest heaves as I catch my breath.

"Must have been an impressive goal. Olivia looks like she can't believe her eyes," Ivy says in her singsong voice. "But please try to remember that we have to use our inside voices in this complex. Our neighbor with all the cats knows about my taxidermy business and is looking for any excuse to have us evicted." Ivy takes her spot on the couch and continues stringing teeth on an embroidery hoop.

Camille introduces her fellow SNN contributor Erik Parker as a pillar in the hockey community and Tori has to hold me back. As much as Brody annoys me, he's got nothing on Erik Parker. Erik grins cockily into the camera like he's the one signing the handsome six-year deal. Then the entire picture-perfect Parker family fills the frame. The NHL's First Family, as they're often referred to by ass-kissers and fans who don't value back-checking. Decorated legendary NHL forward Erik Parker, his perfect petite wife, Hannah Parker, and the prodigal son, Brody Parker. Their smiles are as lifeless as the animals in my new room. The hockey world might not be able to clock their act, but I know the tells.

Brody gushes to Camille that he's excited to get to Minnesota and win hockey games, but it's Erik who hogs the camera. "I always enjoyed visiting the Twin Cities and taking on the Freeze. I know the great state of hockey will be just as accepting of Brody as he heads north to carry on the Parker legacy. It's been years since the team was decent enough to crack the playoffs and a Parker is just the player to resurrect some life into that franchise," Erik says.

SNN shows an image of the 2000–2001 Minnesota Freeze Stanley Cup winning roster. It was the beginning of their dynasty run—and the year after an injury ended my dad Kevin Hinckley's professional hockey career.

Camille cuts back to the Minnesota Freeze preseason game coverage, but the only thing I'm watching is the lack of reaction from my sister. Sometimes grief hits you like an open-ice body check, and sometimes it's as subtle as a tip. The news of the Parker legacy spreading to Minnesota is a hit from behind.

"Don't tell me you're happy about this." I knot my arms over my chest and pace the room.

Tori shrugs. "Team's got a shot at being decent now."

"I can't believe a Parker is going to wear Dad's jersey," I say, my jaw straining under the tension of disdain.

"It's not Dad's jersey anymore. Hasn't been for a long time." Tori takes a seat next to Ivy on the couch. She pulls a long slurp from her can of Diet Pepsi.

Smashing the TV briefly crosses my mind, but instead I stare my sister down. She's the spitting image of our mom—forgiving hazel eyes, soft mousy-brown hair just long enough to gather into a ponytail, and a sweet face that always got a second helping of dessert from our grandparents. She even identifies as two-spirit. How am I ever supposed to compete with that? I hardly have one.

Everything about me is my dad. It's all a bit darker—my hair, my eyes, my complexion, my moods, my jokes. I'd say I'm the black sheep of my family, but ever since my dad died, I feel like a completely different species compared to my mom and sister.

"Don't tell me to let it go," I snap.

Tori huffs. "I didn't tell you to do anything." I sulk back into the kitchen and clean my mess.

The Parkers get called a lot of things: hockey royalty; an athletic dynasty; the father, the son, and the hockey spirit. Call it what you want, because I'm calling bullshit. It doesn't matter if you dress it up in a nice jersey; it will always be bullshit.

March of 2000 was a record-breaking frigid winter in Minnesota. My mom was pregnant with me, Tori was learning to walk, and my dad was playing in his 200th NHL game. It was in that game that Erik Parker laid a dirty heavy hit from behind on my unsuspecting dad. Not only did it take my dad out of the game, but he never returned to the ice that season. With lingering post-concussion symptoms, my dad never played another hockey game in his life. Erik Parker on the other hand went on to play over a thousand NHL games. Now his son is picking up where he left off.

As I pass by the living room on my way to an early bedtime, the Freeze's play-by-play and color analysts discuss Erik Parker's bid for a Hockey Hall of Fame induction. They call it an egregious oversight that he's yet to receive the call and say that this is his year.

Maybe it's the sweetgrass Ivy's burning or maybe it's the hot spite that courses through my veins, but in a rare moment of clarity, I'm inspired. Lots of people think they hate a player, but few do anything about it. "I'm going to kill him." The words flow out of my mouth as calmly as a pleasant miigwech. The idea and its consequences wash over me like a wave of relief, and I settle into a closed-mouth smile. This must be how people feel at the end of yoga.

"Which one?" Tori's gaze remains fixated on the game.

I sit down beside her and kick up my feet on the coffee table. "You're right. Why pick when I can take down the whole family."

"That sounds like a lot of work," Tori says, peeking over at me. "I know you're really hurt that mom sold the house, but are you sure you don't want to cut bangs and text a toxic ex instead?"

"I have scissors!" Ivy interjects.

It's too late for their meek suggestions because I'm already lost in my phone's contacts, frantically typing a small novel that I will likely regret the moment I press Send.

"It was a joke! Don't text any of those losers you dated in college." Tori grabs at my phone, but I turn out of reach.

"I'm not texting an ex." My thumbs tap frenetically to keep up with my train of thought.

"You're not putting a hit out on him, right? Right?" Tori asks.

"I'm texting Uncle Derek," I say. "I bet he'll be able to get me a part-time job with the Freeze."

Uncle Derek played with Dad for years—he's not our actual uncle, but it's what Tori and I have called him our whole lives. Ever since Dad died of heart disease seven years ago, Derek carries some guilt. Hopefully enough to help me land a gig with the team.

"This is great. I'll kill two birds with one stone. The extra income will make finding an apartment easier and I'll have access to the Parkers." I hit Send without proofreading. I'm sure the Freeze need part-time people to sell popcorn, shovel ice, or scan tickets this season.

"What do you mean by *kill*?" Tori leans in, trying to get a look at my screen.

"He's typing back!" I scoot up higher, giddy with anticipation.

"Just to confirm. You do mean figuratively?" Tori's concern continues to fall on deaf ears.

Since my dad died, my relationship with hockey has been anything but healthy. Playing hockey became an impossible chore once he was gone, but I had to keep my roster spot on my college's Division I women's hockey team if I wanted partial scholarship. It's been years since I've been to a Minnesota Freeze game. The only feeling strong enough to overpower the pain I experience being around the game is the promise of revenge—and the thought of enacting it on the Parker legacy has me practically salivating.

Erik is not getting inducted into the Hockey Hall of Fame. Not if I have any say in the matter.

"Uncle Derek says to come into the office tomorrow. He's got something for me." I jump up and pump my fist in the air as the Freeze lose a face-off.

Tori gives me a look, the same one she would give me as kids when she caught me doing something I shouldn't. Like the time I snuck a stray dog into the house, or pierced my ears with a sewing needle, or tried making moonshine and ended up in the ER. She wants to yell *stop*, but she can't. So instead, she distracts Mom, sterilizes the needle, and makes sure the vomit doesn't get in my hair.

"I'm not going to kill anyone," I say convincingly. "I'm not trying to watch the world mourn the death of hockey's biggest jerkwad father-son duo. I just can't let the Parkers' legacy intertwine itself into the Minnesota Freeze. I can't let them finish what Dad started."

"Well then what's the plan, genius? How exactly are you going to sabotage the Parkers by selling popcorn or ushering fans to their seats?"

I huff. "Tori, you have no sense of whimsy or mischief at all."

"And you never think things through."

"That's the advantage of an entrepreneurial brain—I'll figure it out as I go. One step at a time." I tap the side of my head, like I've got a whole plan unfolding already.

Tori lets out a heavy sigh. She's known me long enough to know that when I set my mind to something, it's best to get out of my way.

TWO

Brody

My name always precedes me. Before I ever stepped on a sheet of ice, a legacy of expectation was dropped on my shoulders and stitched across the back of them: Parker.

I'll do anything to get away from it, including moving to the middle of America where the snowbanks are as high as the waves I grew up riding. I baked under the Florida sun for as long as I could stand the heat, but eventually I got the hell out of there and away from *him*. The pressure that comes with following in my dad's footsteps was never as heavy as the dread I felt being his son.

Everyone thought I was holding out in free agency for the Tampa Storm to offer me the right contract and bring me back home. The price was right, but I've been running from that place ever since I was good enough at hockey to get away. I can't even stand playing in that arena on the road, his retired jersey number looming over me in the rafters, casting a cold shadow too big to outskate. In fact, I turned down a handful of lucrative offers from more skilled teams to be here. Minnesota was the only one with a winter cold enough to shock the

Florida tan right off your skin. Cold-blooded animals need heat and I'm trying to freeze my dad out.

I receive a text from my dad as I walk into the rink for my first ever Minnesota Freeze practice.

DAD:

Did you get an apartment yet? Make sure it's got a guest room. I'm flying in for the season opener. Everyone thinks you've made a big mistake signing with Minnesota, myself included. Your game better not suffer. It's my reputation too.

It appears he's still pissed that I turned down the opportunity to play for his former team, a deal that would have given him unlimited access to me and would have guaranteed I'd have to see his disapproving scowl in the stands every night.

The pit in my stomach intensifies. Since the deal with the Freeze took so long to work out, I've missed the entirety of training camp. These guys have spent the last month practicing, completing on- and off-ice testing, and even attending team bonding events. With only a few preseason games left, I have to hit the ground running today. A contract as big as mine comes with a lot of responsibility.

I bury my phone in my back pocket for later. Maybe an excuse as to why Dad can't visit will come to me while I'm out on the ice.

"Parker!" A voice echoes down the hall.

I flinch hearing the name. Like a reflex, I yell back, "Parker's my dad. Call me Brody." My tone is ruder than necessary. These guys think they know my dad, but they've only seen the highlight reel. They don't know the real him—and for the sake of my reputation, I hope they never do.

Behind me is the Freeze's starting goalie, Devin Hamilton. He goes by Hammer and depending who you ask, you'll get a different story on the origin of his nickname. I choose to believe it's because he's known to whack you across the back of your ankles if you get too close to his crease, but I guess I'll know for sure after today's shower. I'm not trying to get on this guy's bad side already because he's a Canadian farm boy and strong as hell. He left a bruise on my ankle three seasons ago that spread up my entire calf. Must be something in the bagged milk up there. I force a smile. He matches my energy with a goofy childish grin that makes me wonder if he's mocking me.

Aaron Jordan, the backup goalie, seemingly spawns out of nowhere. They stand side by side like *The Shining* twins. "But that's your name," Jordy says.

I've been told these two are like SpongeBob and Patrick: always together. Last year for Halloween they went as Cher and Dionne from *Clueless*—it was all over social media.

"Exactly." My hockey bag drops to my feet with a thud. It's still branded with my old team's logo, the Washington Federals. I'm hoping a locker full of green-and-gold swag awaits me today.

"I don't think I've ever called someone by their government name before." Hammer scratches his head. He bends down and grabs my hockey bag by the handles. Before I can object, he swings it up on his shoulder with ease. *Okay, now he's definitely mocking me.*

"We'll think of something better to call you," Jordy says, wrapping his arm around me.

"Please don't," I say, already feeling uneasy by the intense comradery.

My last team was a bunch of old veteran players who wanted nothing to do with the few young guys on the team. It was all stretching, long steak house dinners, and bed by nine. I had to smuggle my gaming console on the road like contraband. This team is currently the youngest in the league and with that comes stamina and pregame music from this decade.

The boys all welcome me into the dressing room with rowdy applause warm enough to have me believing I made the right choice signing here. Team captain, Leo Andersson, gets up to shake my hand. Although "Andy" looks more like a Swedish DJ than he does a hockey player, the only remixes he'll be serving up are game-day time checks over the pregame music. He'll be on my right side feeding me beauty passes all season long.

As I stand there in the middle of the dressing room, illuminated by the glowing Freeze crest hanging from the ceiling, I know what they want from me: confirmation that they have a Parker on their team. They want to know that I'm going to be the guy who leads them to the playoffs this year, just as my dad did back in his playing days. I need to give them the Parker performance. It's showtime and the puck hasn't even dropped.

I clear my throat and the room quiets. "I had a lot of offers this summer, but I told them all to fuck off because I'm winning the Stanley Cup this season with the Freeze." I grab my jersey from the stall. Number ninety-one, an inversion of my father's famous nineteen—my own secret way of telling the world we are total opposites. I lift the Freeze jersey into the air as the cheers intensify. Nothing like getting all fired up before my first practice of the season with my new team. The boys all holler, accepting me as their own.

I take my time after practice, lingering around the facility. It will take me a while to get familiar with the layout. After meeting more people today than I can remember, my social battery has less juice than my legs. That's saying a lot, considering the intensity of this afternoon's practice.

I don't mind hanging around when it means avoiding the missed call from my dad and my tiny hotel room. Eventually it's only Hammer, Jordy, and me left in the locker room—goalies always take forever and these two are particularly slow.

"So, Brody, got a date for the big season kickoff party after the first home game?" Jordy asks. "Andy said you can bring whoever you want."

"Seriously, we're very open to *anyone* coming." Hammer gives me a loaded look.

I don't know if they're digging to find out if my dad will be tagging along or if they're trying to get to the bottom of the regular rumors about my sexuality—which have never bothered me enough to speak on anyway.

"What we're trying to say is we're very supportive," Hammer continues.

Ah, I see. I interrupt them before they confess to accidentally attending a pride parade after-party. "I get it, guys, you're very accepting. That's great, but I'm not gay."

This rumor's been around as long as I've been in the league; I think it's because I'm the only guy in the NHL with a proper fitting suit, and I've never had a serious relationship. I've had my hands full with hockey and family drama my entire life. I've never been brave enough to throw a public relationship into the mix.

"Oh, no it's not like that. I mean, my brother is gay, so we're all cool," Jordy blurts, shaking his head and starting over. "My point was, if you don't have a date, you *should* bring your dad."

"I'd love to get his autograph," Hammer agrees.

Jordy digs his elbow into Hammer's ribs. "Be cool," he says through his teeth.

“Right. Of course. I’ll bring someone—not my dad—but I can find someone,” I say.

“Sounds good, Bro-nado.” Jordy pulls his long dreads back into a bun at the crown of his head.

“Who?” I ask.

Hammer and Jordy’s motions are in sync as they slip into their jackets’ sleeves. “I’m trying out new nicknames,” Jordy says.

“We’ll keep trying. The right one is out there,” Hammer adds.

Once the goalies finally leave, I pull my phone out and text my dad.

BRODY:

Still searching for an apartment. Team’s hosting a party after the game, and I should bond with them. Let’s hold off on the visit for now.

DAD:

I like to party . . .

I know he likes to party. It’s one of his many hobbies tearing our family apart.

BRODY:

I’m bringing a date.

My dad has been on me for years about settling down and starting a family. “The Parker legacy doesn’t include gay rumors,” I’ve been told. Producing superstar hockey-playing grandchildren to carry on our legacy into a third generation is an uncomfortable discussion he loves to bring up. He says that's what men do.

DAD:

Well done, son. About time. Can't wait to meet the lucky lady. I'm coming before Thanksgiving, so get house hunting!

I hate that getting a "well done" text from him makes me feel good. The challenge to meet his expectations for perfection feeds into my competitive nature. It doesn't matter how old I get or how much success I achieve on my own, there will always be a part of me that craves his validation.

Quickly my guilt is replaced with panic. Where am I going to find someone on such short notice? They don't need to be good enough to bring home to Dad, but I do need them to be available the night of our first home game. If I show up to this party alone, these guys might think I can't seal the deal—and Parkers always close. A good teammate is a man of their word, but I don't know anyone in this city.

As I round the corner, standing under the glare of a single pot light is a blur of disheveled chestnut-brown hair. I've met a lot of people today, but from behind she looks unfamiliar.

"Hey," I call out down the hall. Looks like I have to tap into my social battery reserve and make nice with one last team employee.

She doesn't respond. Instead, she unsuccessfully hides behind a handful of sticks. I call out again. "I can see you. Do you need some help?"

She fumbles with the sticks, and then they collapse like a pile of Jenga blocks for a full body reveal. She's got the type of face you spend all day thinking about. Sharp features and eyes so dark I'm sucked in like a daydream. I search for a name, but there's no employee badge around her neck or clipped to her hip.

"Are you trying to steal our sticks?" I point to the floor, attempting to break the ice with a joke. About fifteen twigs lie scattered on the ground like the beginning of a game of pickup hockey.

"No." Her voice is shrill. She folds over and starts to frantically collect them.

"Let me help," I say, approaching. Her body is turned away from me, her face covered by a sheet of long thick hair. This is starting to feel like *The Phantom of the Rink*. "Do you work for the team?" I ask, prying for any information. I don't care about the sticks; we can get new ones. I want to see her face again. I inch closer.

"No." She keeps her head hung.

"Do you know any other words?"

"No." She continues to gather the sticks, pulling them into a pile across her lap.

We reach for the same stick and our hands momentarily collide. As our fingers intertwine, I realize mine are trembling. She looks up at me and our eyes lock into a stare. Like déjà vu, there is something about her passionate glare that makes me feel like this isn't the first time we've gotten this close to each other.

She pulls away, and in one swift motion she's on her feet, aggressively shoving the sticks back up against the wall before sprinting down the hall. I stare as she scrambles out the double doors back into the lower concourse of the rink, hoping she glances back at me before the doors swing shut, but she doesn't.

So much for Minnesota nice.

THREE

Olivia

I sprint through the hall like I'm being chased. Every step feels like a bad dream and I'm running through sinking sand. It was supposed to be a quick peek, to see for myself that a Parker had touched down on Minnesota ice. I crank my head over my shoulder, looking back like the final girl in a horror movie keeping tabs on the killer, but I've lost him.

Suddenly, I find myself crashing into a big body and ricocheting off with force. I nearly fall on my ass, but they wrap their arms around me and steady my feet. I open my eyes to find Uncle Derek preventing my fall.

He sets me upright. "No running in the hall, sport."

"Shit. My bad." I straighten out my outfit, retucking my shirt into my wide-leg slacks. My clammy palms smooth down my flyaways in one sweep.

"No cursing either." Derek gives me a stern fatherly look, one so paternal that I think I've just seen my dad's ghost. In an instant, we both break into laughter and embrace in a warm hug.

It's been so long since I've stepped foot in the Freeze Dome that I got lost trying to find the offices. A lot has changed since Derek used to take my sister and me to Freeze games as kids, my dad always declining the invitation to join us. Some hockey injuries are visible; most are so deep they're hidden to the naked eye.

One thing that hasn't changed around here is Derek. He's still missing a bottom tooth and his nose sits sideways on his face, pointing both left and right. There's a giant line running from the corner of his eye down his cheek. Back then they didn't have to wear visors. He looks like he's been on the losing end of one too many bar fights, but this city knows the truth. He was a protector out there. He took care of my dad the best he could, and now he's taking care of me.

I follow him back to his office while I try to wrap my head around running into Brody Parker. When he smiled at me, I could have sworn I was staring at Erik. I can't believe I came face-to-face with a Parker and didn't knock his front teeth out—even with several weapons handy. As I looked into Brody's eyes, it was hard to repress the years of disdain that have been quietly burgeoning beneath my skin. All I could think about was Erik Parker holding up a Freeze jersey on national television. The need for vengeance was oozing out of every one of my pores. My skull is still steaming.

But Brody's not Erik; he's only his son. If my plan is going to work, I need to control myself. First, I need to get a job. Then, I can figure out how I'm going to ruin the Parker reputation and make sure Erik isn't inducted into the Hall of Fame. With confirmation that Brody has no clue who I am, it shouldn't be hard to get close enough to him to learn all their dirty little secrets.

"So, data science isn't all it's cracked up to be, is it?" Derek asks as I trail him down the hall.

"It's a tough market for freelancing right now," I explain.

He nods. "Well, I'm happy to help you out for the time being. Actually, you'll be helping *me* out. Your timing couldn't be better."

With the season about to start, I'm sure there's tons of demand for extra concessions workers, bar staff, even information desk employees. "Whatever you need, I'm your girl."

"I was hoping you'd say that." Derek leads me into his office. "You're about five foot nine, right?" He pulls the leather chair out from his desk for me.

"I'm about that." I plop down, immediately noticing the photo of Derek and my dad framed on his wall. My dad and I have the same face-contorting smile—the type that's mostly eyes. What I wouldn't give to see it in person one more time.

Derek takes a seat across from me. "And there wouldn't be anything preventing you from climbing stairs or carrying over fifty pounds?" he asks, interlocking his hands and anchoring them to the desk.

"I don't see why not." I lean forward, gripping the arms of my chair. A shock of anxiety shoots up my spine and tingles all the way down to my fingers. Something about the way this place smells is a haunting nostalgia trip. I feel carsick.

"And you're legally allowed around children?"

"Legally, yes, but I can't guarantee that they won't pick up a few new curse words from me."

Derek pushes his chair back and bends down, disappearing beneath his desk. "You'll have to be mute. Is that a problem?" he grunts out of sight.

Did Tori put him up to this? Even for a loose cannon like Uncle D—who is known to enjoy giving my sister and me a hard time—these questions are getting weird. What job does he have planned for me? Whatever it is, it can't be worse than modeling for Ivy's taxidermy website; she says I have beautiful hands. It's bad enough sleeping with all those carcasses. I can't stand touching them too.

Derek pops back up from underneath his desk wearing a comically large lynx head. Like a surprise gone wrong, I shriek, flinching so hard in my seat that I catch air. I recognize it immediately as Chilly the Lynx, the Minnesota Freeze's mischievous mascot. My petrified expression reflects back at me as I stare into the mascot's glaring golden eyes. Its pointy white teeth revealed in a friendly open snarl taunt me.

Derek quickly takes the mask off and places it on his desk. "You're not still scared of Chilly, are you?" He lowers his brow.

"Of course not. That was a reflex." I put my hand to my heart. It beats like a drum. That *thing* used to always visit our section and steal my hat. I would cry so loudly that Derek had to tell the mascot's handler to keep it away. Around eight years old, I finally warmed up to Chilly, and by ten I was too cool for it.

"The guy who's usually in the suit was injured in a stunt gone wrong. He sustained third-degree burns to eighty percent of his body and is out for the season."

I gasp. "That's horrible."

"It was a pretty standard mascot injury. Felix will be back better than ever, but in the meantime, we need a temporary replacement." Derek lifts his hand toward me and I want so badly to believe he's giving me directions to a popcorn stand looking to hire.

I glance around the enclosing office, and then behind me. It's only us in the room. "Me?" I dig my index finger into my clavicle.

"It's yours for the season." He pushes the lynx head across the desk and into my lap. "Please don't make any kids cry."

"You're kidding." I quickly set the head down on the ground next to my chair. I'm not scared of it; I just don't need to hold it on my lap like the beloved family pet.

"No, I'm being very serious. If you're going to be the team's mascot this season, you cannot make kids cry. That's rule number two of being a mascot." Derek pulls out a manila folder from his top drawer and begins riffling through paperwork.

"What's rule number one?" My leather chair squeaks beneath me as I lean in, trying to get a peek at what he's holding.

He slams a document down on the table. According to the header, it's an employment agreement—mascot specific.

"Your true identity has to remain a secret from everyone. Fans, players, coaches, staff . . . I mean everyone." He readies his pen with an echoing click and hands it over.

"It's Chilly, not Spider-Man." I scan the contract. It's lengthy, but none of the rules seems too outrageous: don't punch any kids, don't tell anyone outside of your immediate family that you're Chilly, don't put on the mascot costume and hang out in bushes at night scaring the locals, etc., etc. I guess great responsibility really does come with great power.

"This job is perfect for you," he says.

"What part of terrifying giant cat spectacle is perfect for me?" I look down at the lynx head and shudder.

"Showmanship is in your DNA—so is athleticism. And you're an excellent gymnast." Derek gets up from his desk and drags a giant unmarked black duffel bag to my feet. It's the rest of Chilly's mutilated body.

"Gymnast? You mean the uncoordinated dance performances Tori and I used to put on for family and friends when I was five years old?" I take the pen in my hand but stop shy of touching the contract. The money is good and it's only a temporary job.

"I thought you needed a job." Derek leans in, tapping on the signature line.

I twirl the pen between my fingers, buying myself time. "I was hoping to usher people to their seats or sell mini donuts."

"Look, sport," he says, sitting down on the edge of his desk. He folds his hands across his lap. "I know you've got complicated feelings about hockey, about this team. Hell, I do too. Why not get back into it in a meaningful way? As the mascot, you'll be able to connect with the fans, the game, and even the players."

Connect with the players.

Uncle D is right. The mascot position gets me closer to ice level than any other job in here and I get to do it anonymously. The Parker dynasty is going to crumble at the hands of a cat.

I don't need any more convincing than that.

After I've signed on every line, I set the pen down and turn to Derek. "I'll take the costume," I say with a newly acquired sense of purpose. Money, power, and the promise of revenge are intoxicating.

"They prefer the term *suit*. *Costume* is offensive," he says.

FOUR

Olivia

I haven't been to the rink this early in the morning since my last year of collegiate hockey. As a yawn engulfs my face, it's obvious that I'm still not a morning practice person. With the Freeze's home opener quickly approaching, I'm here bright and early before team practice for mascot orientation. In the email, I was instructed to wear athletic clothes and comfortable footwear, which was ominous enough to consider quitting before my first day. It was the bold and highlighted last line of the email that ultimately got my ass out of bed: "Social media content needed with players after practice."

The shadow of a dark arena paints the ice a cool purple tone. Thousands of empty seats tower over me. The clock hits 7:00 a.m., but I'm still sitting alone on the bench.

"Chilly!" a voice bellows from behind. It echoes up into the stands.

I turn and wave at the approaching shadow. As she gets into focus, her face drops with disappointment. "You just failed your first test, rookie," she says, embarrassingly loud.

"I thought . . ." I begin to stutter as I rise to my feet. The bedazzled employee badge around her neck says Quinn Wilson, Talent Management. She's the mascot handler, the one I'm here to meet for my orientation.

"Aren't you Quinn?" I ask, pointing at the badge.

"Of course I am, and I'm here to teach you everything you need to know about sports entertainment."

"Just the basics will suffice," I mumble.

Quinn anchors her hand to her hip. "There's no use in being cute with me. I have the hearing of an owl. Can even spin my head a full three-sixty when needed." She forces her eyes real wide as she gives me an intense look.

I gulp.

She bursts out laughing. "Grab your things. We're already behind schedule," she says, pivoting on her platform sneakers. I jog to keep up.

Quinn leads me to the team's gym and the pit in my stomach grows at the sight of my past life. Weight racks, exercise bikes, ropes, medicine balls, and any other piece of equipment needed to train for the CrossFit Olympics are stocked and ready to use. My old hockey injuries prematurely ache at the sight of what's to come.

"Before you can become Chilly, you must first become a cat." Quinn says it like it's an old proverb.

"I'm actually more of a dog person," I say jokingly.

"We'll need to fix that." She blows the whistle around her neck and starts pointing a laser pointer around the gym. "Chase it, Chilly," she shouts.

The neck strap of Quinn's whistle is thoughtfully decorated with baby blue, pale pink, and white beads. The speed in which she whipped it out and started blowing lets me know she keeps that thing on her and that she isn't afraid to use it.

"Let's go, girls!" She meows at me.

She has the energy of an overzealous camp counselor. One who knows how to braid the shit out of some gimp plastic and run a game of capture the flag like a drill sergeant. Her hair is tied up in a tight spunky updo like the quirky best friend in a Disney channel show and her outfit is vibrant enough to steal the spotlight from Chilly's fur suit. I don't know if I fear her or want to be her best friend.

On the second whistle, muscle memory takes over and I chase the red dot around the room. The faster I get this orientation over with, the faster I'll have access to Brody. After a tiring game of laser tag, Quinn makes me get in a cardboard box and tear my way out. When I think I've experienced the worst of it, we play a variation of dodgeball with yarn balls. The entire thing is as humiliating as it is tiring.

We finish off with a snack. Quinn feeds me a breakfast of milk and canned tuna while we grab a seat on a couple of exercise balls. I pass on the tuna, but sip the milk. Quinn sits, wobbling around on her exercise ball, giggling to herself. She wipes away a milk mustache with the back of her hand.

"What?" I ask. She giggles harder.

She sets her milk saucer down next to her on the rubber matted floor. "I can't believe you did all that. Most people quit the initiation when they're told to get in the box."

I finish my milk with one big gulp. "Initiation?"

Her eyes bulge. They're as green as the team-spirited forest-green-and-gold glitter she has coating her eyelids. "Did you really think brushing your hair with a metal pet comb was part of your official orientation?" She laughs again, this time almost rolling off the back of the exercise ball.

I knew coming back to this arena was a bad idea. I don't have a single good memory in here. I've been through team initiation before, but Quinn was so committed to the bit that it was believable. Who was I to question what she called *traditional mascot values*?

"Ha ha," I mockingly laugh. "Very funny. Forgive me for actually trying."

Quinn's laughter dries up. "Oh, you better try. I know you only got this job because you're a Hinckley." My body stiffens. Quinn looks down at my balled-up fists. "Relax, I won't tell anyone. I mean, technically I can't tell anyone."

"Thanks," I say, relaxing my knuckles. "Derek's like an uncle to me."

"Which is why I promised him I would take good care of you. It's also why I'm overlooking the fact that you showed up the same week as Brody Parker."

I flinch at his name. "I don't follow."

Quinn doesn't skip a beat. She's as fearless as a fourth-line fighter. "I know everything about this team. I'm a mascot handler. I see everything, even the unseen."

What does that even mean?

Quinn reaches into her bag and pulls out a thick spiral-bound book. The cover reads *Official Mascot Handbook*.

"This is my *actual* orientation?" I ask. My balance shifts as she hands it to me.

"It's your everything. Study it. Know it. Live it." Quinn goes digging in the bottom of her bag again and for a second I worry she's about to pull out some catnip. Instead, she gifts me a handful of glitter gel jars. "Sorry I tricked you into being a cat. Yarn dodgeball was really fun."

"Yeah, I was pretty good at it too," I tease. Her laugh is so contagious even I join in.

I get to the second page of the handbook when the sound of sticks tapping the ice and pucks crashing into the boards interrupts my reading.

"We have to get out of here," Quinn says, gathering her things.

From the top corner of the stands, Quinn gives me the game-day rundown while I watch practice. Periodically, I nod my head in agreement so she thinks I'm listening, but I'm watching Brody. He's as good as they say he is and it's maddening to witness in person. He's even faster than last season and hasn't missed a shot on goal yet. *Practice how you play*—that's what my dad always told me. Looks like Erik gives his son the same advice.

"And then if the third period ends in a tie, you and the other team's goalie will meet at center ice to fight to the death," Quinn explains.

"Great," I reply mindlessly. Brody effortlessly snipes bar down and I have to stop myself from giving it the reaction it deserves.

Quinn huffs. "You're not even listening to me." She kisses her teeth. "You're watching him, aren't you?"

I pull up from my hunched-over lean and scoot my butt back from the edge of my seat. "I'm watching practice," I reply.

We sit and listen to the game. Blades carving in ice, sticks slapping pucks, and bodies crashing against the boards; it used to be my favorite song, but now I hardly recognize the melody. I look up at the banners hung from the rafters—two Stanley Cups and three Cup Final appearances in five years is no easy feat. While my dad's name was never etched onto the prized trophy, he was there for the growing pains that preceded a well-functioning dynasty.

"I'm sorry about what happened to your dad and his career," Quinn says. There's a genuine glimmer of sadness in her eyes.

The first time I heard the word *CTE*, I thought it was a

local news station's acronym. I would come to learn that in death there are lots of acronyms. My dad had chronic traumatic encephalopathy, a neurodegenerative disease linked to repeated trauma to the head. Apparently, brain injury increases the risk of cardiovascular disease—a fact I wish I hadn't learned my senior year of high school. They said he endured approximately twelve concussions throughout his hockey career. Two were documented by the NHL. One was the hit that would send him into early retirement and end his hockey career entirely—the one that would have him locked up in a dark room for my formative years, unable to escape the ringing.

My whole life I've been told how much I remind people of my dad. His eyes. His smile. His drive and determination. When I watched him begin to unravel, I worried I would start to splinter at the same soft spots to the point that I began writing everything down on Post-its so I wouldn't forget. I didn't want my memories to fade the way his did. For a month, I ate as many carrots as I could get my hands on because I didn't want my vision to blur; I have his eyes, after all. It never did but my skin started to turn orange and my mom made me stop.

I can't do this with Quinn. Not now. Not here. "Let's go over the in-game routine again." I stare down at the ice in a trance.

"His teammates should be watching him as attentively as you are." Quinn points to a group of players gathered by the bench for a water break. They're leaning and kneeling while Brody goes back-to-back on the drill. "Look at them. Probably talking about the home-opener party when they should be getting ready for the game. Going to be another long season if they don't come together as a team."

"What party?"

"It's been a Freeze tradition for the last ten years," she says.

"I've only heard rumors about what actually goes down after the game. Matching team tattoos, sushi served on naked bodies, a camel entrance. I'm sure it's even crazier than that, but everyone is really secretive about it."

"Does Chilly ever make an appearance at the party?" I kick my feet up on the chair in front of me, but Quinn is quick to bat them down.

"Nice try," she says. "But no."

Coach blows his whistle and gathers everyone at center ice. Quinn jumps out of her seat and gives me a playful punch that nearly knocks me over. With much pleasure, she says, "Practice is almost done. Let's get you in that suit."

FIVE

Brody

I try dipping out of practice before the team's social media admin finds me, but I'm not quick enough and she intercepts me before I reach the locker room. Doing cheesy social content is practically in the job description nowadays. As long as I keep getting roped into the team's content, my dad will have something to say about it; back in his day, players weren't doing free advertisement. Every time he sees me in a video, he reminds me that he had a major equipment deal—billboards and everything.

My linemate Ethan Cook—or Chef as he's known in an ice rink—stops me in the hall. "I know you don't like doing this social media stuff, but just because you're a Parker superstar doesn't mean you're getting out of it."

"It's alright. I get it. Sex sells."

Chef barks out a laugh. "Yeah, that's why I'm here." He gives me a playful shove to the chest. "You're here because they're getting their money's worth out of you."

He and I have easily picked up our friendship where we last left off. Our paths have continuously crossed throughout our hockey careers since playing opposite each other in the Ontario Hockey League as teens. We've also played with each other in a few international tournaments—World Juniors and the Olympics—representing team USA.

Chef slips off his helmet and shakes his long hair free. He's a surfer boy too, just grew up riding waves on the opposite coast. His blue eyes pop against his impressive off-season tan. If it wasn't for Jordy's sick dreads, Chef would have the best flow on the team, a sun-kissed shoulder-length mop that all the local kids try to re-create with bleach and a prayer.

"How do I look? Am I camera-ready?" he asks. "I've been stealing your Korean face cream and I've already noticed a difference in my skin. Must be the peppermint in it."

I stare at him blankly for a few beats. "That's my organic toothpaste, but I do think it's working."

Chef's got a penthouse downtown with a couple extra rooms and an impressive home entertainment setup. He invited me over after practice one day to watch *Love Is Blind* and I haven't left since. I enjoy his company, but selfishly I'm also prolonging getting a place of my own while my dad still hounds me for a visit.

Andy comes barreling down the hall. "Let's get this over with," he says as he blows past us. We know better than to make our captain wait.

When Chef gets a glimpse of the team's mascot, he nearly jumps out of his skates—here he goes again with his irrational fear of mascots. I swear every team has one player like this. While Chef darts out of the way, Andy and I awkwardly pass by. Usually, the team's mascot tries to mess with you or at least give you a high five, but this guy's as unamused with the media request as we are.

The team's social media admin directs us to our designated

spots on the bench. Once we're seated, Chilly slips on the bench beside me. The video concept, we're told, is the team's major sponsor welcoming a new player to the starting lineup. After the nameless player is announced, the camera pans to Chilly, who attempts to take a shift. Instead, I step up and join my new linemates out on the ice.

While the admin finds the best angle to film, Andy sticks his head out. "You stoked for tomorrow, Bro-meo?" he asks.

The boys stopped calling me Parker and have settled on a new nickname—Bro-meo. A book accidentally fell out of my jacket pocket at practice and they haven't let me forget. You would have thought I dropped a giant bag of illegal drugs in the middle of the locker room with the way they gawked at me in total shock. Romeo must be the closest thing to a book reference these guys have in their repertoire. Safe to say, I won't be starting a Minnesota Freeze book club this season.

"Hell yeah," I say with forced bravado. "I'm sick of playing against AHL plugs in preseason tryout games. I'm ready for the real thing." It's a cocky response—something my dad would say—but I can't let him know I haven't given our first game of the season much thought.

Even today, I tried to distract myself with practice, but with every stride I remembered that I told the boys I'm bringing a date, and with every shot I thought about my dad showing up as my plus-one.

"Easy champ," Andy says. "Save that intensity for the game. I meant the after-party."

"You guys really take this party seriously," I say.

Chef and Andy side-eye each other before giggling like children. Chef composes himself enough to say, "It sets the tone for the whole season." He lowers his voice and adds, "Did you secure your date yet? Some of the guys are still holding out hope that your dad's coming. Hammer keeps his hockey card in his wallet just in case he can get it signed."

I force a laugh. "Sorry to disappoint Hammer, but I'm bringing a date." Chilly inches closer to me, so I scoot down the bench a bit.

"Bro-meo, living up to the nickname. Nice," Chef says, giving me a fist bump.

"What's her name? Is she local?" Andy asks. "You need to make sure she isn't *friends* with the goalies."

Something bumps into my skates. Chilly's feet are practically touching my blades, so I angle away. "I'll tell you when I meet her," I say.

"Time's running out." Andy gives me a stern captain's look of warning.

"Good thing I don't need much time on the clock to score." They laugh, but I can't even get myself to fake one after that gross comment.

I hear my dad's voice in my head. *Don't be soft. Don't be weak. Parkers don't chase.* Even though we're miles apart, I can never shake the feeling that he's always watching me, hovering over my shoulder, making sure I don't trip up, making sure I'm Parker-perfect.

Out of the corner of my eye, I see green-and-gold fur, inches from my face. "Should he be this close to me?" I shout to the admin.

"A little to the right, Chilly." She motions with her thumb and Chilly backs off. "Perfect. Now, everyone, look at me!" We all hold our positions. "Three, two, one," she counts us down with her phone in hand.

Chef and I drove separately to the rink today because I've got a few errands to run after practice—including touring a couple places to rent. Some of the boys are trying to convince me to get a place out in the suburbs where most of the team resides. I'm not so sure I'm ready to settle down in a quiet neighborhood like all the married guys. I like living in downtown St. Paul. It's a quick commute to the rink with lots of good food nearby, including my favorite Korean café, a city staple that serves the best carbo-loading pasta, and a burger spot open late.

I'm rolling out of the underground parking and typing the first apartment's address into my phone's GPS when out of nowhere there's a loud bang. A blur of dark clothes and hair collides with my car. It comes tumbling up the hood, crashing into the windshield and bouncing off like a slap shot rebounding off the boards.

"What was that?" The car jerks as I slam on the brakes. I shift the car to Park and jump out. "I'm so sorry, I thought it was clear. Are you okay?" Panic grips my breath as I rush to the front bumper.

My victim groans loudly, rolling on the pavement in the fetal position. *I'm so getting sued for this.* She flops onto her back like a fish on land. A forceful exhale blows the disheveled hair off her face, and suddenly I'm looking down at the girl from the stick rack.

"It's you again," I think out loud. I couldn't forget that face if I tried—and I did try. All week I've been beating myself up over my uncharacteristically bad first impression. I should have introduced myself last time, because this is an even worse impression than the first one.

"It wasn't supposed to hurt that bad. Am I dead? Is this hell?" She continues to roll around in agony with both hands gripped to her hip.

"This is the Midwest, so I mean, depending on who you

ask . . ." I chuckle at my own joke. Remembering the loud thud her body made rolling up the hood of my car, I briefly glance over to assess the damage. No dents, no cracks, but her makeup is smudged across the hood, an extreme contrast against the pearly-white paint. Nothing a car wash can't fix.

She stops flopping and sits up. "Are you going to help me up, or what?" She reaches for me.

I scramble to get to her. With our hands interlocked, I pull her up to my level. Nearly face-to-face, I get a closer look at her. She must be in a lot of pain because she's practically shaking as she stands before me, biting her lip in a way that looks agonizing. I wipe the bit of smudged lipstick from her chin, and she gulps. There's a light sheen of sweat coating her face—she's practically glowing. She must be feeling the same physical attraction I am. I have great instincts—I'm never wrong about this stuff.

"Can I give you a ride somewhere? Maybe to the nearest hospital?" I ask.

"Home is fine." She takes a step, shifting her full weight to the side of her body I hit with my car, and winces in pain.

The collision must have really thrown off her equilibrium because her legs wobble for a few steps before she collapses onto my shoulder for balance. I swing her arm around my neck, and she leans into me like a book to an end. She smells like the beaches back home and I discreetly turn my head into her hair for a closer salty tropical whiff.

I help her hobble over to the passenger-side door where I attempt to lift her up into my arms. Her rigid body protests and for a few beats we both struggle against each other. "You're hurt. Let me help you." I grunt, bearing her weight in my arms. With a painful groan, she willingly folds into my embrace, and I lift her into the seat.

"Nice car. Is this a Toyota?" she says, fastening her belt.

"This is a Maserati." I cringe. There's really no way to say that without sounding like a dick. I adjust my rearview mirror, sit up straight, and steady my hands on the wheel—ten and two. It's a miracle she's still standing after I literally ran her over. I'm not letting anything else happen to her; I'm about to drive like I'm taking my driver's test.

"Hmm, I think Toyota has a similar model." Her eyes scan the interior of my car, from the overflowing bag of clothes in the back seat, to the hairbrush and bottle of leave-in conditioner in the cup holder, and then to my Nintendo Switch 2 balancing on the dashboard.

I quickly toss the handheld gaming console in the back on top of a pile of dirty clothes. I'm not usually this messy, but I've got nowhere to put everything. Looking around at the chaos makes me realize it's a good thing I'm apartment hunting this afternoon because even if Chef is too nice to say anything, it's time I get my own place.

The radio cuts to commercial and a jingle for a personal-injury lawyer begins to play. Someone sings, "Run me over and I will sue. Hit me with your car and legally I'm going to come for you." I slam the power button on my console.

Cutting through the silence, I say, "I'm Brody by the way."

I keep my composure on the outside, but internally I'm sweating more than that time I took a cheap penalty during a double overtime in my first playoff appearance. *Oh no, she is totally going to sue me over this. And then, after she sues me, my dad's going to kill me.*

"Olivia," she says, glancing over at me with a coy smile. As it breaks into a toothy grin, I feel like the one being hit by a car. She's beautiful.

"Olivia from the stick rack," I say, hoping I'm not the only one who remembers our brief encounter in the hall. It's awkward enough that I hit her with my car; I can't sit here any longer pretending I don't recognize her.

She nods sheepishly. "Brody from the Minnesota Freeze."

"So, you do know who I am."

"The whole state won't shut up about you." Her top lip curls into a snarl before being tamed into a tight smile. "I mean, your deal was major news."

"Do you work for the team?"

"No," she blurts out.

"But when we met, you were . . ."

Olivia interrupts. "I was lost," she says curtly.

"In the authorized-personnel-only section of a locked rink?" My eyes drift over to her.

She shrugs. No longer batting her eyelashes at me, she turns to look out the passenger window as we pass a park. Instead of admiring the changing leaves, I notice her rubbing her neck and wincing in pain as she presses her fingers into her muscle. I white-knuckle the steering wheel.

She knows who I am, but we're ten minutes into this car ride and I only know her name. Why was she at the stick rack? And today, why was she hanging around the underground player parking lot? Paranoia makes my palms prickle.

If she's starstruck, she's hiding it well. She isn't asking me for an autograph or a picture. She isn't telling me some obscure personal hockey story with little to no relevance to my life. She's comfortable enough to let me drive her home, but indifferent enough to not make a big deal of it. The way she's sitting on her hands makes me think there's more to the story.

"You're not a stalker fan, are you?" I force a laugh out, but it's pinched.

"Absolutely not," she says. "Why? Do you run a lot of fans

over with your car?" Her tone is as casual as her emotionless face.

"Only the cute ones." I lay on the Parker charm heavier than a body check.

"Uff da."

"Bless you."

She starts to laugh but restrains herself, painfully clutching at her ribs instead. "If you think I'm some superfan, then you've got the wrong impression of me."

"I don't know what to make of you, which is really intriguing."

Her cheeks dimple. "Fine, I'll tell you why I was down there, but you can't tell anyone," she says. I nod in agreement. "I was at the rink for an interview when I got lost and ran into you. I was back there today to pick up my uniform—I'm selling mini donuts on the concourse at Five-Hole Donuts this season." She winces again, but this time it's her ego.

"Sweet," I say, but she doesn't appreciate the pun.

She keeps giving me just enough to make me crave more. As a man who loves to read, I'm going to get a read on her. No engagement ring, no tattoos, matching athleisure clothing, and nothing with designer labels.

"Are you a college student?" I ask.

"I was for six years. Now I sell donuts and I'm a freelance data scientist."

Beauty and brains. And old enough to be sitting in my passenger seat.

I lean back in my seat and rest one hand on the top of the steering wheel. My other arm lounges on the center console, inconspicuously bridging the distance between us. "Freelance data scientist. That sounds like three words you just put together to sound impressive."

"If you think that's impressive, you should try my donuts." She smirks.

As we near our destination, Olivia's quick wit, undeniable beauty, and indifference to my stardom has propelled her as the front-runner for tomorrow's plus-one. Well, that and the fact that no one else has jumped out in front of my car today.

It's the perfect win-win: I've got an excuse to keep my dad away and Olivia gets an invitation to the coolest party of the year. People who get an invitation to the coolest party of the year definitely don't sue.

"Don't have to twist my arm. Can I place a custom order for tomorrow night?" I ask.

"Won't you be busy tomorrow?" She points out the window, reminding me of her upcoming exit.

"Tomorrow? What's tomorrow?" I play dumb.

Olivia tosses her head to the side. I catch her eyes turn in their sockets. The sight of which I find rather amusing.

"Fine," I concede. "You clocked me. A Parker would never miss a hockey game." Girls usually love it when I remind them that I'm hockey royalty, and as much as I hate my namesake, I can't deny the privilege it's provided me.

"Are donuts part of the Parker pregame meal plan?" Olivia unzips her sweater and slowly peels it off her arms, revealing a tight tank top underneath. I swallow. *Eyes on the road.*

"No, but I'd love for yours to be part of my postgame plan. Can I place a pickup order for tomorrow night?"

"Just so we're clear, *my donut*," she says, wincing, "isn't on the menu for the first date."

"Oh, no." I panic. "Of course not. I meant an actual food order. I'm always starving after the game and donuts would be an amazing postgame snack."

"Oh." Her voice pinches. She wraps her arms around herself in a hug.

"They would actually be perfect to bring to the home-opener after-party, and so would you," I blurt out like a contestant who just buzzed in their answer. *Why did I say it like that? I'm making it sound creepy. Maybe she doesn't like to party. Am I staring at her boobs? Shit.*

Olivia points to an apartment complex on the corner. I slow to a stop on the curb outside the entrance. She fidgets with the sweater lying across her lap, avoiding eye contact. "A party?"

"Don't worry about your food services job, there are no rules against us hanging out," I assure her. "It's the least I can do after—"

"Okay." She nods, looking up at me. "I'll give you my number."

The wave of relief is as instant as flipping a switch. As I get one last good look into her big brown eyes, all I can think about is how this would please my dad.

Olivia puts a heart emoji in lieu of her last name and saves her number in my phone. Grabbing on to the holy-shit handle in my car, she pulls herself up and out of the seat with a grunt.

I roll down my car window as she turns to leave and shout out to her, "It was nice running into you today!" She stares back at me blankly over her shoulder. "Well, you know what I mean."

"See you tomorrow, Brody."

Olivia hobbles up the entrance with incredible agility for someone who was recently run over. She ignores the railing and slips back into her sweater while speeding away from my parked car.

Wow. She's beautiful, funny, and tough as nails—that's a hat trick.

SIX

Olivia

When I got to work today, I didn't think I'd be dangling thirty feet in the air like a piñata above seventeen thousand screaming hockey fans. I feel like a human sacrifice to the hockey gods. *Don't look down.* Thankfully, with my head stuffed inside this comically large lynx head, no one can tell that my eyes are squeezed shut and my face is twisted into a petrified wince.

Despite the layer of protection the mascot suit offers, I'm still doing my best to refrain from shitting my pants—an act which would surely crack SNN's Not a Top Ten and solidify my place in internet-fail meme history.

The crowd cheers as the MC introduces Chilly. This suit is so hot that beads of sweat are dripping down my back and slipping between my butt cheeks. I gulp as I begin my descent. *If I can work retail through the holidays, I can do anything.*

It's not until I feel the firm ice pressing against the soles of my feet that I open my eyes. I'm ice-level in front of way too many people. It's like a nightmare except I'd prefer being naked in front of my entire high school over this scenario. Before I have time to bail and scurry off with my tail tucked between my legs, someone's shoving a pole into my paws. A huge Freeze flag unravels and I start waving it back and forth like the white one I wish it were. The crowd roars.

Not soon after, I hear the MC begin to introduce the team, which is my cue to get off the ice. I yelp as I bang my bruised hip on the edge of the boards on my way out. My plan to jump in front of Brody's car went south when he didn't stop in time and ran me over like an indecisive squirrel.

I pictured a classic rom-com situation where he slammed on the brakes in the nick of time and the momentum sent a gust of wind blowing my hair back elegantly. Except he ran me over like it was *Fast & Furious.* Can't say I'm surprised though; that guy is so full of himself he doesn't even give pedestrians the right of way.

I hobble down the tunnel after my keeper, Quinn. We're briefly huddled—tucked away in a corner at ice level—while she looks me over to make sure Chilly is picture-perfect and ready to hit the stands.

"If Chilly is ready to rock the Dome say, yeahhhh," she screams musically, throwing her arms up. This woman definitely knows her way around a megaphone.

I don't reciprocate the energy. It's taxing to move my arms in this fur suit and I need to save my energy for my big drum number in the second period. Being a mascot takes much more athleticism than I anticipated. I thought looking like a climate change–stricken abominable snowman covered in grass stains would be the biggest hurdle. Instead, it's remaining limber and rhythmic despite the size sixteen shoes and five-inch acrylic nail claws.

"I said, if Chilly is ready to rock the Dome say, yeahhhh," she cheers again, this time giving me a nudge. The stack of rainbow bracelets jangles around her arm.

I pull up my mask and the cold air hits me with a much-needed breeze. My face-framing layers are stuck to the sweat of my brow as I pant in the unrestricted air. "Hey, when do I get a T-shirt cannon?" I ask. I've always wanted to fire a T-shirt across an arena into the gut of an unsuspecting spectator.

"Are you crazy? Why isn't your head covering fastened properly?" Quinn shrieks in terror and slams the mask back on my head. She makes quick work of the straps I found far too confusing to deal with. She snaps me in and gives a pull to make sure nothing pops off. "And as far as a cannon goes, thanks to that killer whale up in Vancouver, never." She grabs my arm and drags me into the elevator before I have time to ask any follow-ups.

It's Quinn's job to make sure I know where I'm going and that I make it there on time. I have a strict game schedule to follow. Plus, if anyone gets too handsy with me, she swoops in and escorts them away. She says since the Philly incident when Spunky—the beloved gremlin of a mascot—punched that kid in the face, handlers across the league had to up their level of protection to a Denzel Washington defense. Quinn is never more than six feet away with a wide smile ready to make a citizen's arrest.

In the elevator ride up to the main concourse, Quinn turns to me. "From now on, use the secret mascot hand signals as outlined in the handbook to communicate with me." She frantically throws up what can only be described as flagrant hand gestures.

That's what those were? I thought it was a how-to on the basics of sign language so I could offer a more inclusive mascot experience. Either way, I didn't read it. I flip her the one hand gesture I know by heart. She swats my paw down as the elevator door dings open.

I follow her through the stands, high-fiving kids with ice-cream-stained mouths, playfully messing up the receding hair of men chugging their thirty-dollar beers, and giving an overexaggerated thumbs-down to the opposing team's fans. I thought I would hate this job, but I kind of like being the menace of the rink. It's a natural role for me to step into, considering my dad was a known menace on the ice. Thinking about what could have been stings more than the bruise on my hip.

Early in the third period, while I play an animated game of got-your-nose with a young fan, the goal horn sounds. I look to the ice and see Brody using his stick as a bow to shoot an invisible arrow into the crowd. One of his many cocky goal celebrations—and a staple in the meticulously crafted Parker branding.

The replay shows him splitting the LA Stars' defense with a move so nice those guys are going to lose sleep tonight replaying it over in their heads. Then he fakes out the goalie and sends the puck flying over his blocker into the back of the net. It's the first Freeze goal of the season and it belongs to Brody Parker.

Everyone is on their feet cheering for him, chanting "Parker" over and over. I press my eyes shut and can almost hear it morph into "Hinckley." The last time I was in this arena for a live hockey game was years ago. I was young enough to be pissed I was missing my own minor league hockey practice for the occasion, but old enough to know attending it was important to my family.

The team invited us to a Freeze game to honor my dad and a few other players from the golden era. We were put up in a fancy owner's suite and given Freeze jerseys and hats to wear—forced team spirit. As if the gesture would soften the blow of cutting my injured dad and leaving our family without health insurance all those years ago as he began the hardest journey of his life. My dad needed help; he didn't need suite tickets to a hockey game. The free jersey was no tourniquet—he still bled out.

While my sister and I preoccupied ourselves with the ice-cream bar, my dad sat politely enduring three periods of play. During a TV time-out, the spotlight shone on him for the last time in this rink, his red eyes wincing under the bright lights. People cheered. He smiled and waved that night like a good sport while the image of the once-heroic Freeze players played on the jumbotron. At home, the confusion, paranoia, and headaches took over. The next time any of us mentioned the Freeze's golden era was at his funeral.

When he died, so did my passion for the game, and no play, no matter how nice, is going to have me on my feet cheering for a Parker goal. My dad didn't deserve the ending he got—none of us did. He didn't belong in that dark spiral, like the Parkers don't belong here.

I feel a tug on my arm and the word "Chilly!" follows. Quinn is at my side, motioning me to our next stop. I let the salty tears spill down my cheeks and soak into the collar of the suit as she pulls me along.

I disassociate long enough to get through the game without crying again, and eventually the final buzzer sounds. The Freeze game might be over, but mine is starting. Right now, Brody feels bad for running me over with his car, and I need to leverage this opportunity. I need to snap out of my grief and put on my game face. Us Hinckleys have been called plenty of names, but unmotivated isn't one.

Instead of reading my mascot handbook last night in prep for tonight's home opener, I scoured the internet for any information I could find about Brody's private dating life. There wasn't much to uncover, besides a few blogs questioning his sexuality. The Parkers are as obsessed with their squeaky-clean reputation as they are with hockey. Through an FBI-level deep dive of all of Brody's social media, I discovered that he too has an Aunt Lisa, he's passionate about ocean conservation, and he got really into *RollerCoaster Tycoon* one summer.

It took some sleuthing around the dark web (Tumblr and Reddit) and a lot of sifting through gay rumors (since when is he cool enough for those?), but I eventually found what I was looking for. A handful of conventionally attractive young women on social media claiming to have had interactions with him. These women were all mildly internet famous, sharp-jawed, perfectly physiqued with hair as blond as a show poodle. They all seemed to eventually come to their senses and realize they were out of his league, or they didn't meet the Parker standard. Either way, Brody doesn't bring girls around his family.

Discovering that Brody's "type" was teen beauty queen turned niche microinfluencer should have intimidated me. All my socials are dedicated to my freelance business and I have no special talent. But what I do have is female rage—blinding rage for revenge—and it's all the confidence I need.

So no, his fling this summer with Paige on yachts in Italy doesn't intimidate me in the slightest. In fact, it's all the reassurance I need to know I stand a chance. She never made it to an Erik Parker introduction; Brody is looking to bring something different home to meet the parents.

Safe in the privacy of the mascot's locker room, I finally unlatch my mask. I sit there steaming like a kettle. Slick with sweat, I lick some salty drops off my top lip. Before I can get a look at myself in the mirror, Quinn comes barging in.

Fired up and shiny with a sheen of sweat, she says, "That was an all-timer of a home opener. I've never seen such a triumphant display of athleticism in this building." With her arm propped, she leans against the wall. Sweat is pitting out at her armpits, but I'm in no shape to judge—I look like a drowned rat.

I knew hockey was physically demanding on its players, but I didn't realize it would be so taxing on the employees. Where's our postgame chiropractic adjustment and therapeutic massage?

I can't deny that Quinn's passion for this team reminds me why I fell in love with the sport in the first place. Pure delusional support no matter the effort—it's admirable, almost.

"The Freeze lost," I say, souring her enthusiasm. "They were outshot, outworked, and outplayed the entire sixty minutes. If this game was any indication of the season to come, they'll be golfing in April." I tilt my head back and squirt some water into my open mouth. A few dribbles trickle down my cheek. I need to shower. My swamp-ass sweat is starting to chill, and my lips are getting cold.

"I'm talking about us, baby!" Quinn throws her arms open and for a second I worry she's about to embrace me in some celebratory huddle. "You're a natural-born Chilly. A purrfect entertainer. A cat of the people!" She dances in place.

I've been called worse. "It was something to build from." The bottom half of my suit drags as I waddle over to the door. Opening it, I tuck myself on the inside to remain hidden from arena workers passing by. "Now if you don't mind, I don't need a handler to help with my shower." I motion Quinn out.

"But we haven't done our postgame debrief or mascot meditation!" she shouts as the door shuts in her face.

There's no time for a postgame debrief tonight, not when the real game is about to begin: Facing off against the NHL's hottest center and most eligible bachelor will take my full focus.

SEVEN

Olivia

Brody goes as hard on the cologne as he does into the corners. I've mouth-breathed the entire car ride over out of fear that the intoxicating smell will overwhelm my better judgment.

He rakes his hand through the front of his glossy long black hair. His loose wet ringlets dance into place below the nape of his neck. "Ready for the party of the year?" He smiles out of the corner of his mouth. His canines are sharper than Chilly's. We make a rolling turn down a quiet street.

"Not sure anything can top the excitement of your goal tonight." Forcing a slow sweet voice, I hardly get the words out without bursting into a fit of laughter. My nails bite into my palms. I deserve to suffer for that lie.

He cocks his head to the side. "They let you watch the game up there while you're making donuts?"

I lick my lips, but my mouth goes dry. I swallow a thick gulp while I try to think up a lie. "I saw the replay on social media." My delivery is a bit frantic, but he must be used to girls fawning over his play because he quickly drops it.

Brody parks the car on the curb of a cul-de-sac. The street

is lined with houses that come with mortgage payments large enough to pay off my outstanding student debt. Everyone's outside lights are on. We each grab a stack of donut boxes and make our way up the long driveway together. I might not have made all four dozen of them, but someone at Five-Hole Donuts did. Lucky for me, mascot handler responsibilities extend to personal emergency errands such as needing a tampon, kinesiology taping, and even postgame donut delivery.

A dull bass line audible from the front steps pulses through the grand front door. The lights inside the three-story mansion are dimmed with no signs of any rambunctious guests. *Shouldn't someone be smoking on this front porch? Someone should definitely be keeled over puking in the manicured shrubbery. Why is no one waiting for their rideshare on the curb with their shoes tucked under their arm and mascara sliding down their face?* This is unlike any legendary party I've ever been to. Then again, I don't know how the elite let loose.

We let ourselves into an entrance so dimly lit that I practically trip over the pile of shoes discarded by the door. *What type of house party requires shoes off?* Brody wanders ahead while I struggle with my laces at the door.

He lowers the music using a remote found on the kitchen island; and trust me this thing is so big it could be a literal island. There is a party platter of food laid out on the granite countertop that would easily feed an army—or in this case, a hockey team. We add the donuts to the spread.

Brody wastes no time digging in. He loads his plate with a smorgasbord of snacks, a combination so random it can only be described as an inmate's last meal. He inhales a hamburger slider without breathing. He smashes a fistful of chips into his mouth. After making his way through the snacks, he takes on the ingredient foods, pouring a bag of salad croutons into his mouth before chomping on some radishes he got from the back of the fridge. He cracks open a can of root beer and crushes it like he's a competitor at Coney Island on Independence Day.

He glances up at me and says, "If I don't eat like this, I get too skinny." He wipes his mouth clean before grabbing another slider.

Snacking on a thin slice of fancy cheese, I open the fridge to a stocked selection of color-coded cans. I move right past the muted flavored seltzer and grab two beers—for whatever reason, beer always impresses a guy like him, like drinking something that makes you so full you have to take a crap mid-party is the benchmark of a cool girl who doesn't give a fuck. I slide one across the island toward him and crack mine open. I stomach it, wanting desperately to reach back for some of the wine sitting in a decanter on the countertop. It's not even boxed, so you know it has to be good.

Brody picks up the can but shakes his head. "Thanks," he says. "But, I'm more of a wine guy."

I point over his shoulder. "There's some on the counter behind you."

"It's okay. I'm driving you so I'm not drinking tonight," he says casually before returning to his plate.

We're interrupted by an explosion of lively shouting and laughter. The noise bellows down the grand staircase and throughout the main level. We ditch the food to find the party. Again, another eruption of cheering and commotion occurs. Brody pauses halfway up the first set of stairs, turning back to look for me. When the voices die down, he shrugs and continues the climb. Anticipation builds as shouting seeps through the walls.

"That's three whores! Yes!"

"I've got wood!" another shouts.

"Damn, I'm bricked up!"

Is this a sex party—did Brody Parker take me to an orgy? Brody stops with his hand wrapped around the doorknob before slowly opening the glowing door. I tuck in closely behind him. The door opens and the whole room full of people stop what they're doing and turn to look at us. They're all huddled around a large wooden table in the middle of a game room. On the table is a half-completed game of Catan.

Three ores . . . they said three ORES.

"I thought the big party was tonight?" Brody steps into the room. I sheepishly follow his lead.

"It is, you're late. You'll have to wait for the next game," Jordy says. I recognize his iconic hair immediately. He's Tori's favorite Freeze to root for; he's everyone's favorite to root for.

"I thought I was in for a night of entertainment, excitement, and nonstop party action." Brody throws up his hands in exasperation. Everyone ignores him as they dial back into the game.

"We have all that and more—right here." If his Scandi blond locks weren't a dead giveaway, his authority over the room certainly is. Freeze captain, Andy motions to the board, making a move.

Brody approaches the table. He braces his arms on the edge and leans in, hovering over the sprawling game. "I don't know how to play Monopoly," he says.

A collective groan spreads across the room and everyone shares a look of disgust. Someone throws a fistful of popcorn at him. Brody stumbles back to my side.

"It's Catan, duh." The insult slips out of my unfiltered mouth. I cup my hand to my lips, hoping to trap any other snarky remarks from slipping out.

Brody laughs. "And you know how to play?" He sizes me up with his eyes.

I think about backpedaling and playing dumb. I could pretend I don't know the triumphant highs and debilitating lows of Catan, a game as strategic as it is beautiful. Instead, I decide I have the unique opportunity to impress the entire Minnesota Freeze roster and I take it. After all, I'm sure the approval of his new teammates means a lot to Brody.

"I was the captain of my high school's Catan team." I push my shoulders back and stand tall, pausing for everyone to gawk at this impressive admission.

"That's a thing?" Brody laughs again. I'm not surprised he's not familiar with eccentric high school clubs; the Parkers only care about hockey and their legacy. Some of us can manage athletics *and* clubs.

"We won the state championship my junior year," I say proudly. "Wait, you really don't know how to play Catan?"

"No, of course not. I had sex in high school," he says, laughing too loudly at his own joke.

Glaring over at him, I reply, "What part of Catan team don't you understand? Catan players and board gamers in general are notoriously horny. Even more so than the glee club. A mono outbreak almost derailed our push for the state championship, but I pulled through. The high dose of cough medicine really expanded my mind and relaxed my nerves." With a sassy hair flip, I turn my back on Brody and get a better look at the board.

"She's on my team!" someone shouts.

"No chance, Hammer, she's mine," Brody says. He wraps his arm around my hip and pulls me closer. My body goes limp in Brody's grip. His bare skin is soft against mine and he smells expensive. I subtly lean into him before realizing my hand is resting on his stomach. As if I've just touched a hot iron, I quickly recoil.

While the current game of Catan drags on, Brody takes the

time to introduce me to his teammates and some of the significant others as his "friend." An ordeal that I find incredibly agonizing. It's bad enough I have to put on a performance around Brody; now I'm doing it for the entire roster and their beautiful plus-ones.

This much exposure puts my plan at risk, but luckily no one here knows who I am. It would appear not a single one of the players recognizes the similarities between my dad's face and my own. The juxtaposition between the devastation I experienced losing my dad and the ease at which none of these guys have the slightest clue about his existence makes my knees weak.

Brody introduces me to Chef, one of his linemates, and judging by the way these two embrace, it's clear with whom he has the closest bond.

Chef shakes my hand. "So you're the girl Bro-meo was talking about."

My instinct is to deny any association with the Parker family, but I know I have to act like that discovery tickles me. I push out a giggle. "Good things, I hope," I say in a forced cutesy voice so sweet I can feel a toothache coming on.

Chef grimaces. "Oh, not like that. He said he hit you with his car."

Brody steps between us. "Accidentally! I accidentally hit her with my car," Brody says in a panicked tone. "I also said that she looked really beautiful while rolling up my windshield."

I should have sued him when I had the chance. *No, no.* Getting close to Brody gets me close to the Parker family. Erik Parker will answer for his sins, and my bruised hip.

Brody looks over at me with a half-cracked smile as he rakes his hand through his luscious hair—*head lice, I hope?* His hair bounces back perfectly into place.

I tilt my head to my shoulder and with a smirk I say, "He really swept me off my feet."

They both cock their heads back into a genuine cackle.

Hammer—who jokingly introduced himself as Jordy's plus-one when we made our round of introductions—comes up from behind Brody and wraps his arm around Brody's shoulders. "Too bad your old man couldn't make it tonight," he says.

Brody slips out of his embrace. "He's a busy guy, but you can catch him every day on *SNN Recap*."

"I never miss an episode," Hammer brags.

Brody looks over at me, and I quickly muster a warm smile. He turns to Hammer and says, "If you really want an Erik Parker autograph, I'll get you one. I'm sure I've got a signed puck somewhere in my storage locker."

Hammer's eyes go wide. "I appreciate the offer, but I'm hanging on to my worn hockey card until I can get it signed in person. With all the upcoming Freeze team events, I'm sure he'll be able to make it to something soon."

Brody nods along pleasantly as Hammer recites an extensive list of team events and Erik's possible participation. I stop listening when Brody's cheeks flush and he grips at his stomach as if the concoction of food he foraged has soured in his gut. Our names are called before I can ask if he's feeling unwell.

We're up to play. I roll up my sleeves, ready to impress. It isn't easy, and I'm rustier than I care to admit, but we win in what I'm told is record time in the history of Freeze Catan tournament play—fifty-five minutes, despite Brody's indirect efforts to sabotage us at every turn. I think he had a bet going with the other team because I not only carried us entirely, but I also worked overtime correcting his boneheaded moves. This guy has no strategic bone in his body, which is shocking because he plays such a strategic game on the ice.

As Andy clears the board and sets up for the next game, Brody hoists me on his shoulders in celebration. Unlike Sean Astin in *Rudy*, I have never been told I'm too small for anything and worry he's about to topple over with the both of us at any moment. To my surprise, he's steady on his feet as we make our way through the room, dishing out high fives.

"To the kitchen! Kicking ass makes me hungry!" he shouts, carrying me to the door.

I wiggle out of his grip and back on my own two feet before my head smacks into the doorframe. "You did so good back there," I lie—I'm really getting the hang of this fawning business.

"That's very sweet of you to say, but I'm a pro athlete," he says peering back over his broad shoulder at me as we descend the long staircase. He flashes a cocky grin before skipping the last few steps to leap down like a child would in the school halls when a teacher isn't looking. "I can recognize success, but I'm also familiar with failure. You carried me through that game like a dead body," he adds.

"A dead body wouldn't have made such boneheaded moves," I say under my breath. I lean against the counter, watching him grab another plate and stack it high with food. Would be a shame for him to wither away from not carbo-loading every two hours. "The team seems as obsessed with your dad as they are with Catan." I peek up at him, gauging his reaction.

He might as well be sculpted from marble the way he doesn't move. "Don't tell me you are too."

"I'm too young to remember when he played, but I'm sure he's a great guy," I force myself to say.

Brody sharply exhales a puff of air out his nose. "Yeah," he grumbles to himself before swallowing his bite and resetting his face. "Hey, what was that thing you did with your hands up there?" He fans his big hands out in front of his face and blows on his fingertips like they're birthday candles.

"I don't know what you're talking about."

I know exactly what he's talking about—he's asking about Hot Hands. I must have done it after we won the game. It's a family inside joke. It was my dad's thing and is now my habit.

Brody does it again, this time with more passion. Too cocky for my taste, but it's undeniably Hot Hands.

I bow my head. "It's stupid. A habit, really. Hot Hands. It's nothing."

"Hot Hands?" He chuckles.

"It's a family thing." I grit my teeth.

"Teach me," he demands. He wipes the orange chip dust off his fingers using his baggy pant leg.

Giving Brody Parker a step-by-step tutorial of one of my most sacred memories of my father was not part of my plan tonight, but I can't shut him out now. Instead, I fan my hands out in front of my face, shimmying each finger individually, building enough suspense, before blowing them out like they're ablaze. Brody giggles and claps like an amused baby.

"That's why I like you," he says, serving himself a donut. He slides another across the kitchen island to me.

"You like me?" I slowly chew my donut while considering an appropriate reaction to his comment. Nothing comes to mind, so I bat my eyelashes.

"I mean, I don't know you that well, but I would like to continue getting to know you. You're funny and smart and tall—and winning that Catan game up there earned me locker room bragging rights." He cracks open another pop.

"I'm not that tall, but um . . . thanks," I say. "In the past, men have been intimidated by my ruthless Catan skills."

"Real men aren't intimidated by impressive women," he

says, dropping what's left of his donut. He turns to me and takes a step. At first, I rock back on my heels, but I force myself to step forward. Staring at my lips, with a low voice he says, "So, are you going to let me take you out again? I'd love a real date. You know, one without board games and an audience."

I hum. "Unfortunately, those are my favorite types of dates," I say. I bite my lip, trying to rein in my widening smile, but it's no use. I love nothing more than victory and tonight I've tasted it twice. "But for you I'll make an exception," I add.

EIGHT

Brody

When I told Olivia to meet me at the Demo Rage Room for our date, I didn't realize it was in the middle of the biggest mall in America. I think I've passed the same hat store six times already. Or have they all been different stores? I'm nervous enough as it is; I don't need to be late and ruin the date too.

I learned at the team party that Olivia has an impressive, potentially borderline neurotic competitive edge. If I want her to take me seriously, I need to show her that I'm strong and capable too. Because her work schedule syncs up with mine, I can't invite her to one of my hockey games. This is the next best thing to watching me tear up the ice.

Finally, I get to the top level of the mall. Olivia is standing outside the entrance waiting for me. Before I have the chance to wave to her, my phone buzzes in my pocket. I discreetly check the notification on my way over. To no surprise, it's my dad.

DAD:

Saw your postgame presser. Next time, speak more clearly and don't look so happy—your team is on a five-game losing streak.

BRODY:

My bad. Was just trying to keep morale high.

DAD:

Winning keeps morale high.

BRODY:

Okay

DAD:

SNN says I can take off work and get out there whenever I want. Let me know when you're free.

BRODY:

Busy this month. Things with Olivia are getting serious, and I'll be spending a lot of time with her.

I regret the lie as soon as I press Send, but ever since he found out I signed the lease on a condo, he's been hounding me to fly him out to visit.

DAD:

Parker greatness requires balance. You need to work on that.

Never mind balance. I need to put this phone away and deliver an unforgettable date if I want to keep my dad away.

The teenage girl behind the counter gasps when I step up to check in for our reservation. "Y-you're Brody Parker," she says, stuttering over her words. She isn't moving; even her pupils are locked in on me.

"I get that a lot, but it's Cole Slaw." I press my hand to my chest and lean forward, trying to get a look at her screen. "Should have a reservation for two p.m."

Olivia kisses her teeth. I know the fake name is corny. It's not because I think I'm so famous that I can't go anywhere without being hounded by hockey fans. I use it because my dad used to call places looking for me so he could keep tabs on my location.

"My family and I are Freeze season ticket holders," the employee says, ignoring my fake-name ploy. "Is Erik Parker going to come watch a game?"

Olivia takes a step closer to me and links her arm around my biceps. I take a breath. "Not anytime soon, but how about an autograph?" I offer. Her sullen face rebounds into a smile. After signing some receipt paper, I lead Olivia inside.

After adorning white painting jumpsuits, we fasten clear safety goggles around our heads for extra protection. I reach for a bat, ready to show off, but Olivia swoops in before I can grab it. She chocks up on her grip and releases a feral yell. What happens next is cinematic. Like one of those viral catastrophic zoo videos where something spooks the animals into sheer primal terror. It's happening faster than I can comprehend, and yet it looks like she's moving in slow motion.

I don't know what that old fridge did to Olivia, but she's showing it who's boss. She smashes and thrashes her way around the room like a tornado. I stand back out of fear that I might become collateral if I get too close—I'm dressed as white as a lot of these old appliances, after all. She doesn't tire; she must have played softball growing up, or chopped a lot of wood. I start clapping and cheering her on as she demolishes a case of old beer bottles. Finally succumbing to fatigue—or boredom—she drops the bat and wipes the sweat off her forehead with the sleeve of her jumpsuit.

"Impressive stuff, Wreck-It Ralph," I say, picking up the bat and swinging at some bottles. Glass smashes with a loud crack.

"I prefer Link, thank you very much." Olivia selects a crowbar next, slicing it through the air a couple times before jabbing the end through an old stove window.

"Really?" I push my glasses up on the top of my head.

Olivia's arms drop, but she keeps a tight grip on the crowbar. "What? Because I'm a girl I can't like video games?" She juts her hip out.

"Not at all what I meant. But since you mentioned it, I know who you remind me of," I say.

Olivia's mouth hangs open. "Really?"

"Yeah. I knew you looked familiar and I just figured it out."

"Um. I get that a lot," she says, taking a half step back. "Usually, people are wrong. They think I look like someone, but I don't." Her chest heaves as her breathing becomes labored.

"No, I've seen you before . . . Lara Croft," I say with a cocky grin. I slide my glasses back into place before smashing another bottle.

She rolls her eyes at me. "Down boy." She smashes the table in front of us.

"Would Master Chief have been better?" I say between slugs.

She laughs—a real one—and it's the sexiest thing I've ever heard.

"Maybe we could play *Mortal Kombat* or *Mario Kart* sometime. Or *EA SPORTS NHL 26* if you're brave enough." I'm laying it on heavy, but mentioning I'm featured in a video game usually works for me—even if they have me rated ninety-three when I'm clearly at least a ninety-seven.

"Are you masochistic or something? Isn't it bad enough your team is oh-and-five to start the season? You want to carry that losing energy over to our dates too?" Olivia roundhouse kicks a computer monitor into the cement wall across the room. Who knew a rage room could be so hot?

"Have you been watching our away games?"

She shrugs and heads over to the screen to finish it off with some overhead high-striker chops.

"We don't suck that bad," I say, flipping the bat around in my hand. Whatever rage and bravado I thought I had disappeared as soon as I saw her. Now I'm just here to watch her kick ass.

"*You* don't. For your size, you're agile as hell on the offense. And somehow your backhand is as lethal as your forehand. How is that even physically possible? And you can find the back of the net no matter the amount of traffic the other team's D is dishing out. I think you've got X-ray vision or something. If you didn't care so much about always getting the nicest goal, you'd have like five more of them this season. Just get the puck on net," she rambles while tossing up bottles and smashing them midair with the crowbar. I stand back, taking it all in.

Olivia throws her last bottle and turns back to me. "What?" she asks, hands anchored to her hips.

"That's like the nicest thing anyone's ever said to me." My glasses fog.

Olivia uses her safety glasses as a headband. Her high cheekbones are sharper than the shards of broken glass littering the floor. She takes a step toward me, crushing broken glass into the cement. "What if I told you your game isn't the only thing about you that's hot."

"I might kiss you." I reach for her hip and pull her in the rest of the distance.

"I know a lot of people like to see you score because they're big Minnesota Freeze fans, but I like it because I get to see that smile on the big screen." Her lips tease me with every word.

With our mouths inches away from each other, I can't help but smile.

"Yeah. That one right there. When it gets real wide, I can see your perfect teeth," she says.

I cut her off before she can say anything else, locking her bottom lip between mine. She hums a moan that reverberates into my mouth. Her lips part and our tongues meet in a gentle embrace, one far more timid than the raw physicality that just wreaked havoc on this room. Her lip gloss is a treat almost as delicious as her chest pressed against me and I can't help but nibble on her bottom lip. She drops her crowbar to the ground and runs her fingers through my hair. As our bodies press closer together, our kissing becomes fervent. It's like I'm gasping for air; I devour her. She meets my passion, letting me in deeper, and the room is hotter than ever. I'm not normally this reckless in public, but I can't pull away from her. My hands tickle down the small of her back and grip her ass—even through the painter's suit, her body is incredible. She's an even better kisser than she is demolisher. Without warning, she immediately jumps back from my embrace. While she catches her breath, I try to figure out what I did wrong.

"Are you okay?" I reach for her hand, but she pulls her arm back. Was it too much? I shouldn't have rushed it.

"I'm good. That was good. Should we get out of here?" With swollen lips, she rushes for the exit before I reply.

Olivia leads me through the maze of a shopping center. Past the amusement park, past the movie theater, past the aquarium, past the six hat stores again until we're stopped outside a hair salon.

"I think your hair looks great today," I say. Her long brown hair hangs to her waist and looks like a shiny layer of protection from the harsh Midwestern winter.

"I know. I washed it this morning, but we're not here for me." She brushes her hand down the back of my head, tangling her fingers in the curls at the nape of my neck.

"Then why are we here?" The growing pit in my stomach is getting hard to ignore. I should have stopped at one of those Cinnabons along the way.

"There's a long history between hair and hockey in Minnesota." Olivia points across the mall to a group of teenage boys. Dressed in their hockey team warm-ups, they all have matching poorly bleached blond mullets. "Beliefs wrapped up in superstition and tradition. Even my peoples, the Anishinaabe, believe hair holds memory."

"Your hair must have an excellent memory because it's so beautiful."

She must not have heard me because she doesn't acknowledge my compliment. Most girls love when I say things like that to them.

"If you want to put an end to the team's losing streak," she explains, "you need to shed the negative energy and start fresh."

"Cut my hair?" The whole mall seemingly stops and turns at my outburst.

"Shed the negative energy," she says, invading my personal space. Her eyes are mesmerizing. My lips still sting from our kiss, and I can taste her on my tongue. "I think you'd look amazing with a buzz cut." She slicks my hair back, using both hands to flatten down the top. Her eyes squint as she looks me over before nodding approvingly.

I glance across the mall where another group of teens walks by in matching hockey team hoodies. This time they all have buzz cuts with stars shaved into the sides of their heads. I'm trying to fit into the culture of Minnesota hockey and appease her, but there's no way I'm shaving a giant snowflake above my ear.

I think about my signature flow. If I close my eyes, I can feel the breeze of the rink's cold air flying through my wings as I speed up the ice with the puck. My beautiful salad, long enough to spill out the bottom of my helmet yet short enough to never tangle. Curls for the girls.

At the same time, I want to fit in with my team. I knew coming to Minnesota to carry on the Parker legacy would be a bigger challenge than going to Tampa. Being oh-and-five isn't the start to the season I was hoping for, and it sure as hell isn't what's expected of me. I'd do anything for the legacy—that's the Parker way. Hockey over everything always makes Dad proud.

I wince at the thought of steel scissors chopping at my beloved locks. I hesitate at the entrance, but Olivia slips her hand in mine and gives me a reassuring smile. I know I can trust her. I let her lead me into the salon. Cutting my hair won't sting nearly as much as tarnishing the good Parker reputation with more losses.

NINE

Brody

My legs feel like cooked spaghetti after today's practice. With every deep breath, I still feel the frozen burn in my lungs. When Coach whistled to signal practice was over, I almost cheered. The relief is short-lived as I leave the locker room.

I wish I could say I'm surprised to hear my dad's inconsiderately loud voice carrying down the hall, but I knew this day would come. I'm shocked he lasted this long, that he wasn't here on day one leading me onto the ice like I was a child showing up to their first day of kindergarten. Of course, his intentions aren't protective in nature. He rarely shows up for me; he's here to get his ego stroked, gathering compliments like hockey cards to add to his legacy collection.

My dad's got Coach Carol cornered. It immediately gives me horrible flashbacks to youth hockey—that one time things went too far, got too public. In an instant, I revert to that same fourteen-year-old boy who wants to run and hide. Unfortunately, both men notice me immediately and Coach waves me over. I gulp, almost choking on my saliva and the memories of a childhood spent chasing an unattainable greatness.

"Jesus. That hair. You look like you're about to enlist," my dad says, wasting no time on pleasantries. He's tanner than I remember. The wrinkles separating his eyebrows deepen as he scans me up and down.

Coach laughs his comment off as if it were a joke. I know it wasn't. I run my hand over the top of my new buzz cut; it's a sensory dream. I think of Olivia every time my head gets cold out on the ice. She was right, shedding the past was therapeutic. I'm sure the wins will follow. Any game now. We're due.

"Hey, Dad." I keep it brief. Small talk is as excruciating as a bag skate.

He smiles his made-for-TV sportscaster grin. "Coach Carol and I were just talking about you," he says, cheerily.

This is not a compliment. The statement doesn't warm my heart; it stops it. It's as scary a thought as it's intended to be. My dad's words are often like rip currents—they appear harmless to the unsuspecting, loving even. But it's not calm and it's not something you can swim through. His words are dangerous, and they swallow me whole.

I grind my teeth, chewing on all the things I can never say.

"You're so lucky to have Erik as a mentor," Coach Carol says to me, his hand firmly kneading my dad's shoulder. They're already friendly—most people in hockey are wooed by his charm.

In that moment, my entire body is more tense than it was at any point during today's practice. Even my knees are locked, which I only notice because as my heart rate increases, my vision pinholes. I remember to release my breath and shift my weight in time to force a smile before things get awkward.

"I should get back to work." Coach's hand falls off my dad's shoulder. "Good job out there today, Brody," he adds before heading to his office a few doors down.

As soon as he's out of earshot, I say to my dad, "I didn't know you were coming."

"I saw a picture of the new hairdo online and knew I needed to stop by."

"Did Mom come with you?" I keep my tone neutral, but my dad always sees through it.

"I'm traveling for business—hockey business. Your mom's at home."

I knew better than to get my hopes up. My dad insists that us Parker men handle the hockey business, but when it's all hockey business, there isn't much time for anything or anyone else. He searches my face, looking for any splinters. I tighten my jaw, narrow my eyes. No weakness, especially not in a hockey rink. But it's not enough. His head still shakes with disappointment.

"Seriously, your head looks like a thumb. Is this a cry for help?" He grabs my arm, feeling my biceps in the process. Body checking me to make sure I'm measuring up to his expectations.

"It's a haircut," I say, wiggling out of his grip. I'm in good shape, probably the best of my career.

"You should have run it by me first. Let's hope it grows out in time for my Hockey Hall of Fame induction ceremony because you look ridiculous." The names won't be released for months, but he's already planning his victory lap.

"It's not about looks," I quietly reply.

"Everything is about looks. We have an image to uphold." He shimmies up the sleeve of his blazer to check his signature Rolex watch—a gift from the Tampa Storm when he played his thousandth NHL game. "We should get out of here. I've got a bit of time before my next flight, and I still want to see your new place."

"How much time?"

"Not much. Maybe a few hours. I'm headed to Toronto to film an SNN feature story on the recent Hall of Fame renovations. This is my year, Brody. I can feel it." He puffs out his chest and for a moment I admire his confidence. "So, no more rash decisions," he adds, waving his finger in my face. "Or emotional breakdowns."

"I wouldn't dare."

I also wouldn't dare spend the afternoon with him. I'm not ready to give him my home address and along with it unlimited opportunities to pop in on me whenever his work schedule so conveniently allows. I need to keep my head in the game, focused on the Freeze—it's the only way I'm going to play well, and the only way this team is going to win any games. Dad even said so himself; we have an image to uphold. The best thing for the Parker legacy is if he stays away.

"Is your phone vibrating?" I ask. But all that's vibrating are my trembling hands.

While he checks the pocket of his designer sport coat, I discreetly call Olivia and pray she picks up. Her "hello" comes through and I quickly bring the phone to my ear. "My bad, it was mine," I tell my dad. "Hey, Olivia. I'm still at the rink so I'll be about ten minutes late to our date."

"Hello? Who is this?" she asks.

I turn away from my dad. I can't lie and maintain eye contact with him. "You're so funny. That's why I love hanging out with you. Anyway, I'll see you in about thirty minutes at the Korean café, just like we planned. Cool?" I hold my breath and cross my fingers that this works.

"Sure."

"See you soon." There's nothing fake about the current smile on my face. I hang up the call before my ploy is spoiled.

"You probably overheard that. I've already got plans this afternoon," I tell my dad.

Without missing a beat, he says, "That's fine. I'll come. I should meet her. Make sure she's up to par."

"Oh. Isn't that a big step in a relationship?" I stare at my feet. He's angling for the exit, but I know better than to get in a car with him. As scary as a public meltdown is, I feel safer inside these walls than I do being alone with him anywhere else.

"Are you serious about this girl or is she a distraction?" he asks.

"No!" I panic. "I mean, it's serious."

This is a disaster. I can't have my dad crashing my coffee date with Olivia. He thinks it's a serious relationship, but we've only known each other for two weeks.

"Actually, I'm meeting her parents today. It might be weird if I brought you. I don't want them getting starstruck." As I try to decipher the expression on my dad's face, Coach Carol interrupts our conversation.

"Hey, Parker." Coach Carol pops his head out of his office.

We both turn. At the same time as my dad replies, "Yes," I'm reminding Coach that, "It's Brody."

"Birds of a feather." Coach chuckles. "Erik Parker, wouldn't want to go over some game tape with me, would you?" he asks.

Neither of us speak. My dad looks over at me with a disappointing glare that lets me know however this afternoon shakes up, I'm about to fall on the sword for it.

Coach rubs his hand over his salt-and-pepper beard. His nervous tic is usually only reserved for our penalty kill; he must be really starstruck. "Forget it, you two are probably catching up this afternoon."

"You're in luck," my dad announces. "Brody's got other plans this afternoon, but a guy like me is always ready to talk hockey strategy."

A classic Erik Parker response. If he leaves it at that, he's letting me off the hook easy this time.

"Let's watch last night's tape and start with Brody's goal in the first," my dad adds, glaring over at me. He waits for me to break eye contact first before walking over to Coach's office.

I hardly feel like I've dodged a bullet. I'm not sure which is the lesser evil, but I'm too panicked to give it any more thought. I need to get out of here. If I stay any longer, I know I'm going to get dragged into that room and be forced to face my dad's critiques in the presence of my coach. I check the time. If I stay any longer, I'm going to be late for my date.

By the time Olivia arrives at the Korean café, I'm halfway through my coffee. I've hardly calmed down since coming face-to-face with my dad's attempted ambush. If anything, the caffeine is making me more anxious, but seeing her walk in and smile at me from across the room reminds me that I have a layer of protection from my dad. I'll make this date last until he leaves for the airport. I hope he has enough sense to keep up the supportive-dad ruse around Coach Carol and the rest of the Freeze's coaching staff while they pick apart our most recent game tape.

"Sorry I'm late. I just left a meeting with a potential new client," Olivia says through winded breath. She swings off her shoulder bag and drops an armful of paperwork on the table. The stack makes a thud as it touches down.

"How did it go?"

"Waste of my time," she says, shedding her jacket. "Everyone wants data research, but no one wants to pay for it."

Looks like I wasn't the only one who had a bad morning. I feel some guilt over the fact that I have everything most people dream of. I should be more grateful for my life. I've never needed a résumé and doubt I ever will. Her disappointment sobers me up.

"I don't know your order, so I got you an Americano, an iced Americano, a green tea, and a peach fruit-ade. If you'd prefer a smoothie, I'll go grab you one."

She eyes the four beverages lined up in front of her as she slips into her chair. "No. No need. I usually slam about five coffees a day to keep a pulse, so this is perfect. Thank you."

She slurps from the iced coffee first. A chill travels up my spine; Minnesotans really are built different. We're well into fall, and I'm still struggling to acclimate to the local temperature. With windchill like this, I need to invest in a good winter hat. I take a drink of my steaming Americano.

"To be totally honest, I didn't realize we had a date today," she says, chewing on her straw.

"About that." I lean back in my chair. I hoped all the drinks would be a big enough distraction to not talk about it, but looks like I should have gotten her that smoothie too. "I thought I had asked, but when I went back through our text messages, I saw it never sent. Cell service is brutal in arenas."

She smiles softly, and I feel terrible lying to her. "Well, I'm happy you called. A bit surprised, but happy to be here with you."

"You shouldn't be surprised. Our last two dates were a lot of fun."

Her face flushes and she giggles into her palm. "I'm surprised you're not spending time with your dad."

I cock my head back. "Where did you hear that?"

Olivia gulps down more of her coffee. "Word travels fast in the Five-Hole Donuts employee group chat," she says with the straw between her teeth.

Olivia pulls out her phone. After a bit of scrolling, she shows me a screenshot from Hammer's Instagram of him with his arm wrapped around my dad's shoulder. Hammer grins from ear to ear like he was just announced as the first star of the game. My dad, as always, basks in the attention.

"His visit is more of a layover."

"What did he think of your new hair?" Olivia bites into her pillowy bottom lip.

"It didn't come up."

Her face falls. "Is everything okay?" she asks.

"Now it is," I say. "But practice was tough. Both physically and mentally."

Right as Olivia winds up to ask me a follow-up question, my phone rings. I flinch on instinct. The screen lights up on the table with my agent's name; it's an incoming call from Lamar. Last time I ignored his call, he sent me five follow-up text messages and a couple DMs. I put him through the ringer this offseason with my free agency antics. He about had a stroke when I turned down that offer from the Tampa Storm.

"This is really rude of me, but my agent is calling." I flash my phone screen as proof.

She shrugs. "I was late to our date. Answer it and we're even?"

"Hey, Lamar," I say, cupping my mouth to the phone. Olivia politely drops her eyes and gathers up her stack of paperwork to shove into her bag. "I haven't turned down any record-breaking contract offers, so to what do I owe the pleasure of this impromptu call?"

He huffs loudly. "Don't mention the Tampa thing, Brody. I'm getting heated just thinking about it." I try to turn down the volume on my phone, but this guy's got one volume level and it's practically speakerphone decibels. "I've got a brand deal for you. I'll be honest, I didn't know what that woman was talking about when she offered it. Body-something? But my fourteen-year-old daughter knew the brand right away and she said you got to do it. After looking into it more, I agree. The money is huge, and the exposure is even bigger."

"That's great. Listen, I'm in the middle of something here," I say, glancing up to check on Olivia. She's in her own world, scrolling on her phone. "If the deal seems legit, let's do it. I trust your daughter Zuri's advice on what's cool. Email over the contract."

"Will do, son," Lamar says before hanging up.

I silence my phone and tuck it in my pocket. "Sorry about that. Where were we?"

"You were about to tell me why practice was so tough today."

"Was I?"

She nods. For a split second, I think about telling her the truth. But it passes as quickly as it comes. If I want to keep this thing going between us, then the less she knows about my family, the better. If a haircut got my dad to make an emergency trip to the Midwest, then I'd hate to see how he reacts to me airing out our family's dirty laundry.

"The guys were giving me a hard time about my Catan skills." I reach under the table and pull out the Catan game I borrowed from the player's lounge on my way out of the rink. "Help me out and teach me everything you know? I'd rather be an asset than a liability."

She sighs. Her eyes flicker back and forth between me and the red box sitting between us. "You might be underestimating how horrible you are at Catan. This could take us all afternoon."

"I don't have anywhere else to be, do you?"

"Considering I didn't leave today's meeting with a new client, no. I don't," she says flatly.

Olivia pulls out a pen and notepad from her bag, and I settle into my seat. As she begins a long-winded introduction on the basic premise of the game and the many variants available, I know that I'm safe from my dad. Learning all the hexes alone will buy me enough time to dodge his visit. My instincts about Olivia were right. She is smart, but perhaps more impressive, she is very strategic and an excellent coach.

TEN

Olivia

I should have never let Brody touch me like that at the Demo Rage Room. What's wrong with me? He looked at me with that same primal glare he gets when he's on a breakaway and I couldn't help myself but let him score. I wanted it—even worse, I liked it. Our most recent date wasn't much better. He somehow tricked me into a last-minute coffee date that lasted longer than a trip to Target. Spending time with him is like getting lost in all the aisles: thrilling, but I know better than to buy another candle. I'm not sure what's worse, the physical intimacy we can't seem to fight when in private or the emotional connection he's so determined on building over four coffees. By the fourth beverage, I thought my bladder was going to explode. *Teach me Catan?* Buddy, I'd have better luck teaching a moose to skate.

I stuck through it—all five hours—hoping Erik would show up. My haircut suggestion—the universal signal that Something Is Wrong—was successful enough to spook his dad into a visit, but wasn't enough to get me any closer to Erik or the Parker legacy.

Thanks to that little interrupting phone call he took during our coffee date a few weeks ago, I'm currently staring down in disbelief at my phone reading a tagline for the newest face of Bare. "Brody Parker is so hot he'll melt your ice."

Surely, no one is reading a cheesy headline like that when the photo below is a suggestive pose of Brody with a pair of skintight black briefs hanging off his hips—it appears they let him keep his cup on for the photo shoot. He's flexing so hard it looks like he's on the verge of farting.

My plan to sabotage Brody's incredible good looks backfired. His new buzz cut has been the talk of the internet since its debut. He even scored two goals in his first game with the new hair. "He's so young David Beckham–coded," they're saying. "I want to rub his head like a genie lamp and use all three wishes for him," I've read.

I can't believe he looks better than ever. In hindsight, his messy shag and loose curls feel childish compared to his dangerous new chop. With his hair off his face, his cheekbones and cut jaw take center ice. And trust me, this bulge is putting up a valiant fight for attention. Brody knows it too. His drastic makeover was the viral internet moment that caught the eye of Bare and they knew he was their new leading man. Since the launch of the campaign, Brody's been promising me a special treat as a thank-you—the promise of which feels a lot like a threat.

With Brody hotter than ever, his inflated sense of self has really done wonders to his game. He's becoming the Freeze's most consistent forward despite the team's inability to win a game. Which is why I need to hit the Parkers where it really hurts: Brody's game. And I'm going to sabotage him tonight. It's an SNN national broadcast game; for the first time this season, Erik Parker will provide remote intermission commentary. All eyes are on tonight's Freeze game.

I usually sneak into the rink through a back door after all the players have arrived and are settled in the dressing room; however, tonight I'm early. Dressed in a tight black yoga bodysuit, I channel my inner Catwoman. I sneak down the hall and tuck beside the stick rack outside the locker room. Unlike last time, I don't send them tumbling over like dominos. My brief time inside the Chilly suit has made me nimble and stealthy.

There are three things you should never mess with when it comes to hockey players' equipment. Up first is his stick. A knight is nothing more than a jester without his sword. Brody is currently playing with a ninety-five flex, which is an appropriate whip for a guy his size. NHL.com has him listed at six foot two and one-eighty—a coach's wet dream. It would be a shame if someone had secretly ordered three of the exact same stick in an eighty-five flex—a purchase that ate into my new-apartment funds. I look up and down the hall to make sure I'm alone. With the coast clear, I make a run for it.

Four of Brody's sticks are lined up and marked with the numbers one through four on the taped knobs. Some call it hockey science; I call it a neurotic system of wearing through sticks evenly. I leave the first stick—his warm-up stick—untouched. I quickly swap out the other three, leaving the rack seemingly as I found it before stashing his old sticks in a mess of a nearby janitorial closet.

It took me four hours last night to get the tape job perfect on these things: sloppy and uneven, just as he keeps them. He'll never know what I've done until he goes to fire off a shot in the first period and he sends the puck embarrassingly wide—or out of play and called for a delay-of-game penalty if I'm really lucky. These whippy sticks are my ticket to watching some sloppy hockey tonight.

The second piece of equipment you should never mess with is a hockey player's skates. Like a chef's knife, the sharpness is essential to their craft. I peek my head into the locker room, cupping my hand to my ear. It's empty. I scurry in and find the cubby with Brody's nameplate. His skates hang blade up, freshly sharpened and ready for game time. In about four hours, he'll be unsuspectingly slipping into these booby traps with laces.

I pull out my pocket-size skate sharpener—a tiny nail file–like stone—and get to work sharpening his 7/8" into a blade sharp enough to cut diamonds. He's going to pivot on these blades and fall right on his ass in front of everyone. An embarrassing wipeout with seventeen thousand live witnesses will shatter his confidence for the rest of his shift, and the looming dread of the internet's reaction will take his head out of the rest of the game.

I bring the blade to my face and blow off the excess dust. Tiny steel particles fly like glitter. I meticulously place his skates exactly as I found them and turn my attention to the last order of business. Perhaps the most important piece of equipment you should never mess with: the jock.

It's a trifecta deadly enough to tarnish the perfect Parker reputation. If all three hit, it should be enough to make Erik crash out on live television. He'll be forced to either downplay Brody's brutal game, in turn putting his own credibility as a hockey legend at risk. Or he'll be as harsh on Brody as he deserves, which will beg the question: Is the Parker dynasty a dynasty at all?

I plug my nose and grab Brody's jock off the hook. Pinched between my finger and thumb, I hold it out an arm's length away. *Gross.* I squeeze a giant glob of extra Icy Hot muscle relaxer cream into the inside of his jock. I lather it in gel, inside and out. As I'm reaching to hang it back in place, loud footsteps thump in the distance. They're approaching the locker room and with each footfall the sense of impending danger rises.

There's nowhere to hide; the locker room is all open space. The footsteps get louder, and along with them, the voices and laughter get closer. Down at my feet is Brody's empty hockey bag. I look for a window to jump out of, but we're below-ground.

From the inside of the zipped crusty hockey bag, I hear two men enter the locker room. By the sound of their conversation, it's the equipment guys getting back from break.

"I said to him, 'Look, Hammer, it's fine that you don't want any of your equipment washed—I can even turn a blind eye to the fact that you prefer to play commando—but I cannot in good faith continue to smuggle a dead octopus to the rink for you to kiss before every game,'" a deep voice says with much exasperation.

"I'm proud you set that boundary. It's difficult to do with goalies—especially superstitious ones," someone replies.

"If the team was winning, I'd go along with it, but at this point I think it's bad luck," the deep voice says.

It's a miracle I can hear them rummaging around the room because the scent of this hockey bag is so ripe it's practically dulling all my other senses. Most of Brody's equipment is hung in his cubby waiting for him, except for a few spare pieces crammed against my body.

Something tangles in my hair. It takes a forceful tug to dislodge the mystery object. Bringing it to my face for inspection, the smell hits me—mouth guard. An old chewed-up unwashed one at that. I gag and jump a bit as I toss it as far away from me as possible.

"Did you hear that?" the one with the deeper voice says. As his footsteps approach, I play dead.

"Not the mouse thing again." The other guy lets out a groan.

I feel a tickle at my ankle. My body goes rigid. As the tickle travels up my leg, I cover my mouth and hold my breath.

What. Is. That?

"I'm telling you, I saw a mouse in here the other day. I swear I did. Why won't anyone believe me?"

"Because you can't read the jumbotron without your glasses. Now come on, let's grab the laundry. These jerseys aren't going to sort themselves."

As the two equipment guys leave the locker room, a tiny mouse makes its way up my body and into my hair. No hockey bag can contain my panic. I bust out of there like the living dead and let out an animated squeal as I swat at my head like my hair is on fire. A tiny little mouse drops to the ground with a smack and lies there momentarily stunned. I let out a few silent gags while flapping my hands. The mouse rolls over and scurries off toward the showers.

I gather up my incriminating evidence, but before I can take another step, I hear someone at the door. There's no time to hide—I'm caught. My breath catches as someone fills the open doorframe.

It's Quinn.

"Olivia?" She stops on the other side as if there's an invisible force preventing her from entering. The force is likely listed in the handbook. "It sounded like someone was ransacking the place."

"There's a mouse in here!" Forcing my distress is easy.

"And you forgot you weren't actually a cat? Get out of there!" Quinn hastily motions me over. "Someone else will catch it."

I dart out of the room, unscathed and innocent.

On the walk back to the mascot locker room, Quinn eyes up my full hands. "Whatcha got there?"

"What? This?" I hold up the skate sharpening stone and drag it back and forth over my trimmed nails. "Just a nail file. Gotta keep the claws looking nice."

"And the Icy Hot?" She reaches for the tube, but I pull away. "You're not injured, are you?"

"No, healthy as a . . . cat." I force a chuckle. "It's for my muscles. Loosens them up so I'm ready for game time." As we pass a trash can, I toss in the empty bottle.

"It is a long season, and rough on the body," she agrees.

Inside my locker room, there's a comically large space bun wig sitting on top of the mascot head. *Star Wars* night. I've got to start reading those emails with the subject line *READ ME*. Next to the wig is a new costume. I'm thankful to see they went with Princess Leia's signature white robe and silver belt look for tonight's game.

"The furries are going to love this cosplay. I'm going to end up on Reddit before puck drop."

"Well, do or do not, or whatever that ugly little green diva said," Quinn says with a sewing needle between her teeth. She's always tinkering with something up until the absolute last minute. No detail too small, and tonight she's making sure my boots are perfect.

As the last of my adrenaline spike leaves my body, what I've done to Brody sinks in. I slowly slide down the wall and fall cross-legged on the floor with a heavy sigh. Have I done too much? Does the jock take it too far? I fiddle with the gold locket and chain around my neck, a gift from my dad for my fourteenth birthday. I wanted a new hockey stick, and at the time I didn't appreciate the sentiment. I've worn it every day since his death.

I shake off the guilt. What's done is done because it had to be.

"Are you okay? You seem despondent, even for you." Quinn startles me.

"I'll be fine," I say. "Hopefully the team can win a game soon. The fans are starting to get restless."

"Any mascot can be entertaining when the team is winning, but it's a great mascot who keeps entertainment alive when the team is losing," she says. "It's in the . . ."

"Mascot handbook," I finish her sentence.

Having completed the boots, Quinn looks to me and says, "We've got some free time before we have to get out there. Want me to braid your hair?"

"It looks fine," I say, dragging my fingers through a lot of resistance.

"Come sit." Quinn gets up from her chair and swings around to the back. She taps, motioning for me to take a seat.

I sit down and let her twist and pull my hair into a cute and manageable style. "Thanks. This will be much more comfortable under the mask."

She places both hands on my shoulders. "The correct term is head covering. Page ten of the handbook."

"You really love that thing don't you."

Quinn nods. "Some of us are going to Hattricks after the game if you want to join." She gives a few finishing tugs to my hair.

"Doesn't that go against some mascot code of conduct?" I take a look at myself in the mirror. Quinn discreetly added some of her green and gold glitter gel to my hair.

"Yes, rule number four." She says this like it's canon. "But rule number twenty-three says you're welcome to join as long as I introduce you as my friend. What do you say, friend?" Quinn extends a tiny canister of hair spray.

"Count me in," I say, letting her spray me in place.

Brody finishes the game with three goals, an assist, and a plus-five rating. It's a natural hat trick, featuring a goal even sexier than his Bare campaign stills. The team barely wins, but it's finally their first win of the season and the media names Brody the first star.

It's like Brody's dad said on SNN during the second intermission, he's shooting harder, skating faster, and his muscles are relaxed and loose. Erik even used his airtime to take credit for Brody's improved play, saying his recent sit-down with Coach Carol was to thank for this incredible display of Parker greatness. Quinn dragged me out of the bathroom before I could hear the rest of his report, but I had heard enough to know my plan B was a failure.

Now I'm hunched over my phone in my locker room watching the postgame presser in disbelief with half the Chilly suit discarded in a frantic mess around me.

Brody takes the first media question of the night. "Parker, your gameplay has been stellar as of late but tonight you were able to find another level. What was the secret to tonight's success?" a faceless reporter asks from the crowd.

"Brody. Parker's my dad," he says, uncharacteristically shaken up. "Um, and I guess you could say the Force was with me tonight." Brody bounces back, quickly finding his signature cocky charm. Pausing for the media crowd to laugh at his joke, he leans back in his chair and takes a drink. The crowd howls. Brody runs his hand over his new buzz cut, exposing his flexed biceps. He's like a parched sponge soaking up every second of the attention and admiration. I almost don't recognize him as the same Brody from our dates. The game ended, but he's still putting on a show.

I grab the mascot head and plop it on. Into the foam and fur, I let out a loud scream of frustration.

Quinn pops her head in the locker room. "Don't tell me you saw the mouse again."

"Out!" I point the way.

"Okay, I'll meet you at the bar," she shouts through a shutting door.

I take the mask off and white-knuckle my way through the rest of the press conference.

"Tonight's game was the best I've ever felt out on the ice," Brody says. "I could sit here and say that it's because of all the extra practice hours I've clocked, or my dad's help breaking down game tape, or even the fresh start I've taken with my career, but this win wouldn't have happened without a full team effort. We all showed up to play tonight."

It's the perfect answer. And he delivered it with no hesitation. No searching on his face to gauge anyone's reaction or opinion. He's confident because he knows it's the perfect answer. Erik Parker has taught him well.

A media member asks what the team has to do to build off tonight's win. After regurgitating another PR hockey answer about playing a full three periods, he adds, "And not for nothing, I hear there's a mouse running around our locker room. Hammer thinks he's a lucky mouse—you know how goalies get—maybe he's right." Brody flashes his perfect smile and the media members all laugh because actually getting on their hands and knees to kiss his ass wouldn't be appropriate for broadcast.

I can't stomach any more. I hate losing. My phone slips from my grip and I hang my head between my legs. This family is unshakable. Brody's only been with the Freeze for a couple months, but he's quickly become a fan favorite. As fans have come to expect a loss from this team, Brody is the sole reason to show up and watch. He's won over the media, the infamously impenetrable Coach Carol, and even the most skeptical Freeze fans.

With each passing game, Brody embeds himself further into the fabric of this team. The Parker name is becoming synonymous with the remaining memory of my dad's legacy. Erik Parker is on intermission reports taking credit for all of it and will continue to do whatever it takes to get his way into the Hall of Fame. I know it because that's exactly how he played the game.

My dad never quit. He battled through a lot. A concussion that spiraled into depression, unemployment, anger, and eventually heart failure. I'm not a quitter either; I'm a Hinckley.

ELEVEN

Brody

The air is heavy in this crowded nightclub, the bass so loud that I can feel it in my chest like a second heartbeat. My head turns, spinning to follow a group of beautiful women with golden sun-kissed skin dressed in what looks to be bathing suits—I fucking love Miami.

About half the team is already so drunk they couldn't tell you their name, let alone their hockey position or jersey number. It's the perfect scene for an epic rookie party. I've been in the league long enough to have survived a handful of these parties—I know the drill. Every year each team holds a rookie party where everyone goes out and gets the new guys drunk and racks up a bar tab large enough to sober them up. *Welcome to the show, boys.*

The rookie party is just as much for the kids as it is for the old guys. Which is why when Andy threatened to cancel it due to our pathetic play at the beginning of the season, I stuck my neck out. Sometimes the best thing you can do for a struggling team is get together in Miami for some unadulterated shenanigans. Some teams drink to celebrate, while others drink to forget, but we're here to bond as brothers and build off the momentum of our first wins of the season.

We started out the night at a five-star steak house where the entire team showed up wearing custom shirts with my Bare campaign photo plastered on them. One of the wives is Cricut efficient. Thankfully, most of the guys ditched the shirts with my abs on them for something more likely to help them pick up a girl to leave with at the end of the night. Except for Hammer, who makes a point to say he won't take his off because he's a proud Parker fan.

I grab a beer from the ice bucket and crash down on the couch beside Hammer and Jordy, who are huddled around a phone reading team stats.

"Put your phone away!" I say, reaching for it, but Hammer's quick to cover it like a loose rebound. "New rule, no NHL app tonight."

"Hold on. Let me check my . . . Ooh, my angel numbers—four-four-four!" Hammer says. He gives the same type of smile you crack when you check your Instagram notifications and your crush liked your story.

"There's nothing lucky about a 4.44 GAA, Hams," Jordy says, rubbing his back.

"Another new rule: no hockey talk tonight." I snatch his phone up. I quickly delete the app before handing it back. "Why don't you two separate? Give each other a bit of space and go mingle."

"I'm not sure . . ." Jordy starts.

"If we could do that," Hammer finishes his sentence.

"Do you two go anywhere without each other?" I ask. They've been known to piss in the same urinal, but they get their own hotel rooms on the road (side-by-side joining rooms, of course). To what extent does this codependent relationship reach?

"Nope," they say in unison.

"We're a tag team." Jordy folds his arms across his chest and smirks. Hammer nods his head reassuringly.

"Shouldn't say that around people," I say.

"No, it's true. When he can't finish, I'll always be there for him, ready to step up and step in." Hammer wraps his arm around Jordy.

"Absolutely. I have no problem getting in there. Sometimes it can be a bit dirty, painful even." Jordy pounds the flesh of his fist against Hammer's chest a few times.

"You're really not hearing the double entendre?" I pinch the bridge of my nose.

"You know we don't speak French, Bro-vember," Hammer says. They giggle back and forth like Beavis and Butt-Head, repeating my nickname of the week. "Bro-vember" in honor of the mustache I've been growing for Movember. He and Jordy high-five while sharing a laugh. The only thing laughable is the sad excuse for a muzzy sitting on Hammer's upper lip.

"My name is Brody," I repeat myself for the umpteenth time. "No more hockey talk. Go mingle." I give them a push off the couch. They slip out of the VIP section together and disappear into the crowd.

My drink sweats in my hand. I'm hot and thirsty, but booze doesn't quench it quite like it used to. I've got enough shit to worry about in my life to add a hangover to the list. I ditch the drink on the table and get up to see what Chef is up to. I find him at the end of the bar talking to four women—an ambitious play, even for him. He spots me in the crowd and waves me over.

"I want you all to meet my buddy," Chef shouts over the music. He wraps his arm around me and pulls me into their tight circle. "If you haven't seen his goals on SNN's Top Ten, then I'm sure you've seen his other body of work in the new Bare ads. Ladies, this is my liney, Brody." He gives me a few pats on the back before tucking his hand back into his pocket. Setting me up to score on and off the ice; what a great teammate.

"He sounds like the whole package," the blonde next to me says. She's been eyeing me from across the room since I got here.

While Chef entertains the other three, I turn to her and say, "I like your sparkly shoes."

"I'm sure."

"Really. You'll never believe this, but I have the same pair at home."

"It's a good thing you didn't wear them tonight, or else that could have been embarrassing." She easily matches my energy and hits me back with some deadpan sarcasm.

"I don't get embarrassed," I say with a cocky smirk that usually works on women at the bar.

"Do you get thirsty?" she says, her bright blue eyes piercing up at me.

"I'm not one to say no to getting a drink with a pretty girl." It's like I'm following a script. We have to run lines for a few drinks before we can both drop the act. I'm sure she's really nice, but I don't have that vulnerability in me tonight. I order a water and another tequila soda for her.

"You do this often?" She sips her fresh drink.

I shrug. I used to. Sometimes I still do. Since moving to Minnesota, my focus has been on keeping Olivia close enough to keep my dad away. I wish I were buying a drink for Olivia instead. She would probably think this place was over the top—and she'd be right. Why am I thinking about her right now? I doubt when she's out with her friends talking to someone attractive, she's thinking about me begging her to play Catan.

"It's fine. I do too, except it's usually basketball players around here." She looks back at her friends.

"You have a nice smile," I say, because I'm starting to feel like a dick. Even saying something nice feels sleazy.

"I'm a dentist." She smiles, showing off her work.

"I'll have to introduce you to Belly. He could use some help." I think of our lovable toothless defenseman. He has to cut up his hamburgers with a fork and knife.

"Well in that case, it's Dr. Conrad," she says.

Commotion at the door pulls my attention away from Dr. Conrad. I hear Hammer and Jordy chanting Parker and my stomach drops. The crowd parts enough for me to see my dad being ushered into the club with a goalie on each side.

"Who's that?" she asks.

"He's nobody. Excuse me," I say, ditching my untouched drink on the bar.

I push my way into the gathering of teammates and strangers formed around my dad. His eyes are already glossy and his salt-and-pepper hair a bit disheveled. As I get closer, I smell the whiskey on him.

"Your dad is so cool. He let me wear his Stanley Cup rings." Hammer lifts his hands and fans them out like Bill Russell.

My dad has three Stanley Cup rings: two with the Tampa Storm and one in his last season of professional hockey with the Carolina Reapers. While they are all being passed around my team for guys to ooh and aah over, I'm reminded that my dad has never once let me try any of them on. When I was six, he told me, *The ring is won, not shared*. The skeletons in our family closet are neatly hung like cherished textile mementos, not even to be removed for special occasions.

"What are you doing here?" I ignore my teammates completely. Careful not to cause a scene, my face is lax, casual even. This is a new team and I have my own reputation to protect. There are too many eyes on us to count, not to mention cameras in everyone's pockets and whiskey in his bloodstream.

"Nice to see you too, son. Since when do you come to town and not tell me?" He lays his heavy hand on my shoulder and I practically buckle at the knees. He just walked in the door but already reeks of booze and has half a glass of something swaying around in his hand. His nice linen outfit and leather loafers tell me this was no impromptu run-in; he's here for a full Erik Parker ass-kissing.

I ignore the fact that he's more than a four-hour drive from home and try my best to defuse the situation. It's important to keep him happy. Good Mood Erik can be fun in this setting. "Sorry, I didn't think you would want to make the drive so late."

While the guys take turns trying on the championship rings, my dad leans in and says, "Are you sure you're not distracted from that bad pass that cost your team the game last night? I had to get over here and tell you in person to get your head out of your ass. I've been trying to get a hold of you, but you've been missing my calls like you've been missing the net." His grip lingers on my shoulder. He holds me in place, digging his fingers deeper into my flesh. Sober Erik is brutally honest, but Drunk Erik is just brutal.

My breathing labors as I suck in hot humid air through my flared nostrils. Right when I think he's going to snap, a smile cracks across his face. He starts to laugh. He places his arm around my neck and pulls me in for a hug. I feel no relief in his embrace.

"You shouldn't be here. It's the rookie party." I slip out from under his arm, tense as a board.

"Don't be rude, ZamBroni," Jordy says, coming up behind me. The guys huddle around us.

"Let's get this guy a drink!" Hammer cheers. Moving in a pack, the boys head up to the VIP lounge.

My dad stares me down, waiting for me to do the right thing. I wish I knew what that was. Flashbacks of our confrontation in a public hockey rink hallway when I was fourteen send a chill up my spine. The dense Miami air has never felt so hot; my palms begin to prickle and my nose beads with sweat.

"I'm heading out," I say, looking for an exit.

"Don't be a pussy, Brody. It's bad for the image," my dad shouts. "No one likes a teammate who bails."

I want to explain that I'm not bailing on my teammates but protecting my own mental health by getting away from him. But I don't. Instead, I say, "I want to be early to practice tomorrow. Work on my shot."

"I know what that means. I saw you talking to that girl at the bar. I remember those days." My dad flashes a slimy grin, and I'm sick to my stomach thinking how similar our smiles look.

"Sure. Yeah. Exactly." I will say anything to get out of this situation.

"I still want a proper visit with you in Minnesota. I need to meet Olivia and make sure she's up to par if she's going to give me the next generation of Parker hockey players. It's my legacy, after all." He finishes the rest of his drink in one big gulp.

While trying to create the "Parker legacy," my mom suffered from infertility for years. It's a miracle I'm here. After two miscarriages, they turned to IVF. Finally, I was born. The whole thing took a heavy toll on my mom, but still paled in comparison to the wedge my dad put between her and I—a wedge that's still dividing us to this day. While my dad ignores my every attempt to distance myself from his control, it's my mom who best respects my boundaries. A perseverant detachment never intended for her, but not seeing my mom often is the unfortunate collateral to avoid my dad's grip. I was never a son to him, always a future hockey player. Hockey above everything is the only way to survive that man.

"You'll love her. She's got great hockey IQ." I force a smile, but it doesn't reach my eyes.

"Good, now go get that blonde at the bar before someone else steals her off your stick. Don't do anything I wouldn't," he shouts back as he disappears deeper into the crowd. I leave without saying goodbye to anyone.

I make a pit stop before going back to the hotel. The rink isn't open at this hour, but there's one other place I know that always helps me clear my head.

I trek through the sand, grains seeping into my sneakers with every step. While seeking refuge from the bustle of the city's nightlife, I plop myself down a few feet from the water. The ocean is an escape that doesn't ask anything of me. Instead, it listens.

I cradle my face in the palms of my hands and let out a long exhale. Physical distance isn't the only measure I'm trying to wedge between my dad and me. I'm at constant war with myself every time he's near. Everyone says I'm like my old man, but how deep do those similarities hide?

What am I willing to do to be a hockey legend? Will I cheat, lie, manipulate, and control my way to the top? Why was I talking to that woman tonight? Was I really going to do something with her? Sometimes I feel like I'm on my own career path, but then I get a bit of fatherly reassurance from him that makes me feel so good I doubt I'll ever succeed without his help.

Every time I close my eyes, I see Olivia's face. I bet she would tell me I had a good game—not great, but nothing to be ashamed of. One shot went wide, but four others hit the net and one went in. My dad noticed one missed pass but conveniently skipped over the countless others that went tape to tape. I pull out my phone and before I can think better of it, I'm pressing Call.

"Hello?" Olivia's voice is hoarse, a bit shaky.

"Shit, how late is it?" The regret is instant. She's going to think I'm crazy.

"I don't know. You called me. Who is this?" she says with more clarity in her voice, and a bit of sass to her tone.

"Are you ever going to save my number in your phone? It's Brody."

"I know. I'm messing with you."

"Are you sleeping?" I give her an out, but I'm hoping she doesn't take it.

"I was. Did you call to ask what time it is?" There's a slight giggle on her end followed by a long pause.

"Maybe." I laugh.

"It's twelve thirty a.m. here."

"So, it's one thirty a.m. here." I dig my fingers into the sand, grounding myself into the beach. A wave crashes and the tide creeps up. It's dark, but between the crescent moon hanging above and the glow of the city's pulse, there's enough light to see the black waves cap.

"Where's here?" she asks.

"Miami."

"Sounds fun."

"It is. Have you ever been?" I slip off my shoes and socks and plant my feet into the sand. I feel at home, maybe even more than when I'm on ice.

"No, I don't travel much."

"I travel too much." I laugh, and she politely does the same.

"I hear waves in the background. What's the ocean like?" she asks before breaking into a loud yawn.

"Alive and yet, calming. It's a pretty standard ocean view." My shoulders, which had previously been curled up to my ears, finally relax back into my familiar poised posture. My jaw unclenches and my chest opens up. With each deep inhale of fresh salty air, my heart rate slowly returns to its normal resting pulse.

"I've never seen one."

"What?" I lean forward, shouting into the phone. I don't think I've ever met someone who's never been to the ocean, let alone never seen one.

"Not a whole lot of oceans in the Midwest."

"Right. Of course." I quiet myself, not wanting to make her feel bad.

"Put me on speaker. I want to hear it," she says in a cute sleepy voice.

I hit the button and hold my phone up. A big wave comes crashing on cue. "Can you hear it?"

We're silent for a moment while the waves loudly dance.

"Yeah. It sounds peaceful."

"It is. I like to come here to block out the noise." I dig my feet in a bit deeper, anchoring myself to this moment, this part of my night I want to remember. More tension washes off me with each incoming wave.

My entire life I've been searching for healthy escapes from my dad and the "Parker legacy." The beach is one of my favorite spots; a good book is a close second. Get the two together and I never want to leave. I gave up my safe space to go play for the Freeze in Minnesota, but Olivia has quickly become a nice replacement.

"Bad night?" she asks.

I've already confessed enough for one evening. "You could say that."

"Should we listen to the ocean together?"

"Yeah. I'd like that." I set my phone down beside me and we sit in silence together, listening to nature's orchestra.

TWELVE

Olivia

Two firm knocks at the front door pull me away from my game of *Zelda*. I drop my Nintendo Switch on the pillow without saving my place and jump out of bed.

"I've got it!" I shout across the apartment.

My epic failed attempt at a sabotage proved to be the turning point in the Freeze's losing streak. An unpredicted pivot that left me feeling so defeated I started preparing myself for Erik Parker's welcome parade into the Hockey Hall of Fame. Erik's been all over SNN doing his Good Samaritan press tour as he makes his final push for a Hall of Fame induction. Apparently, Erik loves donating his time and money, which is strange because I've never heard of a single Parker charity initiative until this season. With all the photo montages of him golfing or standing awkwardly beside what seems to be a paid child actor, I've decided it's time someone finally called him out on his bullshit.

I tousle my hair at the root for volume and breathe into my palm to check my breath on my walk across the apartment. Pausing in front of the door before I open it, I reach into my bra and tug the flesh of my boobs up, fluffing them like pillows for a bit of extra volume. I force a big showgirl smile.

With the turn of a knob, Brody Parker is standing in my doorway. Before I can say hi, Ivy pops out from around the corner with a long cloud of smoke following her like a shadow. She wedges herself between us, waving her bundle of burning sage all around him from head to toe. Brody looks to me for an explanation.

"They do this every time a cis straight man enters the apartment. It will only take another thirty seconds or so," I say, standing back because smudging makes my eyes water and I'm wearing mascara.

"It's all good. Need me to spin around or lift my arms like this?" Brody stands in a wide stance with his arms overhead like he's getting searched with a metal detector.

"All clear," Ivy says, retreating back to her spot on the couch beside my sister. Tori nods casually to Brody and then glares over at me.

I reciprocate with a be-cool glare and usher Brody into my temporary bedroom. Stepping into what could very well pass as an oddity antique shop, he gasps, spinning a full three-sixty to take it all in. I've been meaning to ask Ivy if we can move some of the animals into storage, but they got really mad at me for buying the wrong type of toilet paper last week and I'm not trying to ruffle any feathers—or tufts of fur.

"Right, the room. There's a couple of things you should know. My sister, Tori, is letting me crash with her for a bit, Ivy is really into taxidermy, and they're lesbians," I say, shutting the door behind us.

"I figured." Brody takes off his puffer jacket. It's a bit much for fall, although it's right at home next to the taxidermized duck on the floor behind the door.

"I mean, some straight people have wolf cuts and wear cargo

pants. Shouldn't assume." I sit down in the chair next to Ivy's work desk to avoid a Rage Room tonsil hockey repeat. I can smell Brody from across the bedroom and now that I know how good he kisses, I'm not sure I can restrain myself.

"And there's a taxidermized beaver holding the lesbian pride flag next to your couch." Brody lies across my bed on his side. He's splayed out like the Creation of Adam. His boxy T-shirt rides up and I can see the space above his waistline. A trail of dark hair runs down his stomach and disappears into his pants.

I feel my finger lifting toward him intuitively. I sit on my hand. "I forgot about Beverly," I say.

"It's good to see you again," he says. "I've got something for you. A thank-you for suggesting the haircut and helping me with my image. It was exactly what my career needed." He smiles and digs his sharp teeth into his pillowy lips as he pulls himself up off the bed. I don't know if I want to face-plant into the divot he's left on my duvet and inhale until I suffocate myself or if I want to pin him down and take a razor to his head, shaving him as bald as Mr. Clean.

Before I have time to decide, he hands me the gift bag I was politely pretending to ignore this whole time. My cheeks flush with the familiar awkwardness I used to feel as a kid opening gifts in front of family and friends. I pre-plaster a fake appreciative smile on my face and dig in, pulling out white tissue paper like a magic trick.

Not even my best fake smile could survive what I pull out of the bottom of the bag. As a way to thank me for helping him land a Bare campaign, he has gifted me a Minnesota Freeze Brody Parker number ninety-one jersey. I lean in and sniff. A new Brody Parker jersey—it's a faint silver lining, but I'll take what I can get.

"It's the new alternative jersey. Technically it's not available to the general public until the New Year, but I pulled some strings. What do you think?" Brody leans in. His eyes widen with his smile.

I force myself to give him a nod of approval. Hopefully he thinks I'm so moved by the gesture that I can't find the right words to thank him. I mean, I am speechless, after all.

"Put it on!" He's sitting on the edge of my bed, watching me intensely—there's nowhere to hide.

My eye twitches under the strain of a forced smile. Is it hot in here? It's as if every dead animal decorating this tiny room is collectively laughing at me, cackling as they watch me panic.

I slowly rise out of my chair and dive headfirst into the jersey. I can't help but gag as I catch a glance of my reflection in the full-length mirror across from me. Chills run up my body like the type of hot flash you get before realizing you're sick with the flu. The Parker name. The Freeze logo. On my body.

"You okay?" His brows squeeze together much like this jersey is around my neck.

With my eyes pressed shut, I dig my nails into my prickling palms. "The Juicy Lucy burger I had for lunch isn't sitting well," I say. After a few deep breaths, I open my eyes.

"Say cheese." Brody snaps a picture with his phone before I'm ready. He takes a few more while I grind my teeth together and pray it ends soon. While he's looking at the pictures, I tug the jersey off and lay it over the back of the chair.

"I thought about getting you one with your last name on it, but then realized I don't know your last name . . . or any of your social media handles. You're tough to find online—and trust me, I went digging." Brody tosses his phone next to his jacket. Together, we sit on the edge of the bed.

"I only use social media for my data business." *And when I stalk you online.*

"You must have a last name though."

"Of course. It's . . ." Panicked, I try to stall. I can't tell him it's Hinckley or he'll figure out who I am with one quick Google search. I look around the room for help. "Ohhh . . . Chair . . ." My eyes dart around the room in search of something else useful. "Clock . . ." I say. Ugh, why are there so many dead animals in here.

"Your last name is Oh Chair Clock?" Brody leans back, his biceps flexing under the weight of his torso.

I'm not going to let him throw me off my game. My plan isn't going to fall apart over a stupid fake last name. "I said it's O'Chairlock. It's Irish." I lean back to lock eyes with him.

"I thought you said you were Indigenous?"

"I am. My mother's side is Irish," I say without hesitation. My mom's side of the family is Scottish, but what's the big difference? In hindsight, her maiden name—Stewart—would have been a better lie. Touching the Parker jersey really disoriented me.

"That's cool. My mom's side of the family is Korean."

My head practically spins like Beetlejuice. This is the first time Brody is willingly bringing up his family.

"Are you two close?" I ask.

Brody's lips press together in a thin line and for a moment I think I've hit a nerve. He runs his palms down the legs of his pants before cracking a half smile my way. "Of course, she's my mom."

"That's great. I know how hard it can be to balance both cultures and still feel like a whole something."

"I'm a whole hockey player," he replies like it's a postgame press conference. "But, yeah. I guess. Sometimes."

My sister bursts into the room. I startle and Brody sits up straight.

"We're headed to lesbian book club," Tori announces.

"We're reading *The Body Keeps the Score*." Ivy pops her head out from behind Tori's shoulder.

"I could have told you that," I say under my breath.

"We wanted to let you know that we will be gone for a few hours and when we return, we will do so very loudly to alert you of our presence. Understood?" Tori says.

"Ugh, gross." I dramatically grimace. Brody looks at me like he does the ref when they make a bad call—offended. *Shit.* "Not you, Brody. I mean, like the thought of my sister hearing us." I struggle to recover from my grimace and jolt up, scrambling to the door. "Okay, bye!" I shout, shutting it before either of us say anything else compromising.

"I got you something else," Brody says.

Haven't I suffered enough? I let go of the doorknob and turn back to him with a smile. "You shouldn't have," I say so pleasantly it's melodic.

"It's kind of cheesy and now I'm second-guessing myself." He reaches into his pocket, pausing with his hand buried deep in his jeans, building the anticipation.

Having realized it's not a giant signed poster of him and his dad for my bedroom wall, I relax a bit. Intrigued even, to see the reveal.

"Now you *have* to show me." I tug on his arm. It's firm beneath the pads of my fingertips. I want to press my nails into his flesh, but I don't know if it's misplaced anger or passion driving me.

Brody pulls out a handful of unique shells from his pocket and a loose piece of gum. "Oops, that's mine," he says, plopping the gum into his mouth. He gently pours the seashells into my open palm.

The shells are practically weightless, but they're heavy in my hand. Each is unique like a snowflake, meticulously hunted and plucked from the sand. I can't believe a guy like Brody can see the beauty in something as spiritual as nature. He saw my face in the sand and I refuse to save his name in my phone.

"I've been thinking about you a lot lately." His fingers tickle up my forearm until he's grasping my elbow. A trail of goose bumps sprouts up in his wake as he inches closer to me. So close that the heat of his body grips my breath. The passion between us is as ironic as it is hot.

It's been a long while since I've been gifted something so thoughtful, and even back then, I didn't have an appropriate reaction. Face-first, Brody leans into me, and I fall back onto the bed. A part of me attempts to slip away from his magnetic pull by retreating to the mattress. But the thought of his body pressed against mine and the weight of him on top of me keeps me in place, hoping he follows. My eyes dance around his campaign-perfect body. There's no need for verbal gratitude. My lips will thank him for the gift in other ways.

Looking up at him I tease, "Why don't you show me what you've been thinking about."

Brody takes the shells from my hand and reaches across me to place them gently on the nightstand. He stays hovered over me while I lie motionless beneath the weight of everything I want him to do to me. With the flick of his eye, his face hardens with an intensity that tells me he's about to take control just like he did in the Rage Room. He runs his hands along the sides of my body and up my arms until he links his fingers with mine, holding them over my head. His hands make hell feel cold.

The more I think about it, the more hooking up with Erik Parker's son feels like the best revenge ever. Where there's passion there's fire, and I'm willing to play with it.

I lick my lips and look up, daring Brody to do something about it. I part my legs, letting him position himself between them. He presses into me and a trembling gasp slips from my mouth. He takes my face in his palm and kisses me. He's soft at first but as I grind against him, his kisses get harder, deeper, rougher.

I pull away long enough to pull Brody's shirt up over his head. His skin is soft to the touch, but his muscles are firm and flexed. It's nothing I haven't seen before. Like everyone else with an internet connection, I've seen the Bare photos. Looking at him now, somehow they don't do him justice. They don't capture the dewy glow of his skin, or the captivating imperfections of the beauty marks and faint hockey-related silvery scars. I want to trace my tongue against every inch. How will his delicate skin feel against mine? I need to know. Propping myself up, I cross my arms at the base of my shirt and tug it off in one swift motion.

Brody immediately runs his hands over my breasts. He kisses along the cup line of my bra while he wraps his arm around my lower back. He pulls me off the bed and we roll over together. While I'm straddling him, he reaches back, and with a quick pinch, my bra falls off. Before I can admit my amazement, I'm on my back again with him kissing down my neck. He's a bit too good at this.

"Your body is incredible," he says, pausing to take my breast in his mouth.

I know this is where I should say something nice back. Like *nice abs*, or *your biceps are huge*, or *how did you get my bra off in 0.001 seconds?* But honestly, he doesn't need to hear it. He's about to find out how I feel about him right now. His skilled tongue teases its way down the length of my torso as he makes his descent. With the snap of his fingers, he unbuttons my pants.

"Is this okay?" he asks.

"Yes." I help him slip them off my hips, sending my underwear to my ankles with them. He presses his hot mouth against my clit and my entire body flexes.

Brody slides a finger inside me, dragging it over my G spot. He found it quicker than he finds the back of the net. I gasp before covering my mouth with my hands just in time to suffocate a moan.

"You're so wet," he says.

"It's a normal amount."

I grab the back of his head and guide his mouth back over my clit. He can shut the hell up. Talking about how wet I am, like I didn't feel his hard dick against my leg.

Brody presses his tongue against me with hard slow motions while he works two fingers inside me. I no longer have control over the part of my brain that doesn't want to give him the satisfaction of a loud orgasm. My feet are tingling, and my legs are shaking as he touches me faster and harder. I press my eyes shut and I moan out in pleasure as I come.

I open my eyes and see the jersey hanging on the chair. I can't help but laugh manically. I'm no stranger to trouble, but this predicament is extra, um, sticky.

As Brody makes his ascent, he's too distracted by the four-inch scar running down my kneecap to notice my euphoric state of delusion.

"ACL?" he asks.

"ACL and MCL."

He grimaces, tracing his finger over the long scar. It's a weird sensation because the incision has no feeling, but everywhere else he touches me feels like an electric charge.

Before he can ask how it happened, I pull him back up toward my face. "Can I ask you something?" His dark eyes are so intense that I lose my train of thought.

"What is it?" He kisses my mouth and I want to chicken out.

Instead, we lie down together and I tuck myself under his arm. "My cousin is hosting this local charity thing next week. It's educational, for students. No pressure, but does that sound like something the Parkers would be interested in attending?" I ask. With my cheek pressed against his bare chest, I run my nails up and down his stomach.

"Educational?"

"Nothing too studious," I assure him.

"I have been meaning to start volunteering more in the Twin Cities." He hums while mulling over the opportunity. "Sure, count me in," he says, sealing the deal with a kiss to my forehead. It's so sweet that the tummyache is instant.

"Oh, they've requested your dad." I hold my breath.

"Ummm, w-well . . ." he stutters and squirms.

"I don't mean to overstep. I told my cousin this was a bad idea, but he said the sponsors were hoping to get Erik Parker."

This *is* a bad idea; I'm about to push him away completely. Slowly, millimeter by millimeter, Brody creates distance between us. Hardly noticeable physically, but emotionally we're on the opposite sides of the bed.

Quickly, I add, "You're more than welcome to tag along with him."

Brody looks unconvinced as he chews on the inside of his cheek. "My dad's schedule is really busy," he says.

"It's only for a couple hours. He can show up, say hi, and take photos with the students. It's easy-peasy good publicity." That's how the saying goes, isn't it? I peek up to see if he's biting.

Brody lets out a long breath. "You know what, that does sound like something he'd be interested in. I'll let him know."

I should be overjoyed, but I feel empty. "You're the best," I say blankly. I'm too tired to force any more fake smiles.

THIRTEEN

Brody

We're already ten minutes late and he's not answering his phone. My dad said he would do this volunteer event with me, didn't he? Technically, he replied to my request by saying, "We need all the good press we can get." That better count because Olivia is counting on us. He's got five more minutes before I call again.

I open my text messages to make sure I'm at the right location. Olivia's directions sent me to the St. Paul Public Library. Parked on the curb out front, I roll my tinted window down. The old brick building is staggering and hard to miss with its grandiose archway entrance. There must be an outdoor rink around back, and I'm guessing the follow-up fan Q&A will be held inside. I'm where I need to be, but my dad is still nowhere in sight. As my thumb hovers over his contact information, I get an incoming text.

DAD:

Golfing with Richard Green. What do you need?

BRODY:

You said you would volunteer with me in St. Paul today.

DAD:

I said we need good press. I'm golfing a PGA course with Hockey Hall of Fame chairman, Dickie Green. Minnesota is your thing. Had you signed in Tampa, you'd be here right now golfing in this charity tournament too. SNN is doing a digital feature on it. That's a lot of eyes.

I toss my phone into the back seat. There's no point in arguing with him; he's on the other side of the country. The disappointment hollows me. I know better and for that reason it's me I'm most disappointed in. It was foolish of me to have thought this could be something I helped him with. Something positive to come from us working together. A reminder why I don't bother.

I pop my trunk and dig around. My old gym bag from summer training is still jammed in the back corner. There's an old pair of skates and gloves tucked inside; they'll do. Ever since the equipment guys messed up on my custom stick order, I've stuck with the accidental lower flex. That happy accident is why I have a few of my old ones stashed in my car. I grab one. Olivia said today would be educational, and someone is going to help teach these kids the hockey basics.

There's no time to linger in disappointment; Olivia is going to think I'm standing her up. I think of her face—I press my eyes closed and picture it. As the image of her gets sharper, the one of my father disintegrates from my memory. With distance, there is safety. With her, there's added protection. After a couple deep breaths, I'm ready to put on an impressive Parker legacy performance for little hockey fans all afternoon.

I spot Olivia near the front desk. She's friendly with the guy behind it. The way she's leaning over the desk into him jerks my jealousy on impulse. He has soft mousy-brown curls that make me miss my old hair. He seems like the type of guy to go out of his way to hold the door open for you. Is that the type of guy Olivia likes, the type to wear a lanyard decorated in enamel pins around his neck? Disappointment sinks in as I realize I'm acting like my dad again. I push the impulsive bravado out of my mind and approach.

Olivia's face lights up when she spots me. Her smile is contagious. She jogs over to me with earnest excitement that bounces through her body. My moment of weakness passes and I don't feel so much like my dad anymore.

"Where's Erik?" She searches behind me.

"About that." I set my gear down on a table near the front entrance.

Her face falls. "Oh, no."

Nervously, I rake my hand up the back of my head. My hair is slowly growing out, and as it does, our team continues to find their footing. "It's all my fault. I accidentally told him the wrong date." Anything for the Parker legacy, even at the expense of my dignity. I reach for her, rubbing her bare arm. "But don't worry. I've got this on my own. Whatever you need, I'm here for you today."

The creases in her forehead deepen. Is she going to cry? Before any tears spill, she strokes her chin. "The public will know he bailed on this event last minute," she says, deep in thought.

"And I'll tell everyone that it was my mistake and that my dad's donating twenty-five thousand to whatever charity today benefits." I said my dad was donating, but it's my money and time that's being offered up today. And it's the only part of today that I don't feel horrible about. I squeeze my clammy fists, really hoping to make lemonade from these lemons my dad threw at me. I can't decipher the expression on Olivia's face; I've never seen her make it before.

Olivia's friend loudly clears his throat. We both turn to find him approaching eagerly.

"Oh!" Olivia composes herself. "This is my cousin Carter," she says.

I reach out to shake his hand and he lunges to grab mine.

"Oh, my Austin," Carter gasps. "It's Brody Parker, in the hot flesh. His hand engulfs mine. The firm shake ascends up my arm—radiating into my shoulder. Dare I be the first to let go or should we stay hand in hand marinating in each other's presence a little while longer? Would it be a crime to linger?" he continues all in one breath. One hand is palm down, pressed into his chest, while the other is holding mine hostage.

Turning to Olivia, I ask, "Is he going to narrate this entire thing?" Overzealous fans are nothing new, but I like to be prepared.

"Carter, drop the purple prose," Olivia says sternly, giving him the side-eye. We all laugh, and for the first time today, I feel like I'm right where I should be.

"Sorry. We don't get many celebrities at the library, besides Stephen Queen." Carter leans in and whispers, "That's my drag name. Not my first choice but Margaret Gotwood caused too much controversy." He rolls his eyes.

"First Friday of every month is the drag queen readings," Olivia interrupts.

"Cool." I look down at my hand, which is still in Carter's grip. "We're still holding hands," I say.

"It's kinda nice. Your hands are soft," he says, looking over to Olivia, who nods in agreement.

"There's a communal bottle of CeraVe in the locker room." I tug my hand back and stick it in my pocket for safekeeping.

"What's all this?" Carter points to my gear on the table. "Raffle items for the library?"

"Sure, I guess," I say, looking back at them. No real loss to me. I get as much free hockey equipment as I need. My gaping mouth is more a result of my confusion. Won't I need them?

"It's just Brody today," Olivia says curtly. Evading my gaze, she fidgets with her necklace. If she only knew the disappointment was mutual.

"*Just* Brody?" Carter snaps. "Olivia, watch your mouth. He's the main character."

"Then we should show him to his stage," she says.

Stage?

Olivia tilts her head toward the small stage at the back of the library. There's a wooden platform and podium tucked in the corner surrounded by plastic chairs. I try to count them all, but I get to about twenty before I'm interrupted.

Carter wiggles his fingers for us to follow. "The original plan was to have your dad discuss the process of writing an autobiography with graduate students from St. Paul University's creative writing program," Carter explains.

Maybe it's a good thing my dad bailed today—he didn't write a word of his bestselling autobiography, *Parker Perfection*.

"Since your dad can't make it today, you'll handle the event solo. You've read the book, right?" he asks as he leads us through the library toward the stage.

"You want *me* to talk about *my dad's* autobiography?" Now

that's something my dad and I actually have in common: I too never read a word of its lies. I wedged the signed copy he sent me under my wobbling patio table and tried to forget about the chapter he "wrote" on fatherhood.

"Ideally, unless there's another book you'd prefer to discuss," Carter says, taken aback by my resistance.

"These students, are they big hockey fans?" I ask, taking extra-long strides to keep up with his enthusiastic strut.

Carter laughs. "You're funny."

It was no joke. Still, I smile politely.

"They're liberal arts majors, so unless there was a Lorde concert during an intermission, they don't care much about men's hockey. They're more interested in the craft," Carter explains.

"Are some of the students film majors?" I ask, pointing to the extensive camera setup across the room.

"Didn't Olivia tell you? The library is streaming this live on all social media channels. We even got the local news station to pick it up." Carter walks up to the podium and fastens a microphone into the stand. Three thumps echo through the library's PA system as he taps his pointer finger against the microphone.

"Live streamed?" I interrupt his mic check. There's that twist in my gut again. I'm out of place. I haven't had an assignment since high school—back when I was handing in absence slips every other day for out-of-state hockey tournaments. "There's no way. I'll get stage fright," I panic.

Carter laughs, which only makes my eyes bulge more. "Are you messing with me right now?" Carter snaps.

We both turn to Olivia. Her breath catches as she asks, "Is that okay, Brody? I know it's a big ask, but I believe in you. You can pick any book—hockey players are notorious bookworms. Slap shots and reading kind of go hand in hand." Her words are riddled with doubt; even she doesn't believe herself. She runs her hand down my forearm. As her fingers tickle from my shoulder to the innards of my wrist, I get goose bumps.

I pull away. "They absolutely do not. Who told you that?"

"You can't bail too," Carter pleads. "We already promoted it online and the students will be here soon."

The last thing I need is a rumor going around that I lack integrity or that I'm some himbo. My dad would kill me if I was at the center of bad press for our family. How did Olivia know I love to read? It's not something I advertise on my social media. In fact, it's something I try to keep secret from the public. I've gone as far to keep it unknown to my teammates—most of which have finally stopped calling me Bro-meo.

I can handle people criticizing my game. I can't have them criticizing this part of me—the part that considers the beach and a book as much an escape from life's stressors as some consider the rink. This is the part my mom nurtured. Whenever I start feeling too much like my dad, I pick up a book and remember that she had some say in the man I am. We don't talk as much as I would like, but the act of reading makes me feel closer to her. It's special to me and I'm not sure how I'm going to share that with a room full of strangers and an internet full of haters.

"No. It's fine," I lie. "It shouldn't be hard for me to find something last minute." I motion to the shelves.

"Great. I'll finish setting up while you look around." Carter goes back to his mic check, while Olivia sets out more chairs.

Soon enough, a roomful of students who look like they would run a Trader Joe's like the Navy settle into their seats. Reusable tote bags litter the floor. Not a single natural hair color in sight. These starving students are going to eat me alive.

With all eyes on me, I take the mic. "My dad's sorry he couldn't be here today, but not as sorry as I was that time I tried reading *Ulysses*," I joke directly into the camera positioned behind the audience. I clear my throat and continue. "I was going to get up here with *The Count of Monte Cristo* and try to impress you all, but I figured we'd go over the hour time slot with our discussion." My stomach knots as not a single laugh is heard. I power through like a bad turnover. "Um. I kept thinking I should pick some pretentious classic novel to discuss, but they've all been made into movies that aren't as good. Instead, I picked *The Westing Game*. Don't laugh. I know it's technically a kids' book, but it was the first book I read that made me feel like I wasn't a child. Like I had some sort of agency in my life."

They're engaged, but I try not to look anyone directly in the eyes, worried it might cause me to get too flustered. Instead, I look at Olivia, who is at the back of the room with her eyes wide and mouth agape. She's hanging on my every word. Her captivation is my encouragement.

I read a bit of the book. Turns out a few others in attendance have fond memories of it as well. We talk about the power of deception and the pitfalls of greed, which I liken to being a professional athlete. You have to present the best version of yourself, even if it feels like a character because you're so hell-bent on achieving that next milestone or signing a bigger contract. A lengthy discussion ensues after a student says the book is a bit unrealistic, that no one would go to such a length for revenge.

Then I take some general questions about my career, and they are surprisingly insightful. No one asks me what the team needs to do to win the next period or if I have six abs or eight. Instead, they ask about my favorite sports autobiography and if I think *The Lord of the Rings* is overrated. The latter takes up most of our discussion because it's not. When someone candidly asks if reading is a way for me to escape a bad game, I give them an honest answer: It is. The whole thing goes surprisingly well.

While Carter wraps up the event, I linger around the library, weaving through shelves. In the children's section, a mom lifts her small son to reach a book off the top shelf. Together, they collect books that will likely be read at bedtimes in the nights to follow.

I think of my mom coming home from work with new books. As I got older, the books got thicker. She used to read them to me, until eventually I was reading them to myself. Hiding them around my teammates, pretending to hate that my mom would sneak books into my bag before I left for tournaments. The memory becomes too much, and the walls start to close in on me.

I rush out the back exit, throwing up my hood as the wind chill bites my ears. There's a swing set in the park adjacent to the library. It's likely the warmest thing to sit on. I close my eyes and make a run for it.

While lost in my memories, Olivia joins on the swing next to me. "When I couldn't find you, I worried Carter had you hostage in the back room. Thought I'd find you two hand in hand rebinding old books and sorting returns," she says.

"Nah. I needed some air." I push my foot against the frozen dirt, swaying the swing back and forth.

"Dust allergy?"

I shake my head. "Growing up, my mom was a librarian. I told you we were close, but that's just what I tell everyone. Truth is, we don't talk much anymore." My heart races; I'm flustered trying to explain the situation without saying too much. "My family is a bit messed up." I kick the ground, freeing a bit of frozen dirt. My toes start to tingle at the tips. I might have been born for the ice, but I still hate the cold.

"I get that," she says. "My family's been pretty messed up since my dad died." She throws her body back and begins to pump her legs. She's quick to get some height.

"I didn't know your dad . . . I didn't know that. I'm sorry."

"Why? It's not your fault—right?" she says. "Just don't tell me you know how I feel because your dog died or anything heinous like that." She laughs, but it seems forced, like a flimsy mask.

"Did he get sick?" I start pumping to catch up with her.

"In a way. Yeah," she says as we swing in unison. "I'm sorry you don't talk to your mom. You seem pretty bummed about it." She looks over at me briefly, but quickly drops her eyes when mine meet hers.

I'm not ready to talk about that. I can't. Or else I run the risk of not only ruining my dad's legacy but sinking my own reputation before I've had the chance to accomplish anything significant in the league. If people know how big an asshole my dad is, they'll think I'm the same. It's like all the articles say, I am his protégé—the second coming.

"Today was fun. It brought me back to some of the highlights of my childhood," I say instead, riding the swaying wave of the swing until the momentum dies.

"Carter would love to have you back anytime. You did so well with those students. You're like really smart." Olivia's smile is warming despite the frigid weather.

"Don't tell me I usually come across as an idiot." I smile out of the corner of my mouth.

"No. You don't. But in all your interviews, you seem . . ." She leans her head against the swing's metal chain, looking up into the gray sky.

"Different?" I interject.

"I was going to say cocky, but sure."

There's a brief pause before we both start to laugh.

"Isn't that what people expect of a Parker?" I say. "Might as well give 'em what they want."

I like talking to Olivia. I like that she doesn't put me on a pedestal. She's taking her time to figure out if her feelings for me are genuine and not throwing herself at me because of who she thinks I am. It has me asking myself, who am I?

"It's hard pretending to be someone you're not. I mean, I think it would be," she says.

"It's easier to give people what they want. Highlight-reel goals and rippling abs. And if I remember correctly, you said something about my postgoal smile." I stick my foot out and nudge hers. The way she looks up at me makes me want to pull her swing closer.

"I think I said that before I knew you, because whatever that sexy literate thing you had going on back there was, it was way more interesting."

"You think I'm interesting?" I know what I'm doing, and I'm sure she does too. It feels good to be seen by her.

"I think you don't let a lot of people see the real you and I'm starting to feel like one of the lucky ones." She nudges my foot back. The whole footsie-on-a-swing-set thing is very elementary, but I can't deny that it's working on me.

"I'm hiding out here because I remembered this thing my mom and I used to do when I was a kid. It's a good memory—a happy one—but it made me really sad." I let my walls down a bit. This girl has been saving my butt, after all. Don't get me wrong, I'm definitely starting to fall for her, but she's also been the best decoy a guy could ask for this season.

"Memories are complicated like that, aren't they?" A gust of wind blows by and she shivers. I take off my scarf and lean over to wrap it around her neck. "What was it?"

"No way." I hop off the swing, ready to run inside.

"Oh, come on," she whines, in a sexy way that almost makes me instantly cave. "I told you my dad died."

"Does that usually work for you?" I delay.

"Dead dad? Yes. Every time. Please, tell me. I'll keep it safe." She zips her lips shut and locks an invisible padlock before tossing away the key.

As much as I want to run away from this intimacy, I can't. I'm frozen in place and it's not the wind chill. It's her charisma and my dependency on it.

"When I was a kid, my mom and I would leave notes for each other. Usually hidden. She would tuck them in books and my hockey gloves and my lunch box. For a while, it became our secret way to communicate." I hold my breath, waiting for her to laugh, or mock me, or worse, come up with some lame "Bro-" nickname.

"That's a really beautiful memory, Brody." She calls me Brody. Not Parker. Not Bro-ontë . . . Just Brody. "Maybe you'll mail her another one, for old times' sake."

"Maybe. Today was definitely inspiring. I'm sure she'd love to hear all about it." Starting to feel a bit too vulnerable, too stripped, I lower my voice and add, "Play your cards right and you might get one too."

"Ah, there he is. I was getting worried you went soft on me." She smirks, rolling her eyes.

I want to tell her they're the most beautiful eyes I've ever seen but it feels painfully cliché. She's looking over, waiting for me to say something, but I'm stuck staring at her like I'm caught in a daydream. I panic and when I open my mouth, "I can't feel my balls anymore. Should we go back inside?" comes out.

"I'll help you warm them under the hand dryer if you want," she says with a contagious smirk, and leads the way back inside. I know better than to try to say something clever back.

FOURTEEN

Olivia

I skate off the ice and slam the door shut behind me. Fresh legs chase the puck into the offensive zone while I slide down to the middle of the bench. With my head between my knees, I suck air, trying to catch my breath. I forgot how long beer league shifts last when your bench is short. My knee aches, despite the ibuprofen I took before the game. The knee injury that sidelined my college career lingers—like most of my invisible wounds.

When Tori asked me to sub on her queer pickup hockey team, the Barn Muckers, I fumbled over an excuse, but ally guilt ultimately got the best of me. She's been so hospitable to me (save for the time she caught me sanitizing my menstrual cup in a communal cooking pot). The least I can do is help her team secure a couple points tonight.

There's no rust on these skates thanks to Chilly's weekly community skating events. Without the weight of the costume dragging me down, I'm free to move as fast as I did when I was playing NCAA DI hockey years ago—though I'm sure my physical therapist would advise against it.

"Everything comes so naturally to you. It's annoying," Tori says, huffing on the bench next to me.

I shrug. Like I said, I take after my dad. It's a blessing and a curse.

"You would score too if you tried lifting your head before you shot the puck. I'm not sure what you expect when you don't look for an opening. And maybe try choking up on your stick a bit." I could go on like this for a while, but commotion along the boards pulls my attention back to the game.

"Why'd you quit again?" She gives me a playful whack with the knob of her stick.

I quit playing competitive hockey after the knee injury, but I gave up on the sport long before that. After my dad died, I failed to find a purpose to get my ass to the rink every day when I had no one to come home to and talk about my games with. It didn't matter how supportive my teammates were, without him, I always felt alone on the ice.

"My knee, remember." I give it a tap.

"Sure, but that still doesn't explain why you're up every night past midnight analyzing numbers. You belong in the game, one way or another."

We lean over the boards, watching our winger battle in the corner with a much larger defense for possession of the puck. The opposition's D slashes their stick across the top of our winger's hands causing her to drop her stick. The ref doesn't make the call.

"If you had one more eye, you'd be a cyclops!" I shout down the ice toward the ref. He turns and gives me a stern look with his lips drawn in a tight line as straight as the black-and-white stripes on his shirt. That's my warning. I've got about one more before he throws me in the box. A two-minute rest doesn't sound like the worst thing ever, but it's not the ref's punishment

I'm worried about. Tori shoots me a much more intimidating look than stripes ever could.

I retreat on the bench. "You're just being nice to me because you want me to play next week too," I say to Tori.

"And . . ."

"And I can't. On top of data analysis, I've got a Freeze game every other day." I squirt water into my mouth and hand her the bottle. I finally landed a new client: a health tech start-up. The contract expires in a month, but paired with my current Chilly workload, I'm suddenly busier than ever.

"How's that going?" she says, removing her glove to take a drink.

"Better since Hammer decided to mix in a save or two every now and then. Team's getting closer to five hundred." Play moves into the neutral zone and I'm on my feet watching them break out into our end.

"I meant how has it been being back there without Dad?" Tori's all eyes on me, but our goalie just made a save I can't ignore. I lean over the boards and bang my stick in support.

"I don't know. I haven't really thought about it. It's fine," I say, wishing she would drop it like the ref is about to do to the puck at the face-off circle.

It was weird being there at first, but my in-game schedule is so jam-packed that I don't really have time to cry in my mask as much as I would like. Quinn would never allow it either. According to the official mascot handbook, grief and sadness are not allowed. Anger in the form of comedic entertainment or crowd riling is, however, encouraged.

We win the face-off. Our defense clears the puck out of our zone and the center skates over, looking to me for a line change.

"Oh, come on! I just got off!" I say as I jump the boards and rush into play.

Ivy saved us a table at the rink's sports bar for postgame drinks. She has a pitcher of Diet Pepsi and a large basket of cheese curds waiting for us at the high-top. With my nose in my phone, I bump into the table and spill a bit of her drink. I've been scrolling social media for days, searching the Parker name in every search engine I can find.

My efforts to ruin Erik's charitable public image resulted in a very successful Brody Parker rebrand. I finish watching the one hundredth fancam of him from the library and I put my phone—screen down—on the table.

Everyone online is saying he's in his *Good Will Hunting* era. Someone said he reminds them of Spencer Reid and another commented that they wouldn't mind giving him some criminal head.

An athlete picks up one children's book and talks in a few complete sentences and the sports world collectively orgasms. The Parkers are being hailed as the smartest family in all of hockey with Erik being the ultimate dad for raising such a well-balanced son. The worst part is that they're right. Brody did that on the fly with no preparation. Everything he said was from the heart. And those fancams are so hot I've got about ten saved on my phone. I hate that my plan was another total failure, even if my consolation prize is as cute as him.

"I'm not normally one to tell a woman to smile, but damn, Liv, I thought the Barn Muckers won?" Ivy's question pulls me out of my thousand-yard stare but isn't enough to save me from my misery.

"We did!" Tori chimes in.

"And you played so good, babe," Ivy coos, and Tori leans in as the two nuzzle their noses together.

"I had my lucky cheerleader in the stands rooting me on," Tori says, cupping Ivy's cheek.

"I can't fucking believe it," I interrupt.

They both slowly turn their heads to me, annoyed, as I ruin another precious moment.

With an audience, I pick up speed. "This family is impenetrable. Erik's untouchable and Brody's indestructible. Everything I try makes them stronger." I dig my elbows into the table and sink my chin into my hands. Defeated like our opponents tonight, I sulk in my loss.

"Oh, good, we're talking about them—*again*." Tori brings the plastic cup to her lips and settles into her chair.

"I go after their good looks—Brody somehow gets hotter. I try to sabotage their game—Brody plays better. I try to destroy their public image—suddenly Brody's a genius," I say.

"For reading?" Ivy asks, trying to keep up.

"It's actually a shocking feat, considering his profession," Tori adds softly.

"All I've done is strengthen the Parker legacy," I complain.

"If I'm being honest, it sounds like Brody is a decent guy," Tori interjects.

I groan. "And Erik? Let me guess, he was harmlessly trying to get the puck away from Dad? Do I need to remind you what happened to our lives after that dirty hit from behind? The Parkers ruined hockey for our entire family—they ruined me."

"If your life is so horrible, why are you the happiest I've seen you in a long time?" Tori's question feels awfully accusatory. My face strains in a scowl and she attempts a hard pivot. "Come on. You're focused and determined at work. You finally came out and played in one of my beer league games. A month ago, you would have never gotten on the ice. I think you're confused because things are finally going well for you."

I hate being wrong but hate when she's right even more. As a kid, adults used to tell Tori she had an old soul. It sounds like a cute thing to say, but it really means that even at a young age, she gave off the vibes of someone living with a deep crippling perfectionism.

Me on the other hand, I'm Nimkiikwe. Thunder Woman. A disruption. Loud and unruly. I wailed through the entirety of my naming ceremony. White people just call me a free spirit. It's what people call girls they think will end up impregnated in their teens or caught in an elaborate embezzlement scheme before they can legally rent a car. I dodged teen pregnancy and Tori's soul continues to prematurely age.

"Maybe my feelings for Brody have evolved," I say through a locked jaw. Getting the words out is like chewing on glass. I avoid Tori's visible reaction. "But his dad is still a monster who has never answered for his irresponsible actions that night." I link my arms across my chest and lean back in my chair while I let my point sink in.

In the last NHL game my dad played, he left the ice on a stretcher. There was no penalty called against Erik Parker. There was no suspension made after the game. No time served. No justice rendered. Despite the lack of reaction from the officials and the league, my dad thought surely Erik would come forward with a spoken or written apology. My dad died waiting for one. I guess you could say my hatred for refs is a trauma response.

"*That* guy's a monster?" Ivy points across the bar to a TV broadcasting *SNN Recap*. Erik Parker is live on location at the grand opening of a new outdoor roller hockey rink in Tampa, Florida. How much money did he have to pay to get them to name it the Parker Park? After he cuts the ribbon, a swarm of small children coast over, huddling around him, adorned with their new Rollerblades and sticks. He throws his arms around them as they cheer for joy.

"There's no greater gift than the gift of hockey," Erik Parker says into the camera before they cut to commercial.

"You'd be easy to scam," I tell Ivy.

"What now, Liv? Are you going to put yourself through another failed attempt to ruin the Parkers or can we all finally move on?" Tori asks.

"I'm done sabotaging," I say. Both Tori and Ivy let out a sigh of relief. "But I'm not done with Brody. Not until he's done with me," I add.

Tori glances to Ivy out of the corner of her hazel eye. The two share a stifled giggle.

"You like Brody Parker." Tori takes great pleasure in announcing the findings of her research. "Olivia loves a Parker," she says, dragging out every word for maximum enjoyment.

I worry she's about to stand up and start chanting it. *Olivia likes Brody Parker!* Over and over until everyone in here joins in. It doesn't matter how old you get; your sibling finding out about your crush is always humiliating.

"I do *not* love a Parker," I quickly shut her down. "I do however have a unique bond with Brody and a suspicion that he's hiding something. He just needs the right person to confide in."

"Like he secretly communicates with the dead?" Ivy's eyes light up.

I glare over at Ivy with confusion. "Like he's hiding a big family secret."

No longer interested, she sits back in her chair, plopping cheese curds into her mouth.

"This has gone too far," Tori says.

"Which is exactly why I can't bail yet. I need to take things to the next level with Brody. Once our relationship is serious, he will tell me the seriously disturbing secrets his family is hiding." I rub my hands together in anticipation.

"I don't know, Liv. Seems like a lot to balance with everything else you've got going on," Tori says, using her serious voice on me. By now, she should know it only makes me want to do something more.

I don't expect Tori to understand what I'm going through. She has everything: a cool apartment, an interesting girlfriend, her dream job. Dad's death didn't alter any of her life plans. She kept on going so seamlessly it made me feel as if we had experienced two different events. Because me on the other hand—I've lost everything, including my way.

The idea I had of myself—of my future—died with him. No one is going to get it back for me. Just like no one was going to help my dad after his injury. I can't let this go because I can't end up like him.

"I could try convincing Brody to join a controversial cult, but he would likely end up making it a trend. At this point, sabotaging the family is pointless, but getting inside the mess is how I'm going to put this to rest," I say. Tori listens with a lifeless expression. "Don't worry about me, I can manage it all. I'll make sure I let Brody down easy. A couple good months together as a couple and then a gentle breakup when the time comes. He's a hockey player. Those boys cycle girls faster than they cycle pucks."

"You need to worry less about revenge and more about rent," Tori says under her breath. She pours herself a refill, finishing off the pitcher's remaining Diet Pepsi.

"Why don't you go enjoy your last night of being single and

talk to the guy who's been staring at you since you sat down?" Ivy tilts her head toward the bar. A defenseman from the other team is sitting at the end of the bar, peering over his shoulder at me. We lock eyes and he smiles before looking away.

"Him?" I ask, pointing. "I absolutely embarrassed him tonight in the second period with a toe drag."

"Unless you're already in love with Brody." Tori smirks from behind the lip of her cup. Her and Ivy giggle.

"What? No! Shut up." I get up from the table, shaking my leaded legs out while I gather a bit of courage to put up with small talk. "You know if you two want some alone time together, just say so."

"We have been!" they shout in unison as I walk away.

I can't deny that the thought of getting closer to Brody is exhilarating. Not having to sabotage him is as relieving as the reluctant plans you made in a moment of gregariousness getting canceled last minute. I can finally settle more into myself and his company. If I'm at ease, so will he be.

I know firsthand the devastating secrets that can fester within families. There's more to Brody's life than the picture-perfect photos of him as a kid with his family standing next to the Stanley Cup. His smile after scoring a goal is infectious, but I've never seen that same smile captured in a Parker family photo. He wants to talk, and whatever he says might be the thing that brings the family legacy crumbling down. I know the feeling of holding your tongue. Being so full of words but sewing your own mouth shut. It's time to remove the stitches.

I slide into the empty seat at the end of the bar.

"Nice goal tonight," the defenseman says. His sandy-blond hair is still wet from his postgame shower. His cheeks are red-hot, but I don't know if he's blushing or fatigued from the game.

"Which one?" I drum my fingers against the bar top. I force the conversation along, knowing Ivy and Tori are watching from across the room.

He laughs. "The toe drag past me by the hash marks immediately comes to mind."

"Shouldn't have been sitting so far back." I look over at him, batting my eyelashes like a pathetic peacock fanning its feathers.

"I saw your face and got mesmerized. Can you blame me?"

"I think that's how Ovechkin scored so many goals too."

"Don't get cocky. You're not as cute as him," he says, and I laugh sincerely. "Trevor," he adds, extending his hand.

"Olivia," I say, shaking it. "Do you always hit on your opponents?" I try to flirt.

He smiles. I'm out of my element. Even worse, I feel like I'm cheating on a test. I look around the room to make sure no one is watching us. They're not; why would they be. We're in a crowded sports bar—everyone is watching the game on the TV screens. The Freeze are in Seattle to take on the Rainiers. I glance up and see Brody skating up to a face-off against Jaylen Jones. The guilt intensifies. I want to hide under a table in case he sees me. Instead, Brody loses the draw.

"Can you believe that guy? Needs to stop with all the modeling and reading and focus on scoring. We so overpaid for him." Trevor's lip curls as he shakes his head in disgust at the TV.

Seems like my sabotage wasn't totally in vain. I look at Trevor. He's got Brody's old signature haircut, except he doesn't pull it off like Brody did. It's wearing him. It makes Trevor look like he has sunglasses on indoors. He's sporting a Freeze sweatshirt he would likely ask Brody to sign had he been present. He has ice packs on his legs like he needs to get the swelling down in time for his shift at whatever pro shop he manages by tomorrow morning. He doesn't hate Brody; he's jealous of him—which is so much worse.

"Let me get your number, and I don't mean jersey," he says.

His lines feel cheesy now. It's forced like everything else about him. I look back at Tori. She and Ivy are watching me, whispering between each other. I begrudgingly hand over my phone and let him create a new contact, knowing full well I'm going to delete his number on the drive home.

FIFTEEN

Brody

I'm right on track with my game-day routine. Binggrae banana milk in hand, I'm on my way into the rink with perfect timing. It's been a game-day tradition since I was a kid. My mom would always toss me one on my way out the door to the rink. "You need the potassium," she would say. My dad hates the flavor, but to me it tastes like childhood.

My fingers are slick from the drink's condensation, and I struggle to pull the metal tab opening on my delicious pregame treat. I should switch to the juice box milks, but these jars are nostalgic to me—they're the ones my mom bought. As I finally peel the green lid off, I round the corner and come crashing into the team's mascot. The creamy liquid spills down the front of my suit, soaking into my tie, my dress shirt, and the lapels of my suit jacket.

"My banana milk," I whine. Craning my head back, I tip the jar over my open mouth, trying to get a drop of my pregame routine on my tongue with no luck. I toss the empty into the trash can nearby.

Chilly's costume is spared. He can't speak—of course—and

instead is flailing his arms around. With his paws pressed together, he pleads to me for what I'm assuming is forgiveness. I'm not going to hold it against him. Being a mascot can't be an easy job. I saw that thing get fired out of a cannon a few seasons ago.

"It's fine," I say, trying to get past him before the social media admin pops out and snaps a picture of the whole ordeal. Our locker room is down the hall; I can see it through his comically large whiskers.

Someone with two pigtails spinning like propellers barrels down the hallway toward us. "Chilly!" she says, coming up behind the lynx. She's quick to grab his hand and drag him out of my way. "On behalf of Chilly, I am very sorry about your suit. Um, good luck tonight. Bye!" Her voice is as shrill as it is winded. She drags him closely behind her and the two disappear around the corner.

I would never admit this out loud, but mascots kind of freak me out. It doesn't help that they don't let us know who's behind the costume. Some of the guys on the team like to try to figure it out, but I'm more focused on keeping as much distance between myself and the team's mascot as possible. For obvious reasons. The phobia likely started as a child when I caught the Tampa Storm's Gator, half dressed and headless, smoking a cigarette in the parking lot after a game when I was five. The magic's been dead since.

By the time I get to the locker room, it's more than half full. Andy and Chef are shooting the shit while they take their time retaping their sticks. Of course, Hammer and Jordy are stretching each other on the floor in the middle of the locker room. I divert my eyes to not provoke them, but I'm not quick enough. Hammer is on top of Jordy helping him stretch his hamstrings when he looks over at me.

"Master Bro-da, you've got something all over your suit," Hammer says, pulling up on the stretch. They switch legs and Jordy throws his other foot over Hammer's shoulder.

"Thanks, I didn't notice." I force a strained smile.

"Really? It's all over you." Jordy points. The two share a laugh at my expense.

My phone vibrates in my pocket before I get a chance to explain sarcasm to the goalies. It's a text from my dad.

DAD:

If we're going to capitalize on all this good press, then we need to be seen together at a game. I'm coming to watch you play and staying through the holidays. SNN already agreed to give me the time off.

BRODY:

Not sure now is the best time. The team is starting to click. Wouldn't want you showing up to watch and making everyone nervous.

I throw in that last part to soften the blow. I'm sure all the guys would love to have Erik Parker in the stands watching them play. Me on the other hand, I know how passionate he gets, and anything less than perfect is an embarrassment.

DAD:

You can't keep me away from your games forever. We're a family and there's an expectation that comes with all the privilege my name has provided you. You're nothing without it.

You're nothing without it. I press my eyes shut and can hear him shouting the words at me. I'm fourteen and he's storming into the locker room during Coach's postgame talk. My throat closes remembering the tug around my neck as he yanked me out into the hallway. He dragged me by the collar of my jersey as people quietly dispersed, his pockets too deep and persona too large to ever question. My bottom lip quivers thinking about him tossing me against the wall, spitting at my feet, and shouting, "You're nothing without the Parker name."

I wanted to die. Even now with years and miles between the feeling, it's still so raw. That was the moment I knew I needed to get away from him if I wanted to make it. At the time, I didn't know if I meant in hockey or life, but that night it felt like both.

Shortly after that incident, I was approved for exceptional-player status through Hockey Canada and was shipped up north to Ontario, Canada, to play hockey. I haven't lived at home since.

I hate reliving that game, but reading those words stunts me right back into a scared teenager. I text back, wanting the shame to end.

BRODY:

I'm grateful, Dad.

DAD:

Then act like it.

The LA Stars are waiting for us out on the ice, and they're known to play great hockey on the road. I stash my phone in my overhead cubby before I'm late for warm-ups. Away and out of sight.

Our game-winning play has been absent since puck drop. This game has progressively slipped away from us with each soft goal and weak turnover. I'm supposed to be playing by example, but instead I can't get my brain to coordinate with my hands. Despite my best efforts to keep my head in the game, I haven't been able to recover since the unfortunate spill on my way into the rink.

I'm minus two with nine hits and counting in the third. If I can't hit the net, I'm going to hit a body. I lay my tenth hit on a Stars skater. As the guy drops to his knees, my hips start to ache. I'm not sure how the fourth-line players keep this pace all season.

Although my phone is far from reach, my dad's words might as well be etched onto the ice. *You're nothing without it.* Despite my hustle all game, I can't outskate his voice. Not wanting to be his prey, I catch my breath on the bench.

I've been tying and retying my skates all game, attempting to get them right. I'm two shifts into the third period and can tell that they still aren't how I like them, an issue that can't wait until a TV time-out.

The lace digs into my fingers, leaving lasting indentations. I heave up with all my might trying to get them tight enough. Through my visor, I glance up at the time left on the clock, and as my eyes travel across the rink and up into the stands, I see my dad sitting directly across from me behind the glass. A chill colder than ice shoots up my spine. I rub my eyes, trying to refocus my vision. He's gone and in his place is a man similar to my dad, but not at all mistakable for him.

"You good, Broski?" Andy says, giving me a nudge. "You look like you saw a ghost."

"Did you see the mouse?" Jordy says with as much excitement as if we scored. He's sitting on his lonely backup goalie chair adjacent to the bench looking like Steve from *Minecraft* in all his bulky equipment. He tosses a piece of candy into his mouth from the stash of treats he keeps tucked in his pads.

"I'm fine. It's all good. I'm great." I try to convince myself like I'm doing one of those affirmation pep talks in the mirror. I finish retying my skates, but it's no use; I have to accept the fact that it's not the skates. It's me. I'm off tonight. I'm playing like that scared fourteen-year-old boy.

I scan the rink again, like a child checking under their bed before crawling in to sleep. My dad's a few rows up behind the goalie, drinking a beer. I keep looking. I find him up in the upper level, standing over me, giving me a look so dirty it's as if he's shooting daggers from his eyes. I turn around and he's sitting right behind the glass eating popcorn. Then an entire row morphs into Erik Parkers like *Animorphs*, angered and yelling, but I can't hear what they're saying because it's all white noise.

Faster than my brain can process, every fan in attendance turns into him. He's beside me on the bench glaring over at me. He's on the ice reffing, pointing at me to get in the penalty box. He's even standing on the bench where Coach should be. They're all speaking in unison. I steady my breathing enough to listen. *You're nothing without it.*

I press my eyes shut and hang my head. My heart thumps in my ears like a marching band. The banana milk spill was unfortunate, but this is devastating. I thought keeping my dad physically away from my games would get him out of my head, but he's still haunting my conscience.

As the panic closes in on me, I'm incredibly grateful for Olivia. I think of her striking deep brown eyes. Her contagious laugh. The way she sticks her fat bottom lip out when she's deep in thought, hovering over a Catan board, plotting her next move. I steady my pulse and squirt water all over my face. The warm thoughts and cold shower snap me back into reality. My dad is gone, and I am up for my next shift.

The second my blades touch ice, this plug from the Stars is glued to my side. We've been on each other all game. Usually, I don't let pigeons like him get under my skin. It's not worth jacking up my hand over a guy who's probably getting sent down to the AHL next week. There's an expectation that I hit a hundred points this season—at least. This game aside, I'm on pace for it.

We go hard into the corner together. His shoulder gets me a bit high and it's my final straw. I snap my head back. "Fuck off!"

"Hockey nepo baby bitch." He spits each word at me and then takes his stick in both hands and cross-checks me across the chest.

The adrenaline coursing through my body acts as a pain blocker so I hardly feel his stick smack across my collarbone. The impact jerks me back, but I'm quick to step up on him. All my frustration comes to a breaking point, and I can't skate away.

I drop my gloves and lunge for his jersey before I can second-guess myself. It's been a while since I've fought anyone, but today has me fired up enough to try. There isn't enough time to be intimidated by the fact that this guy's main purpose on the ice is to throw his body around in a human sacrifice for his team. I know I can hold my own against a fourth-line guy—I have been all night.

Our helmets come loose in the tussle. He gets me in the jaw with a right hook and I taste hot copper. As if I've been hit with the defibrillator, electricity shoots through my body. Charged up, I catch him on the nose with a hard left—southpaw surprise. He wasn't ready for it. They're never ready for a left. He's got tears in his eyes from the blow.

The crowd—which spent the majority of this game quiet and groaning in their seats—is alive. It's louder in here than it was after Andy's lone power-play goal.

This guy—whose name was likely pressed on his jersey last week when he was called up from whatever small-town American minor league team he came from—lands another, this time on my cheekbone. It will be a nice black eye by morning. The tender flesh of my cheek throbs instantly.

I smile because it feels good—nice and wide the way Olivia likes. My teeth coated in blood add to the intensity. The guy looks up at me and his flared face softens. I cock a right this time and catch him in his jaw. He drops before I retrieve my fist. I might be a hockey nepo baby, but I still punch switch.

I fan my arms up and down to the chanting crowd as the ref ushers me off the ice. I'm missing my elbow pads, helmet, stick, gloves, and a few other pieces of equipment, but I don't care. With blood still spilling from my mouth soaking into the collar of my jersey, I can't help but laugh. From the locker room, I watch the guys rally a comeback in the last four minutes of regulation. We sneak out of that game with a three-two victory.

The first thing I do when I leave the locker room is check the results of HockeyFights.com—any fighter who says they don't is lying. So far, the polls have me winning tonight's fight with 99 percent of the vote. I screenshot the results as I'm about to head to the underground parking garage. Before I get too far through the underground concourse, the sound of sneakers squeaking against the slick concrete gets my attention. It's Olivia with a duffel bag slung over her shoulder. She sees me and quickly tosses the bag like a sack of potatoes into a random closet. It crashes down with a heavy thud like my KO tonight.

"What are you doing down here?" I extend my arms to welcome her with a hug. She looks around before walking into my embrace, tense and reluctant, like she's hugging a creepy uncle. Her hair tickles my cheek and I inhale, anticipating a whiff of sugary donuts, but she smells as beachy as ever. She stands in my arms like a plastic doll. This is probably weird for her because technically she's still at work. I don't want to get her in trouble, so I back off quickly, dropping my arms and putting some distance between us.

"Finishing up my shift," she says, petting the ends of her hair.

A couple guys pass by on their way out. We all share a quick mumbling of hellos and goodbyes.

"Fels-Naptha should get that banana milk out of your suit," she says sympathetically, pointing to the now-dried milk stain.

"How do you know it's banana milk?" It's not overly visible now that it's dry. Did the social media admin get a clip of the accident and post it online? I swear they've got hidden cameras rigged all over this place.

Her eyes go wide and her mouth agape, but she quickly fixes her face. "I . . . I . . ." she stutters. "I can smell it from here. Banana is very pungent. It's a Korean drink, right?"

It hurts to nod my head. "I used to drink them as a kid, and it somehow became a part of my pregame routine. Ended up wearing most of the drink tonight." When I take a sip of the Gatorade in hand, the liquid stings the cut inside my mouth. I wince.

"Is that what threw you off tonight?" She touches her cheek in the same spot where I've got a bruise forming, looking at me like you look at a maimed animal—sympathetic and cautious.

"You should see the other guy." I smile, rubbing my thumb along my fat lip.

"I did. I saw the replay of you beating him up." She laughs softly as she tucks a sheet of hair behind her ear. "Didn't know you had that in you."

Our eyes lock in the quiet hallway and she reaches up to touch my cheekbone, but I intercept her hand and grab it firmly in mine. I'm feeling reckless tonight.

Still buzzing with adrenaline, I ask, "Want to get out of here with me?"

Without giving it a second thought, she nods.

SIXTEEN

Olivia

While Brody bangs around the kitchen getting us something to drink, I quietly snoop through his condo. I slink around the living room like a snake, stretching my neck to get a glimpse into his bedroom and bathroom. His place is practically empty. There's a cold echo every time he makes a noise, and his furniture still smells like a warehouse.

While his decor is charmless, his gameplay was full of charisma tonight. But the tension on the ice was nothing compared to my internal struggle beneath the mascot head. That guy was on Brody's ass all night laying dangerously dirty hits, uncalled-for slashes, and one final bush-league cross-check. I wanted to scale the boards, put him in a headlock, and drag him to the penalty box myself. Classless play; someone was bound to get hurt. I'm not one to condone violence, but since the refs weren't going to do anything about it, Brody did what needed to be done. And now so am I: patience, restraint, and observation—until the moment is right.

I'm not learning too much about Brody from my current

surroundings besides the fact that he hasn't lived in this condo very long. The stack of moving boxes piled in the corner tells me he's taking his time to settle in. There are no family photos hung on the wall or heirlooms on display. It's like an apartment showroom in here with his unremarkable stock furniture. While I consider snooping through his bathroom, there's commotion in the kitchen.

Brody's phone starts ringing as the microwave whirs. Gray smoke seeps from the humming appliance and circles the ceiling. The smell of campfire hits my nostrils and I approach to help. With his phone ringing in one hand, Brody throws open the microwave door. A thick cloud of smoke releases into the air as he pulls out a blackened bag of popcorn.

"Great." He drops the steaming bag in the sink. With one hand, he stuffs his now-silent phone into his pocket, and runs the other under the tap.

"Can I help with anything?" I hover on standby.

He smiles for me. "No, no. I've got it all under control." I'm shooed back into the living room while he moves around the kitchen at a frantic pace, searching through his drawers until he pulls out a lighter.

Brody returns with two full wineglasses and a lit candle. As Brody sets my glass down on his coffee table, his phone begins to ring again. Frazzled, he accidentally knocks the glass on its side. The red wine splashes against the mahogany hardwood flooring. Had this place been more furnished, a rug could have been stained. We both scramble to clean it up. By the time I flip the glass upright on the table, it's empty.

"Oh, come on," he says to himself, and rushes back into the kitchen for a towel. On his hands and knees, he's desperate to soak up the spilled wine. Nothing is ruined, but his body is tense and there's no sense of relief once the mess is cleaned. "I didn't get it on you, did I?" He looks me over, ready to rub me down with the dirty dishrag.

I grab his hand and pull him onto the couch beside me. "What's going on with you? You didn't play badly enough to warrant a full mental breakdown. In fact, I'd say your little fight at the end of the game is what sparked your teammates to get their heads out of their asses and shoot the damn puck. You were kind of responsible for that win even from the locker room." I rub his shoulder, trying to ease some of the tension.

"You really catch a lot of the game from Five-Hole Donuts, don't you?" He lets go of the rag. "It's not the game that's throwing me off. It's a text I got before I went out on the ice." He pinches the bridge of his nose. On cue, his phone rings, and he pulls it out of his pocket. Before I can get a look at the name on the screen, he ignores the call. To occupy his trembling hands, he pours half his wineglass into my empty one.

"Seems important."

"It's not. It's just my dad."

"Oh, no. Is everything okay with him?" I try to swallow my eagerness with a sip of wine.

I study Brody. Watching like I do when he's on the ice. Looking for any weakness, any bad habits. He's worn tonight—in the face, but also in spirit. He stares in a trance, with his wineglass just shy of touching his lips. It's a familiar feeling. In hockey, we call it a bad bounce and I can't stand to see him fumble any longer.

"What do you normally do after a bad game?" I ask, changing the subject.

"Sulk . . . Read . . . Play video games . . ." He glances down at the TV console stacked with every gaming system available.

"Fire it up then. What are we playing?" I grab a controller off the coffee table and get comfortable on his couch.

"Really?" He sets his drink down.

"Scared to lose?" I ask playfully.

"Look at my face, Olivia." He points to the already darkening bruises he refuses to ice. His cheek is pink and puffy, and his lip is swollen red. His injuries aren't bad enough to make me wince, but he looks vulnerable enough that I want to kiss them better. "Do I look scared to lose?" His eyes narrow.

We spend the next hour and a half working our way through all his favorite games. What his new apartment lacks in homey decorative touches it makes up for in gaming setup: dedicated shelving for multiple gaming consoles, custom-made controllers organized by color, and a state-of-the-art sound system to transport us right into the action. Finally, after beating him in several *Mario Kart* races, Brody convinces me to play *EA SPORTS NHL 26*. Hoping to cheer him up, I let him take the first couple games.

"One more—winner takes all," he says.

"What's the wager?" I might have blown those first couple games on purpose, but I can't turn off my competitive side completely. There's no off switch on the Hinckley genetics.

"Bragging rights, obviously," he says, getting the next game ready.

"Boring." I pretend to yawn.

"Fine. Since you're the life of the party, what's your wild idea?"

"Loser has to do a striptease." It was the first suggestion that popped into my mind. I honestly said it as a joke, but when Brody smiles his signature cocky grin and I see those beautiful canines, I realize that I have to try to win this game.

Brody takes a deep breath and stretches his neck side to side. "My biggest game tonight. You're on." He extends his hand and we shake on it.

I blurt out a nervous laugh as I avert my eyes down toward my controller. Looking into Brody's eyes is like staring at the sun. I know I shouldn't, but his irresistible glow sucks me in, and I risk the irreversible damage. My cheeks heat up and turn the same color as the tiny drop of wine pooling at the bottom of his empty glass. I press Start.

He might be a playable character in the video game, but while he's been practicing on ice, I've been practicing with the controller in hand. The poor guy never stood a chance.

He drops the controller on the coffee table and throws his head back with a long defeated exhale. "I knew you were throwing games on purpose."

"Nothing anyone hasn't seen before," I say, sitting back on the couch with my freshly topped-off wineglass in hand, ready to bear witness to his second performance of the night.

"Should I put on some music? Maybe some Hozier?"

"Are you trying to make me cry?"

"You're right." He fumbles with his phone until The Weeknd is blaring through his apartment. "Is this okay?" He sets his phone down. The tension is as hot as the song selection.

"Less beaking, more streaking." I've got to keep things silly or else I'm going to blush.

"That's not helping."

"Quit stallin', get those pants a fallin'."

"Are you done?"

"Time's wasted, get naked," I say, practically shouting over the music. He gives me an emotionless glare—unamused . . . or nervous. "I'm done," I add.

Brody starts swaying to the bass and thrusting his hips into the open space around him. He'd make an excellent Hula-Hooper. The sight of it causes me to do a spit take with a mouth full of wine. It burns coming out my nose. I throw my head back in an unfiltered cackle. As I refocus on Brody and his moves, I'm hit with the dizzying realization of how drunk I feel from the glass I had while we played video games.

He stops with the cheesy *Magic Mike* moves and rips his shirt off over his head with one swift tug. My laughter evaporates. He takes a step toward me and starts unbuttoning his pants. I swallow what's left of the wine in my mouth with a hard gulp. The back of my throat burns, but I hardly notice.

Brody props his leg up on the coffee table, opening himself up to me in new and exciting ways. I'm mesmerized by the sharp cuts of his body. His muscles flex with every thrust. Revenge has never been so sexy. Or smelly—that campfire smell again. I look to the kitchen but there's no gray smoke circling the ceiling. The popcorn bag was tossed out in the hall almost two hours ago, but the smell is undoubtedly back.

A high falsetto shriek from Brody pulls my attention back to his bulbous crotch. He's no longer posing sexily or trying to seduce me, because his pants caught fire in the lit candle and the flames are burning up his leg. He's stomping his legs around like he's *Dance Dance Revolution*ing for his life, trying to extinguish the flames.

"What do I do? What do I do?" he says.

While he burns, I do exactly what you're supposed to do in an emergency: I scream and panic. With a throw pillow in hand, I begin beating him senseless. Most of my blows hit Brody in the face. "I don't know!" I shout. "What's the saying, drop it like it's hot?"

"Stop with the pillow!" he says, absorbing blows with his already-bruised face.

I look down at my hands and find that the pillow has now caught flame like a torch. *Is everything in this house soaked with gasoline?* I frantically toss it onto the couch, where the flame grows, using the cushions as kindling. Brody stiff-arms me out of the way and waddles over to the kitchen sink like a pirate with a wooden leg.

The fire alarm in his apartment starts beeping loudly while we both harmonize our screams with its piercing wail. Water shoots out of the ceiling sprinklers in a ferocious downpour. I'm positioned directly under a nozzle with my head tipped back and my mouth open. A sensation similar to being waterboarded occurs as the water shoots down onto my face and into the back of my throat. I begin to choke violently. Through blurred vision, I see Brody reach the sink and extend a leg up.

I'm quickly at his side, rushing to help him with the faucet. The water extinguishes his leg in seconds with a loud sizzle similar to bacon on a hot frying pan. Brody lets out a moan of relief, the type of sound I thought we were heading toward when he started dancing.

He winces, pressing his eyes shut. "Is it bad?"

I look around his apartment. The ceiling is still raining down on us and everything is soaked. His entertainment system is destroyed, our wineglasses are shattered, and broken glass is sprawled across the living room. Puddles form on the hardwood floors. There's a hole burnt in the middle of Brody's coffee table and half his couch is melted. It looks like we're in the middle of a natural disaster.

"Noooo," I lie. "I think if you get a really big fan in here and add a bit of paint, your apartment will look good as new." Water beads down my face, but it's the least of my concern.

"No, my leg! How does my leg look?" Brody reaches to pull up his pant leg, but it's melted off. He winces.

I lean in, holding my breath. His leg is hairless, and his ankle is already bubbling into a welt. I pull back. "We should go to the hospital."

"It can't be that bad."

I place a gentle hand on his shoulder. "I think you're in shock."

"Please, I'm a hockey player. I'm fine." Brody brushes my hand off and leans in for a look. A shriek louder than the beeping alarm projects from his mouth, and his eyes roll into the back of his head. He goes ghost white in the face before finally toppling over like a rag doll into my arms.

SEVENTEEN

Brody

I slowly come to, dazed as I regain consciousness with each forceful blink. The fire alarm stings my ears like an unwelcome alarm clock. Friction heats my back as baseboards pass by my line of vision. *Am I being dragged through a doorway?*

"Oh, no. No. No. No. What am I going to do? What am I going to do?" The voice in front of me whimpers. "Tori is *so* not going to believe this was an accident."

Like a sled dog, Olivia pulls me down the hall by my good foot. We're headed for the stairs. I prop up before I'm dragged down five flights.

"Did I faint?" I ask, anchoring myself on the wall. Olivia lets go of my leg and it drops like a log.

"Brody! You're alive!" she cries out, short of breath. She falls to her knees and leans over me, water from her hair dripping on my face. A couple people evacuating the building step over us on their way out. I prop myself against the wall. Olivia didn't get too far with me; we're a few feet from my apartment door. "I'm going to grab our jackets and shoes, but then we should get out of here," she adds.

Sirens cry in the distance as she helps me to my feet, but I'm able to get myself down the stairs and out of the building unassisted. Outside, a fleet of emergency service vehicles pull up in front of the apartment building. With my pant leg singed off and both of us soaked through like a pair of wet dogs, discretion has gone up in smoke. The entire building's residents reluctantly loiter around in the cold dark street, perturbed by the midnight disruption.

I duck my head. Olivia gives a dramatic and performative recap of the evening's events to the firefighters.

"We don't need to know about the striptease. The cause of the fire will suffice," the firefighter says.

I apologize profusely for my fire-safety negligence, but he tells me it's okay. "This is the number one cause of apartment fires," he says.

"Candles?" I ask.

"No, foreplay mishaps."

Great, I'm a foreplay failure.

Once things are settled with my unhabitable apartment unit, a paramedic takes me to the back of an ambulance to examine the sharp throbbing pain at my ankle. I avoid looking at the burn while I sit at the edge of the open ambulance's back door. The sight of my injury knocked me on my ass last time, and I don't think I'll get another chance at foreplay redemption if I pass out into Olivia's lap again.

As the medic takes a look at my ankle, I realize that tonight's sequence of events is much more embarrassing than painful. The medic says it's a small second-degree burn and if bandaged properly with cream, I shouldn't miss any hockey games. No need for a trip to the ER. I look for myself; there's nothing more than a tiny burn bubble the size of a silver dollar on the ankle. My pants and socks bought me a lot of burn time and protected my skin from any serious wounds that would keep me off the ice.

Wrapped in foil emergency blankets like two burritos, Olivia and I walk across the intersection to the pharmacy to fill my burn-cream prescription. Having the team doctor on speed dial is one of the many perks of being a professional athlete. She was able to call in a prescription for me in minutes. Hopefully by the time it's filled I'll have figured out where I'm going to live until my apartment dries out.

While we wait for the pharmacist to return with my cream, I pull my phone out of my back pocket along with my soggy disfigured wallet. I text Chef and ignore the three missed call notifications from my dad, just as I did when they were incoming. As I press Send on my late U up? text to my night-owl teammate, my mom is calling.

My stomach sinks. She only calls when it's an emergency, which means an aging relative is ill, someone has died, or there's immediate Parker family drama. Either way I brace myself as I answer.

I'm not greeted by her soft voice. Instead, it's my dad's bark. Disappointment swallows me up, when I should be feeling a rush of relief that nothing bad happened to a family member. I clear my throat. "Hey, Dad." My voice is so calm that I almost trick myself into believing everything is under control. If he could see me now, he'd have a lot to say. As if I weren't feeling guilty enough about tonight, now I feel flooded with it.

"So, you'll answer Mom's call but not mine? Why haven't you been answering your phone or replying to my texts?" He shouts when he's been drinking. I turn down the volume on my phone, but it doesn't do much to muffle his bellowing voice.

I look over at Olivia, who is staring up at the ceiling, doing her best to pretend she can't hear us.

"I'm hanging out with Olivia." I realize this puts me in a tricky situation. Now she knows that I've talked about her to my dad, which makes things between us a bit more serious than I think they presently are. On the other hand, if I don't give him a good excuse as to why I'm dodging his calls, he'll start reaming me out over tonight's game.

"You're always hanging out with Olivia." I can hear his eyes roll through the phone.

Olivia is an arm's distance away, pretending to read vitamin labels. Still, I cup my mouth to the phone and in a low voice say, "Can I call you tomorrow?"

"No," he cuts me off. "We need to talk about tonight's game. There's no reason a Parker should be fighting a fourth-line nobody. I don't care what excuse you have this time, I'm coming out there for Christmas break to keep an eye on you. I'm worried you're not taking this seriously."

"I take hockey very seriously, which is why Christmas isn't a good time for you to come visit." My body tenses as if my muscles could flex into human armor.

"You're not taking my bid to get into the Hall of Fame seriously," he huffs. "What is it now? Why isn't Christmas a good time?"

"Why?" I repeat, stalling for an excuse.

Once I turned eighteen, I was drafted into the NHL and moved to Washington, DC, to play for the Federals. For a few years, I came home for holidays, but who would want to spend their Christmas break watching game tape with a dad pointing out every little thing they did wrong? Eventually, I made Dad come to me (and he did as often as he could). It was self-preservation—I had to stop visiting or else he was going to destroy what was left of my self-confidence.

Before I can make up an excuse that doesn't involve an

accidental-arson confession, the pharmacist comes back with a tiny white paper bag in hand. "I've got your prescription ready . . ." She trails off once she notices my phone pressed to my ear.

Now I'm being rude to my date, my dad, and the pharmacist. Overwhelmed with limited options, I give her the one-minute gesture with my finger. For once, my dad is silent.

"Instruction for your prescription is in the bag," she says, setting it down on the counter. "Hope you feel better. Go Freeze!" she cheers with an enthusiastic fist pump before disappearing again.

The silence is short-lived. "Prescription? What's going on over there? You better not miss any games."

Olivia clears her throat, catching my attention. She motions to me with an open palm, gesturing to the phone pressed against my cheek. There's no way I'm handing it to her. I shake my head no.

In a low threatening voice, she says, "Give me the phone." While I stare at her perplexed, she says softly, "Trust me."

I slowly hand it over like it's a live bomb. My dad's shrill voice—spiraling to conclusions—continues to project into the store.

"Hi, Mr. Parker, it's Olivia." She grabs a seat on a nearby chair in the waiting area. "I want to assure you that Brody is in top shape. We're here to fill his prescription for ß2-agonists to help increase his power and stamina so he can be quicker on the ice. All the best in the league are doing it, and we can't have Brody falling behind in any aspect of his game, now can we?"

She's lying for me, but there's no way he's going to buy the whole I'm-getting-an-inhaler-at-a-quarter-past-midnight bit. I sit next to her, holding my breath and leaning into the phone so I can listen closely.

Suddenly, my dad's voice isn't so big and mean. "That's great. I think I read an article about that recently. It's big in the NFL too," he says, not wanting to admit he has no clue what she's talking about.

"Totally, I knew you would agree." Olivia leans back in her chair, kicking her leg up and crossing it over the other as if this is some chitchat with a friend. "And, Mr. Parker, I'm sorry for stealing Brody away from you this Christmas, but my dad passed during the holiday season when I was a teen, and I can't face the family festivities without my boyfriend by my side. Plus, he plans to get in extra ice time and work on improving his stick handling." She juts out her bottom lip. With her whole body in character, she sells the lie like a skilled salesman.

I stop eavesdropping after that. In fact, I'm not sure I can hear anything at all. *Is that ringing in my ears? Did she say boyfriend?* More importantly, why would she help me get out of a toxic Christmas visit with my dad?

The calls ends and Olivia hands back my phone. "You didn't have to do that," I say, though my lie is hardly as convincing as hers.

"Yes, I did. You should have seen your face. You were in more shock talking to your dad than you were when your leg was lit up like a birthday cake." She looks down at my exposed shin and the pant leg burnt into Bermudas like I'm trying to start a new fashion trend.

Becoming self-conscious of how unhinged I look, I ditch my foil blanket. "So . . . I'm your boyfriend?" I let the question roll off my tongue. If I forced myself to be any more laid-back about the term, I'd be horizontal.

She smirks and laughs to herself. "Don't worry, I know it's a bit early to make anything between us official just yet, but if it helps get you out of a visit, you can be whoever you want."

What does that mean? Wait a minute—who cares. She basically answered all my prayers: She's Erik Parker repellant. This is the first time I've ever gotten my hands on some and after the scary hallucinations during tonight's game, I'm using it.

"Thanks," I tell her. "My relationship with my dad is really complicated. No one knows this, but I came to Minnesota to get some distance from him. My dad knows no boundaries—except when it comes to you."

"Happy to help." Up from her seat, Olivia grabs the medical supplies from my hands and bends down, beginning to bandage up my leg. I think about stopping her—assuring her she's done enough for me tonight—but after all we've been through, this intimacy is hardly inappropriate.

"Your dad passing around the holidays must have been difficult. I know how important Christmas can be for some families." I avoid looking down at the red splotchy burn on my ankle by focusing on her face. Even with smudged makeup and disheveled hair, she looks angelic.

"I lied." She stops wrapping briefly to look up at me with her signature sexy smirk. "Wow, I was really convincing, wasn't I? My dad died in the spring—April Fool's Day. Sick bastard had to get in one last bad dad joke."

My mouth falls open. "You lied about your dead dad?"

"Please, the least I can do is exploit it for a good excuse every now and then. It's what he would have wanted."

"Was he as good an actor as you are?"

She sits back down next to me and thinks about her answer. "Yeah," she says as a smile overtakes her face. "He would make similar calls to the office at my school, telling them I had a dentist appointment. We would grab butter burgers instead. I can't believe the secretaries never caught on—I was at the dentist weekly."

"My mom never let me skip school. Except this one time when a famous Korean author did a reading and signing at her library. It was a big deal. I got her autograph and everything." I don't notice I'm smiling until my cheeks strain.

"Do you still have it?"

I nod. If I dwell too long on this memory, I'll be angry for days. Instead, I push it aside, back where I keep all my memories with Mom. Compartmentalized with my few and fading good childhood moments.

"You should come to the team's holiday party with me," I blurt out.

Olivia fusses with her hair, tucking it behind her ears. "No, I couldn't impose," she says, making a face. "You should bond with your team or whatever you guys call all the homoerotic behavior you can't stop doing to each other."

"It is a lot of spanking. I know," I say, picturing it. I shake my head and get back on topic. "No, really, you should come. Everyone wants to pick your brain about Catan strategy."

She likes that compliment. I can tell by the way she's fighting her smile.

"Okay. I'll go with you," she concedes as easily as I've ever seen her. "And if you ever want to use me as an excuse to keep your dad away, by all means, inflate our relationship as much as you need."

"You don't mean that. You just feel bad about my leg."

"I don't. You'll have a cool scar and an even funnier story."

My cheeks burn up with embarrassment. I am never doing a striptease again—I'll leave that to the professionals. I hide my face in my hands.

"A story that I will take to my grave," she adds, resting her hand on my leg.

"Never mind Hot Hands, I think I invented Hot Leg tonight."

Olivia cackles at my joke, and it's the most euphoric feeling in the world. "Look at us!" She toggles her finger between the two of us. "We look like we were rescued from a deserted island." She laughs so hard she begins to tear up.

"At least we got a fire started."

We both fold over into a disruptive fit of laughter in the middle of the night, in an empty pharmacy.

EIGHTEEN

Olivia

I let Brody lead me through the arena, pretending I don't know how to get to ice level on my own. When he points out the mascot locker room during his guided tour, I act intrigued.

For the Freeze's Christmas party, the large ice-level suite is adorned with festive holiday decorations. Hot food sits buffet-style against the far wall while drinks are being served by food service employees. Toddlers run around everywhere, while older kids play a lively game of mini sticks in the corner of the room. A grandiose green velvet chair with gold detailing staged near the center of the room awaits Santa's visit—or Liberace's.

We grab some food and take our seat at one of the round tables. Realizing some red wine would pair nicely with my meal, I excuse myself to find one of the employees helping guests with beverages.

I find someone bent over, fishing through a cabinet of plastic cups. "Excuse me, could I please get a glass?" I ask. When they turn around my face drops. "Quinn?" I gasp.

"Finally." She releases a loud pent-up sigh. "I'm so happy to see you. We're short-staffed." She shoves two full wine bottles into my empty hands. "Start serving these."

Before I can get a word in, Brody's at my side. "Damn, you drink more than Belly," he notes, eyeing up my full hands.

I stutter—babbling as if my tongue is swollen.

Brody laughs. "I'm kidding. It's nice of you to help the staff. You're really thoughtful. That's why you're my date and Belly isn't."

I blush and pray Quinn doesn't notice. She gives me a pensive glare. Quinn notices everything—it's her job.

Brody places his hand on the small of my back and says, "I've got to go help the boys with something, but I'll be right back."

My body goes rigid. "Sure," I say to him while maintaining intense eye contact with Quinn, who is looking back at me like she's determined to win the staring contest.

As soon as Brody is out of earshot, Quinn snaps, "You're here with Brody!" She's got a crazy look in her eye—even crazier than Chilly's.

"Shhh." I bring my finger to my mouth. "Be cool." I drop the bottles off on a nearby counter.

"The team's new star forward, really? What, was a secret affair with the coach not an option?" Her tone is as sarcastic as it is disappointed.

I know better than to answer her, so I go mute like I'm muffled by a mascot head covering.

"I can't believe I thought you were here to pick up the extra hours." She juggles a stack of disposable cups and a wine bottle in one hand while fanning her flush face with the other. I haven't seen her this stressed since I tried high-fiving the kid with two broken arms during a mascot hospital appearance.

"What extra hours?" I ask.

"The organization needed people to work this event. Didn't

you get the email?" Quinn says, annoyed. She doesn't pause for my answer, because she already knows the truth. "Girl, you've got to start checking your work email."

"I've been busy." I look over my shoulder. There's enough chaos in the room that no one seems to notice I'm still missing from my seat.

"I can see that," she says. Her smug look turns into one of sheer terror in a quick revelation. Hand to heart, she gasps. "He doesn't know, does he?"

A kid running by flailing around a mini stick bashes it into my shin. I wince and quickly jump out of the way as more plow through the area. Parents shout at their kids to "watch out." I assure them I'm fine. It's a level of attention that makes Quinn and me duck. We quiet our voices and discreetly huddle against the buffet's back wall. I begin picking at the selection of desserts, intentionally lingering on a sugary decision.

"No. He doesn't know our secret. Chilly's true identity is safe," I whisper.

Quinn hovers beside me. Instead of pretending to adjust her cups for the fiftieth time, she begins slowly uncorking a corkless wine bottle. "Still. This is so bad."

"Is it really? I've yet to fully read the handbook." I plop a tiny tree-shaped sugar cookie into my mouth. The green sprinkles crunch between my teeth as the cookie dissolves on my tongue.

"You don't say," she mocks me. "Besides the obvious code of conduct violation, do I need to worry about this?"

The corkscrew sticks out of her knuckles like Wolverine, and I gulp down what's left of my Christmas treat. I've come too far to get caught—especially like this.

"What? No. He'll never know I was the interim mascot, promise." I'm not trying to get fired tonight. The extra money from this job is keeping me afloat while I neglect my struggling freelance business to hang out with Brody. Plus, Quinn and I have a good game-day flow going. It would be a waste to disrupt it mid-season.

She tucks her weapon back into the apron pocket. "You're a very forgiving person."

"We shouldn't talk about this here."

"Just don't let it interfere with the job. Or the team."

My shoulders slump. "I won't."

Quinn turns around and leans against the buffet table, laughing to herself. "I can't believe Brody Parker is in love with the team's mascot."

For the first time, I don't flinch when I hear his full name. "Definitely not. We're just hanging out. It's not like that."

"Bitch please," she says with a confidence I wish I had. "Don't insult me. I'm a mascot enthusiast. I can read people like a psychic. I knew the second he touched you, and the way he's looking at you right now confirms it—you're hockey's Romeo and Juliet."

I lift my head to see what she's looking at. Brody's back in the room and he's looking at me. He winks from across the room. Shockingly, I don't get the ick. Instead, I get giddy and practically giggle to myself.

"Gross. Get a room," she scoffs. "NOT the mascot locker room! And stop talking to me because we're being incredibly suspicious." Quinn's raspy voice pulls me out of Brody's trance. She gives me a firm shove, tossing me a couple steps away.

Brody circles the room, herding all the children over to the large chair. He looks so cute tonight in his hunter-green knit holiday sweater and shaggy hair. His buzz cut has grown out to the perfect length—long enough to run my fingers through, but still short enough to show off his face. And it's a face worth seeing. Tingles swarm through my extremities like pins and needles before settling into the pit of my stomach. I eat another cookie and try to ignore it.

Bells start ringing melodically and two elves enter the room, cheerfully hopping around. It's Hammer and Jordy in green-and-white elf costumes complete with curly shoes adorned with tiny bells. Chef dressed convincingly as Santa follows.

Once the children get wind of the large sack he has thrown over his shoulder, they all erupt into cheers like the crowd at a winning game. Santa finds his seat, and Hammer and Jordy begin an impressively choreographed dance routine in front of Old Saint Nick. With the kids all seated, Brody sneaks next to me.

"Were you back there helping them choreograph this little jester jig?" I ask.

"No, this performance is courtesy of the very talented Freeze Ice Girls, but I did warn them to stay away from open flames."

One of the kids stands up and accusingly points to Santa, saying, "Where's your big belly Santa?" The room erupts with laughter.

Chef quickly says in a forced deep tone, "Ho ho ho, Santa is on Ozempic."

A little girl speaks up. "My mommy lost her belly when she pushed my brother out of her vagina. I watched it happen in a pool in our living room. Did a baby come out of your vagina, Santa?"

The little boy on the end picking his nose says, "I thought babies came from the hospital?"

"Okay . . . How 'bout some presents?" Chef opens his sack and the kids all cheer.

Once Santa leaves, everyone laces up their skates for a public skate on Freeze ice. I don't tell Brody I played hockey; instead, I let him tie my rental skates and give me a verbal skating lesson.

"We'll go slow, and I'll be right by your side. I won't let you fall." He extends a hand, offering to be my balance, and promises to not let go until I feel comfortable on my own.

As sweet as he's being, there's a major oversight on his part: Brody is forgetting he's no longer living in the Sunshine State; he's in the state of hockey. A place where as soon as you learn to walk someone is strapping skates on your feet. Be it on a rink or a frozen pond, skating is a way of life.

"Thanks," I say, standing up and heading out on the ice without him.

He watches me take a few long graceful strides with bewilderment. "You can skate?" he says to me from the bench, his voice growing quieter the farther away I glide.

I look over my shoulder to find he's caught up to me. "I can shoot too," I say cockily.

Brody grabs some sticks off the bench and tosses a few pucks over the boards while I get a warm-up lap in. All the young kids have been carried off home to bed and the significant others already got their photo ops and have moved on to the open bar. There's a lot of ice to play with.

Brody hands me a stick. I stickhandle the puck for a bit—forehand, then backhand. We pass the puck back and forth as we head down center ice. As I near the top of the circle, I wind up and release a loaded slap shot. *Ping*—the puck vibrates against the net's crossbar and slices into the back of the netting. Bar down. Brody's stick bangs against the ice, cheering me on.

"What are you doing selling mini donuts with a clapper like that?" He comes sliding in beside me, spraying my ankles with snow as he stops.

I bashfully drop my head and fish the puck out of the back of the net. He steals the puck off my stick and stickhandles it away from my reach.

"Seriously. Who taught you to shoot and can they teach me?" he asks.

"My dad." With some force, I take the puck back and he lets me keep it.

"You looking for a team because we're weak on the PK."

I rip another shot off, picking the top right corner. "Oh, I know. I watched your game last night." I pick up another loose puck and circle around the net, but before I can get into position for a shot, Brody steals it off my blade and backhands it in. Top corner, bar down.

And cue the cocky smile in three, two . . . There it is.

"Seriously, did you play in college or something?" He's persistent with a stick in hand.

I can't get into the details of my failed hockey career because it could blow my cover, so I think on my feet—or rather, my skates. "Remember my gruesome knee?" I say. "Now I only play when my sister's team is desperate for skaters. That, and when I have the opportunity to impress someone cute."

"Are you talking about Hammer and Jordy?" He points across the rink where the two elves are watching us. They both start banging against the glass and flash a couple thumbs-ups our way. A puck is shot wide and slaps against the glass right where they stand. Like robots, neither flinch.

"Sorry!" a girl shouts.

At the other end of the rink, a pair of young girls are taking turns lining up pucks and firing them into the net. They can't be more than twelve years old. The natural talent is there, but they aren't following through on their shots properly and most are hitting the glass, too high and wide. I ditch Brody to help them. Growing up, I worked a lot of hockey camps to offset the cost of registration.

Mom says helping me with hockey gave Dad his purpose

back. That it gave him the kick in the ass he needed to forgive the game. At least one of us could. My dad taught me everything I know about the sport, about being a competitor and teammate. Even if he couldn't demonstrate it out on the ice with me, he would break the game down strategically on a piece of paper. The symptoms of his disease eventually left him homebound and hollowed, but living inside me is everything he used to know about the greatest sport in the world. A few of those tips will have these girls hitting net consistently.

Brody watches from afar for a while, but skates over once we wave him in for a friendly game of two on two. Eventually, we outskate our welcome and the equipment manager yells at his daughters that it's time to head home. Brody and I slowly make our way off the ice behind them.

"What can't you do?" he says.

His beaming smile fills me with anything but pride. I duck my head and skate off the ice, hoping to leave the shame in the back of the net with a handful of pucks.

NINETEEN

Olivia

Studs is packed. I don't normally spend my New Year's Eve at a lesbian bar third-wheeling with Tori and Ivy, but it was the only place I could watch the Freeze game without some drunk guy mansplaining hockey to me. With two points in tow, Brody and the team are en route back to the Cities to celebrate ending the year with a winning record.

"Let's go around the table and share our resolutions," Ivy says cheerfully. The sparkling fringe draping off her shoulders shimmies as she talks. "I'll start. As you both know, this was a successful year for my taxidermy business thanks to my boy-band rabbits—Hare-y Styles was a bestseller. Next year, I have my sights set even higher with drag queen rats. My working title is RatPaul's Rat Race. My resolution is to be the top taxidermy seller on Etsy. I'm going to dethrone that fish plaque guy once and for all." Her closed fist shakes passionately in the air, pumping to the beat of the blaring music.

How big is the market for taxidermized drag queens? If I don't get my own apartment soon, I'm going to be sleeping next to Bianca Del Rat. I shudder.

Tori, on the other hand, is delighted by Ivy's determination. "Great resolution, babe," she says, matching her energy. "Tough to follow something as revolutionary as that, but mine is to drink more water. Which is why I bought this." She reaches under the table and pulls out a giant stainless steel mug. Gripping it by the handle, she slams it down on the table. The ice cubes in my drink shake from the aftershock.

I push it aside, clearing my obstructed view. "Was the Stanley Cup not available for purchase? You'll be peeing all day if the water poisoning doesn't kill you first."

"The New Year starts tomorrow," she says, leaning out of her seat to reach the straw. "This is Diet Pepsi."

"What about you, Liv?" Ivy asks.

They brace themselves for my answer, flinching before I have a chance to open my mouth. My parents used to give the same look when they'd get called into the principal's office for an emergency meeting with my teacher.

I've never been much of a New Year's resolution type. The whole thing feels so performative. And even though I love the attention, I lack the necessary patience needed to outwait the countdown. Why wait on a calendar to give me the go-ahead when I can sneak in undetected?

"Seriously?" I say, flabbergasted. I look back and forth between them waiting for one to clue in. *Ugh.* "I'm avenging my dead dad by fake-dating a pro hockey player so I can ruin his family's legacy. Not to mention, I'm busting my ass every day in a fifty-pound cat suit so I can eventually afford to move out of a guest room that doubles as an oddity shop with a pop culture obsession." I bring my glass to my mouth, but it's just ice. My frustration grows as I slam it back down on the table.

Tori grabs Ivy's face and looks so lovingly into her eyes that I sink in my chair a bit, wanting to hide behind the mug. "Ignore my sister. You're the most creative person I've ever met." The two begin to passionately make out.

"Ew, gross!" I shout right as someone walks by. They stop and cock their head back, giving me a look of judgment so appalled that I have no choice but to give my testimony. "Not in a homophobic way! She's my sister," I explain.

Tori bursts into laughter and the confrontational stranger continues on their way. "Stop being such a prude. Be a better ally because technically you shouldn't be in here." Tori smirks.

There's thirty minutes left of this year, and everyone is paired up (or grouped up). I feel like a wet rag. My phone vibrates against the table, and while Tori and Ivy continue to examine the back of each other's throat, I check the notification. It's Brody. The team landed back in Minnesota, and everyone is heading to the club to make it in time to watch the live broadcast of the New Year's Eve ball drop in Times Square. He sends me the location. I let out a loud exaggerated sigh, discreetly slipping my phone into my purse.

"I think I'm going to call it a night," I say, forcing a loud fake yawn. "I don't have another hour of listening to Reneé Rapp in me."

Tori gasps. "Just because your sister is a lesbian, doesn't excuse you from saying homophobic things like that." Her pursed lips fight a smile.

I slip out of the booth and into my jacket. "Love you guys. Have fun."

"Have fun with your *fake* boyfriend. I hope you know your denial is starting to sound an awful lot like Aunt Lisa and her *roommate* Holly!" Tori shouts as I head for the door.

Brody's directions lead to a trendy club with a long line wrapped around the building. I don't have to wait out in the cold in my short skirt and heels for too long because he assured me my name is on a list. I sneak past a gathering of people near the entrance, and the bouncer lets me inside. With the team still on their way, I park myself at the bar with a drink while I wait for everyone to show up. I'm hoping secrets of the family sort will spill as Brody and I share drinks.

I keep to myself, sipping my espresso martini at the bar. *New Year's Eve Live* plays on the TVs mounted above the alcohol selection. There's just over ten minutes left on the countdown. An anxious energy hangs in the air as people shuffle around impatiently. I take another sip, hoping to catch a buzz and maybe whatever delusional optimism fills people when they ring in the New Year.

Some guy slides in beside me, rudely knocking my arm as he pushes closer to the bar. "Here I am. What are your other two wishes?" he says.

I look at him dumbfounded for a few beats. "What?"

I squeeze my crossed legs together tightly at the sight of his predatory smirk. He finds a way to get closer. The beer stench seeps off his body like cologne. "I'm hitting on you. Don't act like you don't like it." He slurs his words.

Despite giving him every physical tell that I'm *not* interested, he brushes my cheek with the back of his stubby fingers. I swat him away like the bug he is and lean so far back in my chair that I practically fall off.

"Oh, gross. Don't touch me."

"Don't be a bitch." With the way he lingers on the word *bitch*, I can tell he takes great pleasure in calling me one.

As I search through the crowd for security, I spot Brody making his way over. Maybe it's the martini or maybe it's the lighting, but he looks better than ever. There's a casualness to his appearance that highlights his natural charm—he's just got it and doesn't have to try. A T-shirt, jeans, sneakers; effortlessly cool. A guy like him will always be in style.

"Is everything okay?" Brody asks, stepping between us.

"Bro, I called dibs."

I tuck my chin into my chest, feeling self-conscious of the growing attention.

"She's not interested." Brody places his hand against the guy's chest, stiff-arming him out of my personal bubble. Every muscle in his arm flexes under the strain of the guy's resistance.

The guy looks down at Brody's hand on his chest. "And who are you, her boyfriend?" The guy looks back at me with newfound disgust. Denial has soured his evening and ruined the illusion of me. It's a much better feeling than when he was looking at me like something to claim.

I panic a bit hearing the word *boyfriend*—so loud and so public. But he's right, Brody is acting like a boyfriend, in the same way I acted like his girlfriend at the pharmacy. Maybe this is what we do for each other?

I step up on the guy, filled with a sudden bravado and confidence that comes with being linked to Brody. "Actually, he's Brody fucking Parker and you're nobody." I point at him aggressively, my eyes narrowing. This guy will take the hint any second now and back off like he should have from the start.

The guy's shoulders drop as he relaxes into a smile and eventually a bit of smug laughter. "Parker? You're the hockey player," he says. He looks Brody up and down before snarling into a shitty grin. "What are you going to do? Karate chop me?"

Before Brody can respond, I'm lunging forward. "He's Korean, you idiot!" I cock my fist then release it through the air, slamming right into the guy's face.

Commotion erupts and I feel someone grab my body and toss me over their shoulder. I kick and scream, trying to resist the pull before I realize it's a bouncer three times my size. As I'm being dragged away like a toddler throwing a tantrum, I look up to find that asshole being helped to his feet with blood leaking from his nose. I'm quickly dumped outside on the curb like trash. Brody shoves his way out the door, rushing over to me.

Helping me to my feet, he says, "Olivia! You absolutely dropped that guy." With his face lit with adrenaline, he asks, "Did your dad teach you to punch too?"

I straighten myself out, raking my hair back into place and pulling the hem of my skirt down my thighs. "No, but I'm pretty sure I inherited it from him."

"As awesome as it was, you didn't have to do that. I was going to take care of it."

"And risk messing up your hand? The Freeze are on a hot streak. I don't want to be responsible for taking you out of the lineup with a broken hand."

Brody's face falls into a bewildered stare. His blinking slows. "I wasn't going to punch him. I was going to have him kicked out of the club." He points back to the giant bouncer standing guard at the door. The two share a friendly wave.

"Ohhhhhh," I say, sheepishly waving back.

Tonight's midnight chill is brisk enough to cool my hot head, but not the racing of my pulse. Drunk smokers gather on the curb for their fix. I look into Brody's eyes and crave him.

Brody takes my hand in his. "Is your hand okay?" he asks.

I shorten the distance between us with a step. Tiny pressure cuts decorate my red knuckles. Brody pulls my hand to his mouth. It throbs in concert with my heart. He blows gently across the wounds and my knees buckle.

"It's fine." My voice cracks as I take back my hand. "I love punching racist assholes. They usually don't have much going on upstairs, so they drop pretty easily."

I close my hand into a fist and flinch as a wave of pain shoots up to my wrist. I immediately relax it.

"We need to ice your hand."

"Yeah. I think it's broken."

I look down at the snowbank beside me and think about shoving my fist in it, but my knees are already quaking from the frigid temperature.

"Come on, there's a convenience store a couple blocks away. Let's get you a Bomb Pop." Brody pushes the crosswalk button and wraps an arm around my shoulder.

"I prefer Dippin' Dots."

"It's not to eat, silly. It's for your hand."

Hand in noninjured hand, on a quiet sidewalk in the middle of the night, my sometimes boyfriend and I take in the New Year.

TWENTY

Brody

The harsh fluorescent lights hum while I peruse the 7-Eleven aisles for snacks. We had dinner on the plane after the game, but that was hours ago, and I can feel my stomach eating itself. I tuck a bag of chips under my arm and go looking for Olivia. She ran off to use the restroom when we first got here, but now I find her lurking around the candy section. She's got a half-melted popsicle held to the back of her hand while she scans her options.

I back up, brushing against a shelf of personal care items, and watch her for a moment. My longing stare starts down at her stacked heels that put her at eye level with me and slowly travels up to where the hem of her skirt falls. Her legs look so long in that tiny skirt. I can't think of much else besides them being wrapped around me.

She flips her silky hair over her shoulder. Like pulling back the curtains at sunrise, her profile is breathtaking. I always knew she had a face men fought over—and tonight I was proved correct. It's unbelievable someone as hot as her is so low-key. Most girls I meet expect to move in with me after a month of talking. It's not an issue exclusive to me—it's an NHL thing. None of them cared to get to know the real me. They were much more interested in being a hockey girlfriend. They wanted free Nobu dinners and suite tickets to every game—I can't fault them for that, but I never like being used. And yet, being used for a free meal was always better than when they wanted to get close to the Parker legacy. Olivia doesn't want any of that.

"Choose carefully, it will be your first treat of the New Year," I say, coming up behind her.

She startles and her face falls when she sees me. I worry I've done something wrong.

"We missed the ball drop," she says, stomping. Jutting out her bottom lip, she whines, "That's like the whole point of tonight."

"Admit it, you just wanted to kiss me."

She scoffs. "I don't need an excuse to do that."

"I was in Utah playing this afternoon, so technically we're right on time." I take a step toward her.

"Five," she says, taking a step to me.

"Four." I sweep her hair behind her ear.

"Three." She bites her bottom lip.

"Two." I wrap my hand around the back of her neck and lean in. Our lips now only inches away. I feel her breath tickling my mouth.

"One." She presses against my lips. Her mouth opens and I slip my tongue inside.

The chips drop to the floor as I wrap my hands around her waist. There's tension in the front of my pants as her body presses against mine. Her tongue tastes like coffee and her lips like sugar. I want to lick every part of her, consume her, but the door chimes open, and I remember we're in the back of a convenience store. She pulls away from me, wiping the corners of her mouth dry.

While Olivia bends down to get the chips, I get a peek up her skirt at her lacy black underwear. She looks up at me from her crouched position. "Let's go back to your place."

No open flames tonight. I'm not making the same mistake twice. My hands are tangled in her soft hair as we enter through my apartment door, mouth to mouth. We bang around the kitchen in each other's embrace while I lead her to my bedroom. My apartment took weeks to repair, and I still don't have a couch. We're not here to play video games in my living room tonight; I want to pick this thing up right where we last left it.

I dim the overhead bedroom lights and kick off my shoes. Olivia bends down, fussing with the straps of her heels.

"Don't," I say. "Keep them on."

"Whatever you say."

She stands up. Pushing her shoulders back, she slips her jacket off her arms and it pools at her feet.

My eyes lower. "Take your underwear off and lie on my bed."

She shimmies up the sides of her skirt and slowly slinks out of her lacy black thong. She kicks it off her ankle and walks with her back to me, pausing right before the mattress to bend over. I practically buckle at the knees at the sight of her bare from behind. She slowly crawls across my bed and props herself up on the pillows. Her gaze drops to the tent I've pitched in my pants, and she smirks while biting her lower lip.

"Now what?" She pouts, twirling a lock of her hair between her long thin fingers.

I lean against my bedroom doorframe with the perfect view of her. I discreetly adjust my waistband, so my cock sits a bit more comfortably against my stomach. "Take off your shirt."

She slowly runs her hands over her full breasts until I see her nipples harden through the thin material.

"I said take it off," I repeat myself.

She lifts her tank top over her chest, the hem momentarily getting caught on her breasts. I can see the weight of them as they fall out of her top and bounce down into position. I take a long breath. They're perfect. She smiles and thrusts them forward a bit, but I'm not going to touch her yet. She's not the type of girl to take anyone's shit. She's independent and knows she can get whatever she wants. As much as I want to give it to her, I want to make her beg for it first.

"Now the skirt. I want to see that pretty pussy." My voice is low and controlled, but inside I'm ready to explode.

She slips off her skirt. Without being asked, she spreads her legs open for me. She's got the type of body you'd see in an old painting hanging in a museum. The type of art so beautiful people endure long crowded lines just to get a glimpse of it. The type that makes you stop and stare. I don't know how to paint, but Olivia makes me want to give it a go. I have to make this as good for her as it is going to be for me, because there are so many things I want to do to her and we can't fit them all into one night together.

"Come here," she says in a sexy whisper.

"Touch yourself," I counter. She watches me pull my shirt off and does as she's told—rubbing her fingers back and forth over her glistening clit. "Good girl, just like that."

I undo my belt and drop my pants, never taking my eyes off her. She moans, and the pace at which she touches herself increases. I ditch what's left of my clothes on the floor and take my hard cock in my hand.

"Please," she says, looking over at it.

I smile and gently stroke myself.

"Fuck me." The words practically fall out of her ajar mouth.

"Is that what you want?" I say in a low voice. She nods and makes another whimpering moan. "Say it," I command.

"I want you to fuck me."

In a couple steps, I'm on the bed, crawling up to her. Suddenly, I can't get to her quickly enough. I reach for a condom from the nightstand and quickly unravel it over myself. Gripping the shaft of my cock, I rub the head of my dick up and down over the opening of her pussy. It's slick and ready for me. I ease myself inside her slowly, for her sake and mine. She wraps her legs around my waist and pulls me deep into her core. Her heels dig into the back of my thighs and I feel her fully. "You feel so good," I say.

I need to pull myself together and give her what she deserves. After a steadying breath, I bare down and start thrusting inside her, deep and hard. She tosses her head back on the pillow. I pull up and lift her legs over my shoulders so I can watch her take my dick, the whole thing. Her tits bounce up and down as I thrust in and out of her. Right when I think I can't hold on any longer, her panting gets louder and faster, letting me know I need to keep doing what I'm doing.

She runs her fingertips over her nipples as her eyes press shut. She screams out in pleasure. "Yes, Brody!"

It's never sounded so good. I feel her contract around me, getting even wetter than before.

I don't let up. "You look so hot taking my dick."

She smirks. "I know. Now, come on my tits." She gathers them in her hands and presses them together for me.

With a loud moan, I quickly pull out of her and grab my cock with a firm grip. I slip off the condom, position myself over her chest, and finish myself off on her. While I get a grip on my unfiltered groans of pleasure, she's looking up at me, laughing. I fall over on top of her, kissing up her neck and planting one soft kiss on her forehead.

"Dirty girl," I say, looking down at her chest. "You need a shower. And a real one, not one from the fire sprinklers." We share a laugh as I toss her some tissues from my nightstand.

She quickly cleans off and our bodies tangle together, still shaking with pleasure.

"More? Already?" She looks down to find my dick, still hard, pressed against her inner thigh. She smiles and thrusts her tongue into my mouth.

I pull away, bringing my hand to her throat. I gently squeeze and she whimpers. "There's so much more I want to do to you," I say.

She wraps her hand around my dick and looks into my eyes. "Then what are you waiting for?"

TWENTY-ONE

Brody

Tom Armstrong, the team's general manager, pops his head in the locker room after practice. His entrance is as subtle as Darth Vader's. Conversation instantly dries up and the room falls silent. Well, everyone but Hammer and Jordy, who both continue to loudly share an inappropriate story that involves a couple bartenders from Hattricks and a shared jockstrap.

Armstrong clears his throat and points to me. It feels as if I dropped a barbell on my chest. "Brody, I'll see you in my office before you head out," he says.

When the general manager wants to talk to you, it can mean one of two things, the first being your official goodbye. Trading me now is unlikely and wasn't an SNN trade deadline prediction, which means I'm being called into his office for the second thing. Across the room, Chef is smiling as he unlaces his skates. He tips his head to me, and it becomes clear what is waiting for me in the GM's office. This is a huge moment for my career and more importantly, the Parker legacy.

Armstrong's office is lined with hockey relics. Reminders of the long hockey history that binds this city to our team. He welcomes me in and motions me to take a seat across from his desk. "How are you liking the Twin Cities so far?" he says, sitting down in his plush leather chair.

"Winter is harsh, but last weekend they had a waterskiing squirrel at the giant mall, so that was cool." Unlike Twiggy the Waterskiing Squirrel, I'm not playing this very cool.

"You know what they say? You're not a local until you know your way around the Mall of America."

"It took me two hours to find where I parked my car the first time I went. Only took me thirty minutes last weekend."

"Impressive. Just like you've been for this team," he says, and I begin to relax. "You've been instrumental in the turnaround season we're having, and I want you to know that we've all noticed not only how great you are out on the ice, but how much better you make everyone else around you with your strong leadership and positive attitude. I think you know where I'm going with this." Armstrong is one of those hockey guys who makes everything sound like play-by-play. He's been in this industry for so long it's the only way he knows how to talk.

I clench my fists tightly, squeezing an invisible stress ball to keep from showing the internal excitement I feel so strongly. "It's starting to sound like I'll be heading to California next weekend."

He nods. "I wanted you to be the first to know," he says. "Congratulations, you're the Minnesota Freeze's NHL All-Star selectee."

For the past five seasons, Chef has been Minnesota's selection. I now understand why he was so excited to contribute ideas in the team's group chat about where we should all go for vacation during the break. That's the thing with All-Star Games for a lot of these guys. The first is an honor, the second is a favor to the league. His smile today gave it away; no hard feelings because that guy is excited to be on a yacht. Me on the other hand, I needed this. Brody Parker, NHL All-Star selectee, has a nice ring to it. I've been trying to crack the NHL All-Star roster for years, but I was always stacked against my former teammate, aka the best defenseman in the league. Erik Parker—the record-holding four-time NHL All-Star MVP—never lets me forget it either.

I can bring a guest with me to California, and I know as soon as this news goes public, my dad is going to pack his bags. I'd rather pull out and take the suspension from the league than have my dad with me. He will cast a shadow over the whole thing. He will be the story of the weekend. And if I don't live up to his storied All-Star reputation, will Freeze fans doubt my ability to get this team to the playoffs? Our names side by side in print is not on my All-Star Weekend bucket list.

As soon as I'm out of Armstrong's office, I'm texting Olivia to meet me for lunch. I have to get to her before the NHL announces this on social media and the news breaks to the public.

At the back of my favorite fast-casual Italian restaurant, Olivia is waiting for me at a table. Hung in the corner within her sight line is a TV playing *SNN Recap*, where my dad discusses the Tampa Storm's recent ten-game win streak. Across from Olivia, my soft drink of choice is sitting in front of an empty chair. She looks away from the TV and spots me. This time, I let the excitement spread across my face. It's nice having someone to share this stuff with again, someone who won't instantly sour the mood with confidence-crushing commentary. To my dad, achievements are never celebrations, but rather obligations I should have already reached.

When I was younger, my mom was my safe person. She was

the one I trusted to tell everything to first. Like when I was named team captain, or when I learned how to toe drag, or even when kids on the other team said something racist about the way I look. She would listen to the good and bad, and no matter what, she was there for me. She would tell me I was an excellent leader because I led by example. She'd say she wasn't surprised I learned how to toe drag because when I set my mind to something, I was a force to be reckoned with. She'd wrap her arms around me and assure me that my face is perfect, but hateful people would always find something ugly to say. And for a moment, before my dad eventually found out whatever the news was, I felt safe to feel the feelings with my mom. I'm starting to feel the same type of safety in Olivia.

Before I can sit down, Olivia is on her feet to greet me. There's a moment of contemplation where she jerks forward to make physical contact, but she second-guesses herself and sits back down in her chair instead. "I'm so glad you called," she says, but her pinched brows and creased forehead say otherwise.

I shed my winter layers before I break a sweat. "Is everything okay?" I ask, taking a seat.

Olivia opens her mouth, but we're interrupted by our server. With the lunchtime rush fed and gone, he's quick to take our order. I request my usual for us to share. Something I coined "the pastas trio"—their three most popular pasta dishes—and an extra order of garlic bread.

Once he leaves, Olivia leans in, pressing her torso so firmly against the table that it skids across the floor an inch or two. "Brody, there's something I've been wanting to talk to you about and I need to get it off my chest."

"I don't understand." My palms itch and instantaneously it feels like everyone in the nearly empty restaurant is watching us.

"I haven't been totally honest with you." Her eyes glimmer under the overhead pendent light. Tears threaten to pour out the corners of her eyelids. There's a slight puffiness to her undereye that suggests they already have. I want to lean over and press my lips to her tender skin. I want to soothe her.

Instead, I reach across the table for her hand, and she grips on to me with both of hers, as if she's holding on for dear life. In a low voice, choked with panic, I ask, "What does that mean?"

"I don't know how to say this. I'm going to sound crazy, and I hope you can forgive me once I come clean." Her breath catches.

I shake my hand free. "You're starting to freak me out."

In the background, SNN announces breaking Minnesota Freeze news. We both crane our necks and listen to the TV.

Camille Duval says, "I'm hearing Brody Parker will represent the Minnesota Freeze at the upcoming NHL All-Star Weekend. It will be Parker's first NHL All-Star appearance. A well-deserved achievement for the center who recently signed a six-year contract with the once-struggling team. Not only is he producing career-high stats, but after a rocky start, the Freeze are experiencing one of their best seasons in recent years. We now go live to four-time NHL All-Star MVP Erik Parker for his thoughts. Congratulations, Erik. This is exciting news for the family."

Olivia gasps and I tuck my pink cheeks behind my open palm. "Congratulations! Why didn't you tell me?" she says.

"I just found out. I rushed over here because I wanted you to be the first person I told."

The feed cuts back to my dad's setup at the Tampa studio. He sits tall and smiles wide from his desk. "I haven't stopped smiling since Brody broke the news to me," my dad lies. "It's a huge honor to be selected for All-Star Weekend and with

Brody at the height of his game, I know he'll put on a great showcase for the fans next weekend." He loses my interest as he reminisces over his past appearances.

"I'm so proud of you," Olivia says. "Like your dad said, it's a huge honor."

Her excitement makes me flush. I dip my head, not wanting her to see how much her affection affects me. Not since my mom have I seen someone so genuinely proud of me.

Our server returns with a full tray of food. While he unloads the plates onto our table, my stomach growls in anticipation. I dig in before he can offer Parmesan. "What did you need to tell me?" I ask, swallowing a big bite that I should have let cool.

"Umm," Olivia hums, repeatedly twirling her fork in a plate of noodles. When she lifts her head, her pupils search to the right.

"It seemed important." I don't want to minimize anything she's going through just because I made the NHL All-Star team. Whatever's going on in her life is just as significant.

"It was. It is. I prefer pizza over pasta." She drops the ring of noodles spiraled onto her fork. They plop into the pool of spaghetti below.

I release a long breath that trails into an awkward laugh. "Lucky for you that's not a deal-breaker." I raise my hand, getting the server's attention. "Can we get a pizza?" I turn to Olivia. "Pepperoni?" I ask her.

She nods. "And olives, please."

"Sure thing," the server says.

Olivia looks no happier than she did when she thought she had to fake her way through three pasta dishes. *What gives?* Upon my arrival, there was no funny remark about my overly ambitious winter-jacket-and-wool-scarf combo she says makes me look like a tourist. She hasn't mentioned my hat trick last night, which at the very least should have gotten a shout-out within the first ten minutes of seeing each other today. Whatever it is, she's definitely got something on her mind. If it's something about her dad, I know how that goes. You don't want to talk about what's got you down, but you run out of energy pretending like it's nothing.

"That was my bad. I shouldn't have ordered so much pasta for us without asking," I assure her. Anything to cheer her up. "Was that really what was bugging you? You had me worried something was seriously wrong."

She nods. "I'm sorry." She looks deep into my eyes, searching for reassurance.

"So, you don't like pasta—noted—but how do you feel about peanuts? You're not allergic, right? Because I don't want our next date to kill you." I take her plate, and start working my way through it.

"Where's our next date? A baseball game?" she says in her classic sarcastic tone.

"The hotel next to the rink in LA makes this incredible peanut butter dessert. Whenever the team's in town, I eat like five of them."

"LA?"

In a casual tone, I say, "Have you ever been to California this time of year?"

She folds her arms and, with some attitude, replies, "No. I told you, I've never been anywhere." After a few beats, she gasps and throws her hands up. "Wait a minute, are you asking me to come to NHL All-Star Weekend with you?"

The smile on her face is sweeter than the peanut butter dessert awaiting us in LA.

"Will you come with me?" I ask.

Olivia's face contorts into an unrecognizable expression.

Discomfort, but excitement—that feeling when you're at the top of a roller coaster and you're about to drop. "Wow. I mean, what other prior commitments could I possibly have going on in my life that weekend? None. Absolutely nothing that would prevent me from going to the NHL All-Star Weekend with you, that's for sure." She smiles, her big wide contagious smile, and I can't help but reciprocate.

TWENTY-TWO

Olivia

This is going to be the weekend from hell. I barely survived the private jet experience. Barfing three times into a plastic bag totally ruined any shot I had at joining the Mile High Club. I can't believe I almost confessed everything to Brody at our pasta date. I was seconds away from spilling it all—my last name, the sabotage attempts, my personal vendetta against his father.

The guilt is rooting itself into the pit of my stomach, deepening its grip on me, and the longer I drag this out, the further it sprouts. A romantic weekend away with Brody is exactly what I need to wrap this whole charade up. Away from the daily grind, Brody will loosen up. He said things with his dad are messy. Well, I'm here to clean up. I'll turn that dirty little family secret into an anonymous tip to the press. Erik Parker's facade of a legacy will crumble and Brody might finally know some peace from his father's ego.

I'm starting to tell myself that sabotaging Erik will do good for both Brody and me—a type of revenge that will serve the

Hinckleys and the new generation of Parkers. Brody seems to really trust me, and I hate to admit it, but . . . my fake-dating scheme is starting to feel less and less fake as we spend more time together. I can't lose sight of my goal, but any kind of real relationship with Brody will have to wait until I take Erik down for good.

I left Brody napping in the hotel. He's got to get ready for a day full of media before the skills competition tonight. He's assured me that while the day is filled with press and promotion, the real party starts after the skills competition ends.

He thinks I'm headed to the pool to work on freelance data research while I bask in the sun. Little does he know, I'm double-booked this weekend. I pull my giant sun hat down over my face and secure my oversize sunglasses to the bridge of my nose as I make a beeline through the busy hotel to get to Quinn's room unnoticed.

Winded from taking the stairs, I bang against her door in a pattern mimicking the tune of a previously agreed-upon song until she opens the door and pulls me in.

"That was not Beyoncé's 'Run the World,'" Quinn says, shutting the door behind me.

"Then you should have picked an easier song for me to knock along with." I sit down on the end of her bed. Making myself comfortable, I ditch my disguise and fluff out my hair.

Quinn drags out the mascot duffel bag from the corner of her room and plops it down at my feet. "We don't have time to go through Beyoncé's legendary catalog spanning over two decades and numerous genres right now. You're late. You need to be dressed and in the lobby for the Mascot Showdown in ten minutes." She checks her watch. "Nine minutes," she huffs.

I made a promise to Quinn that I could manage this weekend, and I plan on keeping my word. I dive into the bag and start sorting out my suit.

"This Mascot Showdown, it's like the WWE, right? It's about putting on a show for the audience, there's an agreed-upon winner, people are having fun and playing safe?" I say, fiddling with my tail.

Quinn erupts into a startling villainous laugh. "Is that what that loser Ava from Dallas told you? I keep telling her she needs to take Hubert the Horse out back and shoot it because she's never going to beat us. We've won it five years and counting, baby!"

A hot flash engulfs my face. "Do you have money riding on this?" I drop the tail.

Quinn steps up on me. She brings me to my feet with one forceful tug of my arm. Face-to-face, inches away, she says, "I have so much more than money riding on this. I didn't want to tell you the rich history Chilly has with the All-Star Mascot Showdown because quite frankly, I knew you'd find a way to screw it up. And you have, in an interesting way I couldn't have predicted, but that's not going to stop us from once again winning this showdown. Because if we don't get out there today and kick some furry ass, I'll tell Brody."

Her finger is still in my face. It's a side of Quinn I've never seen, a side I'm not trying to disappoint. And I'd be lying if I said I wasn't a little bit fired up to kick some mascot ass. Quinn's an incredible pep-talker.

She turns, giving me privacy to slip into Chilly's main body piece.

"You wouldn't. That's mascot rule number one." I antagonize her a bit, perhaps feeling too revved from the weekend's excitement.

Quinn turns, mustering a smile both terrifying and sexy. In

her signature raspy voice, she says, "Oh, I won't tell him you're Chilly. I'll tell him you're Kevin Hinckley's daughter."

My jaw unhinges. Damn, she really is pissed I double-booked myself this weekend.

Quinn shoves her finger in my face. "I knew it!" Her rejoice is short-lived. "You're up to something."

"I don't see how my last name is relevant. I usually keep it hush because once people find out what happened to my dad, they start acting weird around me." I stare her down for a beat. Maybe she'll take the hint. "Obviously, Brody and I are cool with each other."

"So cool you're Icy Hot?" she says. My throat burns with bile. "I told you I see everything. I also found Brody's sticks stashed in a janitor's closet. Then they oddly went missing. Maybe you know about that too."

Fighting back tears, I slip into more of the costume. "It's not your place to say anything."

"For what it's worth, I think you deserve to be mad at them—the Parkers."

"It's complicated." I search my bag for the mascot head. When I can't find it, I start scanning the floor.

"I bet," Quinn says, cradling the missing costume piece in her hands. "But it can't affect your job, and really can't affect this team. Got it?" Quinn adds, handing me my head. The force from her firm handoff pushes me back a full step.

There's the guilt again, as subtle as a bowling ball in my stomach. "It hasn't yet, has it?" I shrug it off.

Quinn ditches the intimidation approach and settles her face into something a bit less angry, but equally as annoyed. "Just make an effort today. I won't tell him, but you really should."

Quinn's warning shakes me to my core. Thoughtfulness

is being demanded of me but wasn't gifted when my family needed it most. The feeling reminds me of the last time I watched my mom iron. She pressed an old game-day ribbon shirt for my dad to be buried in. She warned me that the iron was hot before stepping out of the room to answer a phone call, but I had to touch it just to make sure. To see for myself. To feel my skin melt. There's pain in lies, but there's pain in truths too.

"I'll give it my all today," I say. "And I plan on telling Brody everything after this weekend. I promise." I slip on my mask, attempting to hide from another empty promise.

Inflatable gladiator jousting wasn't listed in the job description when I signed my contract. Neither was arm wrestling an eagle, tug-of-war-ing a hog, or Hula-Hooping with the devil, but I beat them all and now the only thing standing between me and that championship is a very sturdy-armed moose.

Midway through the first challenge, it became painfully obvious that I should have stretched—fear and determination are the only things keeping me going through this championship round. Every deep breath is accompanied by a stabbing pain to my lung. My biceps feel like they're ripping off the bone. And yet, I plant my numb feet on the tiny pedestal beneath me and brace my noodle legs for balance.

Sweat drips off my brows and stings my eyes. NHL rinks are deceptively warm, and this one is hot. My electrolyte balance has been shot since the flight in, and an hour of physical events isn't helping with my dehydration. If I stare long enough, Biscuit the Moose blurs into a bright shining light. *Gitche Manitou, the Great Spirit? Am I dying?* Biscuit pulls back on his baton and whacks me across the stomach. I dry heave as I'm brought back down to Earth.

The crowd of bloodthirsty children screams from the stands. I tighten my grip. As soon as this is over, I'm petitioning for an event name change because the Mascot CrossFit Olympics of Doom is a much more accurate depiction of what's transpiring today. I'd like to have these mascots tested for PEDs. They're all on the juice, every single one of them—athletic freaks!

Quinn's voice is loud enough to cut through the noise. "Think like a car, Chilly!" she yells.

I momentarily worry she's referencing something from the handbook, but then my Northern instincts kick in. Everyone knows hitting a moose with your car is so dangerous because of their anatomy: long legs and a heavy body. You slam your car into their knees and the body is going to come crashing down on you.

Biscuit tries to shake me with a quick jab to the chest, but a cat always lands on their feet. I jump back a half step and avoid contact. Before he sees it coming, I pull back and land a devastating sweeping blow across his ankles. Biscuit topples over, falling dramatically off the beam.

"We're having moose meat tonight!" I shout into my head covering.

With the little strength I have left, I raise my hands and fan my arms for the crowd. They go nuts, but the relief that it's over is far sweeter than any victory. The same cannot be said for Quinn.

"Six years and counting!" Quinn hollers as she guides me back to our dressing room. "You've got to celebrate with us tonight. Last year, Rink Rat dropped molly and was caught streaking through the hotel in nothing but the rat head."

Away from the crowd, I shed a layer. The cool air is nice on my face, but I'd still dip my face in a snowbank if I could. "So that's why everyone calls him Naked Mole Rat."

I hand Quinn the trophy; it's ours to share. She laughs giddily and brings it into her arms in a tight embrace.

"They're already calling you Puss in Boots. What do you say, Puss? You coming out tonight?"

As a temp mascot, I'm not trying to get involved in any weird hazing initiation. Having to compete in the challenge today was enough. As much as I enjoy hanging out with Quinn, I've got to get back to Brody before he gets suspicious.

"I've got plans, but you guys have fun. You deserve it."

As I maneuver through the packed hotel lobby—deking through press, fans, staff, and the occasional player—I hear my name. I search through the crowd to find a very handsomely dressed Brody waving me down. He rushes over to me and gives me a big public hug, the pressure of which against my sore muscles causes me to whimper like a maimed animal. An Epsom salt bath in the hotel room Jacuzzi tub is just what I need.

"You got a lot of sun today. Your face is so red." Brody cups my cheek with his cold hand. "It's cute," he adds lovingly.

I step back, not wanting him to smell the victory (mascot suit stink) on me. I didn't get sun today; I got heatstroke. My face is still flushed from almost dying in the name of Minnesota Freeze fan engagement. There's a water bottle slick with condensation in his free hand. Before he says another word, I snatch it from him, guzzling it like a cup of room-temperature tap water resting on the nightstand the morning after a night out drinking.

"Sure, it's all yours," he says, watching me chug.

I drag the back of my hand across my mouth, panting as I toss the empty into a nearby recycling can.

"Great suit." I motion up and down to the Minnesota-Freeze-team-green, impeccably cut, double-breasted two-piece he's wearing. "Are you headed to the skills competition red carpet?"

I check the time on my phone. The mascot event ran late and we'll have to settle for this rushed goodbye in the lobby. Someone says a quick hello to Brody in passing, reminding him that everyone is meeting outside the front entrance for a team photo before bussing to the rink. He politely lets them know he'll be right out.

Turning back to me, he says, "Your ticket and VIP pass are on the desk in the room. I should go take this group shot with the team before they come looking for me."

He goes to leave, but I reach for him. "What move are you going with tonight for the shoot-out?"

He shrugs. "I haven't really thought about it," he says, waving to someone across the room.

"Bullshit."

Brody does a sweeping glance of the room before shortening the distance between us with a step. "It's called the Goal Horn," he says in a low voice.

Marty Horn's a former legendary Freeze shoot-out specialist. His signature fake-out move was rightfully coined the Goal Horn because it almost always resulted in one. It's a nifty little move that's as cheeky as it is agonizing for the goalie on the receiving end. Brody is just the menace to dust it off and take it down from the shelf.

"Wow. Has that been attempted this century?" I ask. I'm as turned on as I am confident he'll pull it off.

"Not successfully."

"If you're brave enough to try, be sure you pause long enough on the backhand to make it believable, but not so long that you lose the momentum of the fake-out." Pretending there's a stick in my hands, I show him what I mean.

He looks puzzled. "I was being a smart-ass. Anyone who even attempts the Goal Horn is guaranteed to embarrass themselves. You don't actually think I can do it, do you?"

I nod. "If you do, the fans will love you even more—if that's possible."

He steps back. "How do I look?" He straightens out his tie and adjusts the sleeves of his suit.

"Like an All-Star." I take in the sight of him, knowing full well this weekend is going to send him into the stratosphere of beloved Freeze players. A stratosphere full of hockey stars still celebrated today. A dream my dad played for but never had a fair chance at reaching.

I look Brody over, at the last moment noticing the protruding phone in his front pocket. "Wait, give me your phone. I'll hold on to it while you take the photo. It's messing up the look. It looks like you've got a square boner in your pocket." I hold out my hand, hastily wiggling my fingers, salivating at its deliverance.

"My dick is bigger than an iPhone," he playfully scoffs as he digs deeper into his pocket.

When the phone hits my open palm, I want to let out a victory cry, but instead I tighten my grip.

"Thanks. I'll be right back," he says, giving my shoulder a squeeze.

As he disappears out the sliding doors with the rest of the Western Conference team, I slip into a quiet corner of the room. Hidden behind a decorative faux plant, I drop into a squat and click his phone on. The home screen is a photo of him celebrating a goal with his linemates, his smile lively and contagious even through a screen. Cocky bastard.

My thumbs hover over the numbers, knowing I have six attempts before being locked out. I try the easy stuff first (0000, 1234, 6969, 0420) before moving on to something more personal. It's not his birth year and it's not his draft year. I'm locked out for a minute as I stare down the glass sliding doors, expecting him back at any moment. I've got one more shot before I'm locked out for five minutes and will have a lot of explaining to do when Brody comes back looking for his phone.

When the time expires, I enter 9191 and hold my breath. The phone unlocks and I exhale deeply. *His hockey number, really?* His endearing naivety makes me laugh, until it doesn't.

There are two types of people in this world: those who assume the best of everyone and those who take advantage of the ones naive enough to believe the world is full of the first type. Staring at Brody's home screen, I desperately wish to be the same type of person as him. I like to think I would have been if she hadn't died alongside my dad.

Text messages from his dad are at my fingertips, but I can't force my thumb to click the icon. Of all the boundaries I've crossed with Brody, this feels the most invasive. Before I get the chance to decide my next move, there's an incoming text from his dad flashing across the screen.

DAD:

You finally got your opportunity, don't fuck up the Parker legacy. I've got a lot riding on this.

There it is.

Erik pretends to be Supportive Father of the Year for the cameras, but behind the scenes, he's a bully. I wish I could say

I'm surprised seeing his true nature for myself, but I always knew this was the real Erik Parker.

And I'm sure there's more where that came from if I go looking through their conversation. All the proof I need to make sure Erik's legacy is tarnished is only a click away. I'm running out of time to take a screenshot, to capture the proof and share it with the world. Do I take a photo of the evidence? Do I post it on social media? I never thought I'd get this far, and now that I have, the final step feels like a dive so low I won't be able to resurface.

Before every game, my dad would remind me to have fun. *Hockey is the best medicine*, he would say. Everyone thinks Erik is the type of overinvolved father who wants the best for Brody, but it sounds like he's the type who only wants the best for himself.

This dirty, messy father-son rivalry is exactly what I wanted to find. This text is the official confirmation that Erik Parker is what I've always expected him to be—a dick—but I don't feel much like celebrating.

The culmination of my scheme hits me all at once and the lies have blurred the line of who I am and who I'm pretending to be. I'm far too exhausted to feel any relief. I'm punching strangers at the bar. I'm neglecting my business. Have I gone too far this time? Or have I gone too far to stop?

I close the phone screen without capturing any of the evidence, but I can't turn off the hurt I feel for Brody so easily. My face is flushed, and my palms begin to prickle. Dizzy and disoriented, I rush into the lobby bathroom. Hunched over a toilet, I empty my stomach. Unfortunately, there's no gag reflex powerful enough to rid me of this guilt.

TWENTY-THREE

Brody

The bus pulls up outside the arena. A swarm of fans gathers around the red carpet. It's so crowded with media and attendees that I can't even see the entrance of the building. I tousle my hair and muster up some signature Parker charm. My smile strains. I love the fans, but feeding into the Parker legacy illusion is more taxing than a long shift.

I get about midway through the red carpet when out of the corner of my eye, I see my dad standing next to an SNN beat reporter. I do a double take and almost mess up my autograph on some kid's Freeze jersey in the process. After a quick selfie with the fan, my dad is calling me over.

The closer I get, the louder the crowd cheers. My dad keeps looking over at me while he talks into the camera. Always watching, always making sure I do as I'm told. The walk over feels like it's taking forever, and yet, I would be so lucky to never make it to my destination. As I step into the camera frame, side by side with Erik Parker, the flashes from the crowd become blinding.

An SNN-branded microphone is shoved in my face before I can say a word to my dad.

"Brody, your father is an NHL All-Star Game legend, what does it mean to you that he's here to witness your first All-Star Game?" the reporter asks me her prepped and approved question.

"I'm surprised," I say. My dad's watchful eyes burn a hole in my temple. His face reddens as more flashes snap. "Surprised he didn't bring his skates, because he could probably still win the shoot-out challenge." My dad's arm is heavy on my shoulder. Everyone laughs. "But seriously, my dad's support means everything to me," I add, just wanting it to be over.

"Did your dad give you any pointers for today?" is her follow-up.

I can't tell her and the million viewers that the prolific pointers my dad gave to me were to "not fuck this up for him." So instead, I say, "My dad always has great advice for me and today he told me to enjoy the moment."

There's commotion in the crowd. Some gasps and more cheering. The NHL's media team pushes through the wall of people. They approach, escorting someone onto the carpet. Everyone parts for them. In the negative space stands a delicate frame with shiny long black hair and a two-piece tweed suit.

"Mom?" The word spills out of my mouth. I feel like running into her arms like a reunited schoolchild at pickup, but I know that isn't best for the family image.

"It's a family reunion!" the reporter declares. Dad scoots in close to me so Mom has room to join us. "What an honor to be in the presence of hockey's first family."

My mom greets me with a hug before standing next to my dad. He takes her hand in his and pulls her in closer beside him, but it's the kiss he plants on her forehead that causes me to do a double take. The crowd "aws" at the tender moment, but I feel like I'm on the ice without a stick.

My dad gives me a nudge and I say, "I'm just happy to be here and can't wait to get out on the ice in front of all these amazing fans, everyone watching at home, and of course, my family."

I can't get through the rest of the red carpet schmoozing quickly enough. Out of all the questions I'm asked on my walk to the entrance, the one that's stuck in my head is the one I've been asking myself: *When was the last time my mom came to a hockey game?* She was at my dad's jersey retirement, the NHL draft when I was selected, my first NHL game, but it's been years since then.

Finally, we're ushered inside the building. My dad walks ahead at a pace that requires no direction. We find a quiet corner to gather for a family meeting. I've always hated these. Patiently, I refuse to be the first to speak.

My dad anchors his hands on his hips. "That went well," he says decidedly.

I stand still, waiting to be dismissed. He pulls his phone out from his interior sport coat pocket. While my dad scrolls, my mom smiles at me shyly. One that's nothing like the fake wide grins she was showing the cameras.

"We're already trending online," he says. Her smile drops and she presses her wary eyes shut.

I clear my throat. "How did you get tickets for today?"

"No thanks to you," he says, peering up from his screen. "Bobby got me a seat in the team's suite. You know he's on the committee, right?"

Dave Robertson, LA Stars' general manager and Hockey

Hall of Fame board member. Everything is about the committee right now. I should have known my All-Star weekend was his opportunity.

"Is that what this is all about?" Maybe if I can get him to admit it, he will realize how invasive it is.

He glares over at my mom. "Of course not. We're here because your mother and I are getting a divorce."

The news hits me hard, and I visibly stagger back. I look for a seat, but there's nowhere to sit. "Are you serious?"

"See, I knew you'd be emotional. I wanted this to wait until after the season ends, but I had no choice."

"Until after the induction, you mean," I say under my breath. The back of my neck is damp with sweat. My tie and high-buttoned dress shirt are suffocating, but I'm too stunned to move.

"You agree," Dad says. He finally pulls his nose out of his phone. "Obviously, this should be kept between us. Thanks to my quick thinking, our wholesome TV moment ensures hockey's first family remains everyone's favorite for a little while longer."

"I'll see you back home, Erik," my mom says curtly.

He doesn't look at her this time. A call comes through his phone, and he answers it on the first ring. "Bobby?" he shouts. "You saw the interview?" He takes his call a couple steps away.

I turn to my mom. "You're leaving? But you just got here." I keep my voice hushed.

She locks her hands together, holding them close to her chest. "I know how important this weekend is to you. I want you to be able to focus." In the distance, my dad wraps up his call. "I didn't want to have this conversation today. Let's talk—just you and me—when you're back in Minnesota," she adds. She reaches for my arm but stops short when my dad hangs up.

"Okay," I whisper. There's so much more I want to say, but I hold myself back. I've got a skills competition to attend.

My name is announced through the arena's PA system. I can hardly hear the voice mentioning which NHL team I play for over the crowd's reaction. The headshot I took earlier today lights up the jumbotron at center ice. I'm up next in the shoot-out competition.

Out of all the events tonight, this is the one I'm most nervous for. As long as there's a 250-pound defenseman tall enough to play basketball, I'm not winning the hardest shot challenge. And for three years in a row, the fastest skater has gone to the same centerman who once qualified for the hundred-meter dash at the Olympics. Instead, the expectation for me tonight is to win at my dad's event. To score the dirtiest, greasiest, cockiest shoot-out goal.

Known for his shoot-out skills, all eyes are on me and my attempt. If I can win this, maybe it will alleviate some of the pressure on me to deliver an MVP performance at tomorrow's game. Maybe the dopamine hit will be a big enough distraction to let me repress the bomb my dad dropped on me hours before tonight's event.

I can't think about that. Not now. I'm up.

As I slowly skate across ice to take my place at the center face-off dot, I look up toward the team's suite. I scan the box for my dad's face, but he's missing. My gaze drops from the suite level to the family section in the lower bowl and lands on her. The always cool Olivia is chewing on the inside of her cheek. While others in the section casually chat amongst themselves, her knee bounces vigorously. Our eyes meet briefly. Her posture straightens and she gives me a confident nod. I shrug my shoulders. On the bus ride over here,

I was confident I could pull off this move. But after running into my dad, I'm second-guessing myself. Olivia smiles softly and mouths the words, "Do it."

A puck at center ice awaits. The ref blows his whistle, and everyone is on their feet. Three hard strides get me to the puck. The moment I touch rubber, the goalie is out of his crease, challenging. I hear Olivia's advice replay in my mind. *Pause long enough on the backhand to make it believable, but not so long that you lose the momentum of the fake-out.* From that point on, I let my body take over. I trust I've practiced the move enough. Muscle memory has me dragging the puck for a backhand fake-out. The goalie bites and the puck trickles through his five-hole.

The crowd collectively holds their breath until the goal lamp lights red. It takes everyone a second, goalie included, to realize what I've done. But once they clue in, it's pandemonium.

This feeling is unmatched.

Often people think the physicality of hockey is what makes it such a challenging sport to play. They're not wrong, but I'd take the bruises and breaks over the emotional warfare brought on by the highs and lows of a performance-based sport.

When I'm off my game, I can feel it throughout my entire body. It plagues me and my team. The pressure to never have a shift that's anything less than perfect is crippling. But when I'm on, when the bounces are going my way and I'm buzzing on the ice, the joy I have for hockey exudes out of me.

As I skate back to the bench, thousands of cheers fall on me like flowers on a stage. I pause momentarily to take a bow. A far more subdued goal celebration for my taste, but it is just for fun, after all. My go-to cocky goal celebration can wait for the All-Star Game. I'm so ready to kick ass tomorrow night. I look up to the team's suite again, but my dad is still missing.

TWENTY-FOUR

Brody

Everyone funneled out of the All-Star Skills Competition and into a nearby bar. Work hard, play hard is the hockey lifestyle. The VIP section is over its capacity with more people continuing to pile in: players and their significant others, celebrity coaches, team staff, and a bunch of other people I've never seen before but have NHL All-Star press badges hanging around their necks.

Based on the fact that my dad's left me on read for hours, I take it he saw my shoot-out move. When I play poorly, I get an earful from him about how I'm tarnishing our legacy. When I play just good enough to go unnoticed, he loves to give me condescending pointers on what he did back in his day. Neither are as scary as when I play better than him.

His silence is a warning. I'm in the eye of Hurricane Erik. Storm-chasing his mood is exhausting, but if I bail on this after-party, everyone will get the wrong idea of me. I'm here to live up to my name, which includes showing a happy face.

Olivia makes her way back from the restroom and seeing her instantly grounds me. She looks unbelievable tonight. Dressed in all black, she is like a sexy video-game skin. Her strappy top shows off her toned shoulders and deep cleavage. It's been so cold up in Minnesota that I forgot what she looked like without a winter jacket. She slips in next to me, cradling her drink.

"More people in VIP tonight than fans at a Miami Beach home game," I say, laughing at my own joke. Her attention is glued to the bottom of her glass, like there's something foreign floating around with the ice cubes. She's been stuck in a daze all night. She hasn't even made a snide comment about how corny it is that Kirill Sokolov is wearing a bedazzled version of his own All-Star jersey out to the bar.

"Can I get you another drink?" I ask.

"No, thanks." With the straw pressed between her lips, she sucks up what's left. "Is your dad here?"

"Where?" It's too crowded to see the entrance.

"I meant at All-Star Weekend. I saw online that your parents crashed the red carpet. I didn't realize they were coming."

Me neither. "He had some business to attend."

"He must be so proud of your goal." Olivia chews on her straw like it's gum.

"You'd think."

She raises her glass. "You know what, I'd love another drink."

We find a corner with open sitting space and I top her drink off. The music is good, and the company is even better. Once there's nothing but ice left in our glasses, Olivia leads me out on the dance floor. All it takes is dancing and singing off-key to a couple songs for me to forget all about the divorce. I'm a horrible dancer, but for her I'll try anything. And her laugh is so infectious that I have no plans to improve my rhythm.

"I'm sorry I suck at dancing," I shout.

With her hands interlocked around my neck, she pulls me down toward her face. Her lips tickle against my ear as she says, "You don't have to be perfect at everything."

My hands grip at the fabric covering the small of her back. The distance between our mouths shortens with each pulsating bass beat. Her mouth is hot against my lips, but before I can taste her, my stomach sinks.

Someone in the distance shouts, "Erik Parker!" Everyone turns and looks. Everyone but Olivia, who hasn't taken her eyes off me.

"Quick, follow me." She pulls me toward the back of the club. We wiggle our way through the crowd and slip out the back door together, unseen.

We spill outside, hand in hand, disrupting a couple of employees finishing up a smoke break. Politely, they disperse and head back inside the bar. Muffled music seeps out the open door. It isn't until the door swings shut after them that I appreciate the quiet retreat. Even near the trash bins and parked cars, the breezy California night is a welcome escape. With Olivia, she *is* the escape.

"We didn't have to bail. You were having fun. We should go back," I tell her. I reach for the door handle, but she grabs my arm.

"Brody, stop," she pleads. "You heard his name and your whole body went rigid. Your face went as white as ice."

"But it's All-Star Weekend. I want you to have a good time."

She wraps her arms around herself. Goose bumps spread over her skin. "I know you do," she says. Her eyes glimmer under the moonlight and her hair dances in the wind. "I also know things between you and your dad are complicated."

"Is that what I called it?" I bury my hands in my pockets. "Because it's more like extremely toxic. Like showing-up-to-All-Star-Weekend-unannounced-to-fabricate-good-press toxic. Like giving-me-the-silent-treatment-after-a-nice-goal toxic. Like sneaking-out-the-back-door-of-a-bar-to-avoid-him toxic."

"Don't be so hard on yourself. Sounds like your dad's got that more than covered," she tells me. Easier said than done. The lines between my career and my father's are so blurred that sports broadcasters consistently mix up our names. "I know what you need," she says. "How does a peanut butter dessert from room service sound?"

Nothing's ever sounded better.

Sprawled on her stomach across the hotel's lush king bed, Olivia kicks her feet back and forth as she licks her spoon clean. She moans, licking the remnants off her lips before dipping her spoon in for more. This time her eyes roll into the back of her head as she indulges herself.

"This is the best thing I've ever put in my mouth," she says.

I'm shamelessly gawking as I watch her intimately eat the dessert. "Should I leave? I feel like I'm interrupting something." I lean back in the armchair next to the bed. "It's like a threesome gone wrong." Despite my exclusion, I'm still enjoying the show.

"I hear it's always better to be the third. You can be ours tonight." She eats another spoonful.

I flash her a cocky grin. "In that case, I've got something better for you to put in your mouth."

She swallows a bit of tacky peanut butter cream with a hard gulp. "Don't say your dick. It's beautiful, sure, but it's not this."

I get up from my chair and take the dessert from her.

"Heeey," she snaps. Her pouting is short-lived because once she looks up and sees that I'm ready to take control, she stops whining. I set the dish on the nightstand, but not before dipping my finger in the whipped cream resting atop the decadent peanut butter pudding.

In full control, I turn to Olivia. "Open your mouth," I demand. She does as she's told, and I shove my finger into her mouth. She sucks it off, never breaking our intense eye contact. My knees buckle, and I brace myself on the nightstand for a moment before pulling it together.

Olivia reaches back and unzips her dress. She's in nothing but a lacy red thong as she crawls across the bed toward me. I stand at the edge of the bed and quickly unzip my pants, sending them to my ankles along with my briefs. My dick, throbbing and ready for her, hangs out level to her perfectly pouty lips.

First, she takes me in her hand and teases me with her tongue along the shaft. I grab on to the back of her head for leverage and gently ease her mouth down. She looks so hot on her hands and knees for me as she sucks and moans.

"Choke on it," I say, tightening my grip on her hair. Her back arches and she gags on me. "Now I want to watch you ride it."

She gets back up to her knees and meets me at eye level. Pressing her soft mouth to mine, she parts her lips. Her tongue swirls inside my mouth. It's even better than the dessert. While we kiss, she pulls my shirt over my head, and I get on the bed with her. I prop myself up with pillows as she slips off her thong. Once naked, she straddles me and I rub my hand across her pussy. She's wet and hot, ready for me.

"Come inside me tonight. I'm on birth control," she says like it's a dare.

I help her ease it inside, but no matter how ready either of us are for the pressure, we still gasp as it slips inside her. She rocks back and forth against me gently and I attempt to keep it together long enough to get her off first.

"You did so good today," she says in a slow breathy voice.

My hands drop. I stop moving and look up at her, unable to mask my confusion. Diffidence stifles my libido. *Is she mocking me?* "What do you mean?"

She rubs her hands over her breasts. Circling her fingertips over her hard nipples. "You were so good out on the ice today. Your goal was incredible." She bends down to kiss me.

I duck my head to the side. "Stop."

She stops grinding against me. "What?"

"You're making fun of me."

She grabs my face and leans in so I can't dodge her eyes. "Brody, you had the nicest goal today. You arguably scored the nicest goal anyone has ever scored at any All-Star Weekend."

Libido back. Embarrassed to admit it, but I've never wanted someone or something more in my life after hearing her say that. "You have to say that. I'm inside you."

"Because you're inside me, I probably shouldn't be talking about hockey."

I feel a lump in my throat as I look over her angelic face. She's still like marble, waiting for me to react. Waiting for me to tell her what to do next. I thrust my hips up, pressing my cock deeper inside her. She winces and her eyes roll with pleasure.

"You're a really good hockey player," she says as she starts rocking her hips back and forth, deeply straddled on my lap. It feels so good I can't help but let out a groan of pleasure. "So good," she says, like she's getting off talking about it.

It's embarrassing how nice it is to hear. I start thrusting into her from beneath, slow and intentional. We move together. Our breathing getting harder and louder with each thrust. I grab her waist and bounce her on me. She throws her head back and moans. Her whole body clenches and it sends me over the edge. I relax and allow myself to finish inside her.

Olivia lays her flush cheek against my chest. Our legs tangle as we lie on top of the bedding, too lazy to get under the covers. No need when we have each other to keep warm.

TWENTY-FIVE

Olivia

I didn't sleep much last night. I couldn't. The guilt kept me up like hunger pangs, eating away at whatever integrity I have left. When I'm with Brody, it's easy to forget what brought us together, but I tried to remind myself all night that he's using me too. As if knowing I was wrong about him and right about his dad is all the justification I need to keep this whole charade going. When Brody touches me, I don't care that he keeps me around to keep his dad afar. After seeing those horrible texts, I'm happy to be the person who offers him protection.

I thought the relief would be instant. That I'd uncover the Parkers' devastating secret and my grief would lift off my back like removing heavy chain mail after battle. I feel no lighter now that I've found exactly what I went looking for.

There's another mascot event this morning before the All-Star Game, but even with a fake smile plastered to the outside of my costume's head, I'm not sure how I'm going to muster a happy face.

Quinn is right. I need to confess to Brody my true motives for getting close to him: I'm a Hinckley and Erik Parker ruined our lives. Obviously, I can't tell him before the big game, or it will throw off his performance. Still, if I can't find the right opportunity, then I need to make it. What's a few more days? At this point, what's the harm?

My phone vibrates against the nightstand with a dull buzz. Bright sunrays seep in through the cracks of the tightly drawn curtains. Beside me, Brody sleeps, mouth agape and arms overhead. He looks peaceful. I hit Snooze on my phone before it disrupts his REM sleep.

As I snuggle back under the covers, Brody wraps his arms around my waist and spoons me tightly. Settled back in Brody's embrace, my phone vibrates again. I don't remember setting an alarm this early, let alone two of them. Begrudgingly, I reach across the bed and fish it off the nightstand, this time checking the screen. It's Ivy—*weird*.

I answer the call. "Hey?" My voice is low and gravelly as I attempt to not wake Brody. He has a big day today. The title of All-Star MVP is up for grabs at the Western Conference versus the Eastern Conference game this afternoon.

"Olivia. Don't freak out, but something happened to Tori," she says.

I sit up so forcefully that I practically jump out of my skin. A tightness grips my chest and squeezes me like a tube of toothpaste. I've gotten a call like this before—this is exactly how my mom sounded when she called to tell me she was picking me up early from school. I must have asked if it was some sick twisted April Fool's Day prank at least ten times. Screaming at her to hit me with the punch line—to say "Gotcha!" I still remember the moment the news finally sank in. My mom and I sitting together in the car, the silence of understanding consumed me. Dad was dead and there was nothing else to say.

Wearing Brody's oversize T-shirt, staying in a fancy hotel,

I sit in that same silence, waiting for the worst news ever—again.

When my dad died, I mourned two deaths: the death of him and the death of what he should have been. Tori is the reason I pulled through; she's the reason I always came out of my deep depressive episodes. She's all I have left—I can't lose her.

"Don't freak out is literally the worst thing to say to someone if you don't want them to start freaking out." My voice shakes. Time stands still.

"Tori was in a car accident this morning."

"No! Not her!" Tears immediately spill. Brody is up and by my side.

"I know, it's so scary. She broke her arm and collarbone. She'll be out for the rest of the Barn Muckers' season."

My body melts into the bed as relief washes over me. But it's quickly replaced with rage. "Ivy! What is wrong with you? Next time LEAD WITH THAT! I thought she died."

Ivy gasps so hard she coughs. "That's horrible. Why would you think that?"

I aggressively dry my tears. "Text me the details, please. I'll get on the next flight to Minnesota. Tell her I'll be there as soon as possible." I hang up and jump out of bed. Wasting no time, I frantically toss unfolded clothes and loose toiletries into my suitcase. Who needs a cup of morning coffee when you have anxiety powering your productivity. All I can think about is the fact that I have to get back to my sister.

Brody hits the lights and begins talking into his phone. "Hey, I've got a family emergency to tend to, so I'm going to need that plane to get us back to Minnesota as soon as possible." There's a brief pause, before he says, "Perfect. Thanks."

As I shove my sandals into my suitcase, Brody also starts packing up his belongings.

"What are you doing?" I snap, unable to filter the angst out of my tone.

"I'm getting you back to the Twin Cities and to the hospital." He walks over to the closet and pulls his suits off the hanging rack.

"What about your game?" I'm frozen in place, watching him. My whole body is suddenly struck with too much PTSD to process what's happening or why it's making me panic even more.

"The game doesn't matter," he says like it's the end of the discussion and shoves the suits into his open suitcase.

I storm across the room, taking the suits out of his suitcase before they have time to wrinkle. "Yes, it does matter. It's your first one. And thanks to yesterday's performance, you're the guy to watch today."

"Olivia, please let me charter the private plane to take you to your injured sister. You shouldn't be alone." He holds out his hands and I reluctantly place the suits back in his arms.

I bite down hard on the inside of my cheek as tears trickle onto my lips and find their way onto the tip of my tongue. I can't find the words to thank him, so I'll suck on my salty tears instead.

Rushing through the lobby on our way out of the hotel, we almost walk right past Erik Parker. If he hadn't called out to Brody, we would have missed him.

Stuck in place as if I've seen a ghost, I say to Brody, "Is that your—"

"Dad? Yeah, it is. Go wait in the car. I'll be right out."

Since I'm in no position to object, I do as I'm told. I hold my breath and clench my fists as I walk past Erik. I've never come face-to-face with him. He's much shorter in person. His face is worn with deep creases between his brows and puffy bags sagging below his eyes. His disheveled hair tells me he didn't take the time to look himself over in the mirror this morning. If I had to guess, I'd say he isn't just waking up, but rather he's just getting back in.

Despite his rough appearance, he's decorated himself in a way that lets everyone know he's still got it. While his once-attractive face and luscious hair are fading, he's wearing leather loafers and a tailored designer sport jacket. You'll find the resemblance between father and son, but only if you're really looking for it. Otherwise, it's almost unbelievable someone so villainous could help create a man with so much internal light that it shines through his eyes. One thing's for certain, everything they touch is forever changed.

I try to watch the two of them from my seat in the back of the car-service vehicle parked out front. The valet worker moves to the other side of the entrance, and I get a better view. Erik is very animated, talking wildly with his hands. Brody is still, head hung, and not speaking. I don't need to hear this conversation to understand it—Erik is pissed, and this time it's my fault.

I used to want to destroy the Parkers. Now, without trying, I'm messing things up for Brody. I can't handle all of this right now, not when I need to get home. I need to make sure Tori is okay—I need to see her with my own two eyes—and then I can fix everything with Brody. One thing at a time.

When we get to the hospital, Tori is already in the operating room and will be out of surgery in a few hours. Ivy leaves to pick up our mom and bring her back here while I wait in the lobby for any news. Brody, who hasn't said much since we left the hotel, sits patiently next to me.

My knee bounces as I sink into my chair; there's no such thing as a comfortable position in a hospital waiting room. When I was ten, I broke my ankle playing hockey. I slammed feetfirst into the boards and didn't know anything was wrong until I took my skate off after the game. My dad took me to get an X-ray and then carried me up and down the front stairs of our house for weeks so my cast wouldn't get snowy. When I blew out my knee senior year of college, luckily my dorm had an elevator because by then my dad was dead.

Since we were wheels up, I've been trying to think of a clever way to casually bring up Brody and Erik's encounter at the hotel but the best I could come up with was, *The nice thing about having a dead parent is there's one less person to disappoint*, which didn't seem like the right thing to say. I decide to outright ask him instead. "Everything okay with your dad?"

Brody stops his lips from quivering by drawing them into a tight line. Even for a hospital waiting room, the look on his face is alarmingly somber. "My parents are getting a divorce."

I wince. "I'm sorry."

"That's the good news. The bad news is that we all have to keep pretending everything is perfectly fine. My dad said by leaving this morning, it's my fault if he doesn't get inducted into the Hall of Fame."

I should be relieved to hear that news, but nothing about the situation feels right. "That doesn't even make sense."

"Welcome to life with Erik Parker." Brody slouches over in his chair and cups his hands to his face.

Someone erupts into a coughing fit, while someone else loudly snacks on a bag of vending-machine chips. If these walls could talk, you likely wouldn't want to listen.

"How's your mom doing?" I keep my voice low, to match

Brody's quiet tone. This type of conversation should be had in private, but everyone here is too distraught with their own challenges to care much about ours.

Brody tosses on the hood of his blue sweatshirt and jams his hands into the front pouch pocket. "We don't talk much." His eyes well up with tears and I know I've struck a nerve.

I want to give him a hug—he looks like he needs it. Before I can say anything else, a nurse walks up to us. Tori is awake and surgery was a success. They're keeping her overnight for observation. She's asking to see me.

I get up and gather my stuff. Turning back to Brody, I say, "Thanks again. I'm going to stay the night with her and make sure she's okay, but I'll call you tomorrow."

The next morning, I zombie-walk through the hospital with a sharp kink in my neck from sleeping on a chair beside Tori's bed. I stretch my neck side to side, stumbling my way toward the exit. Out of the corner of my eye, I see a blue hoodie that catches my attention. He's sound asleep in his chair—Brody stayed the night. I crouch down in front of him and gently shake his arm. As his eyes slowly open, a lazy smile spreads across his face.

"I don't want to be your girlfriend when your dad calls asking to come for a visit and you need an excuse," I say. His smile strains. "I want to be your girlfriend when you've had a bad game and need someone to stay up late playing video games with. I want to be your girlfriend when you light yourself on fire and need someone to extinguish the flame. I want to be your girlfriend when you need a Catan partner to carry you to victory and celebrate together with Hot Hands. I want to be your girlfriend when you need someone to sneak you out the back door of a crowded bar. I want to be your girlfriend, no matter what. You did a nice thing for me this weekend and I really like you, Brody." My feelings flow from my mouth like poetry. I've never seen something as clearly as I see him. I want to be good like him. I want to be worthy.

A smile cracks across his face, reaching all the way up to his deep brown eyes. "I really like you more," he says.

"You can't turn off your competitive edge, can you?" I shake my head.

He grabs my cheek in his palm and kisses me in the lobby of the hospital.

TWENTY-SIX

Brody

Grocery bags decorate my arms like that one picture of Michael Phelps with all his Olympic medals. Fourteen bags in one trip; it's a new personal best. Even after I drop them off on my mom's countertops, red lines and tiny indentations remain marked on my arms.

I spent the weekend moving my mom into an apartment near me in St. Paul. A one-bedroom, one-bath, no-Dad unit. I called her after my All-Star weekend was cut short, ready to swoop in and rescue her. She didn't need saving, just someone to help carry all her groceries.

My mom's been quietly making her own money by working weekend bingos at a community center, eventually saving up enough to leave her old life in Florida behind. The press stint at the NHL All-Star Game was her legal way out. She agreed to take family photos and keep quiet if Dad agreed to sign the divorce papers.

When Mom picked up my call, she told me she had secured housing. Of course, I offered the spare room in my apartment, but she declined. She doesn't want to have to rely on anyone and I'm doing my best to respect that while we gently repair our own relationship.

I try to focus on the fact that she's getting out of that toxic marriage and less on the guilt I feel for not being the one to help her leave. I was too wrapped up in my own drama with Dad to notice I wasn't the only one trying to run away from him. I thought Mom hated me, possibly more than Dad hated me. At least Dad talked to me—albeit cruelly.

Together—in the same kitchen for the first time in years—we put away groceries, the mundane task as comforting as a familiar routine. We move around each other like it's choreographed, unloading her choices from the Korean supermarket. *Her* choices, not Dad's. I never knew she preferred tea over coffee, but after helping her unpack a pickleball set from a box of her things, I realized there's a lot about my mom I don't know. The unfamiliarity of my own mother makes it painstakingly obvious how little I know about myself.

I'm just Korean enough to guarantee that at any point in time I can search my name online and find some hurtful social media comment about my heritage. But deep down, I feel like a fraud. I don't speak the language. I don't celebrate the holidays. I mean, my favorite food is pasta. The further my relationship with my mom strained, the further I felt from myself. Clinging to my pregame banana milk like I clung to her hand crossing a busy intersection as a small child.

When I was little, people said I favored my mom, but I quickly became Erik's mini. His protégé. The better I got at hockey, the further my mom and I drifted until there was nothing left but Dad and me and the game. Eventually, hockey was my entire identity. Any shred of individuality was suffocated by the Parker legacy.

My mom's phone rings. As if it were a siren, we both freeze

in place staring down at the countertop, waiting for something bad to happen. It seems my mom has the same reaction to notifications—*what does he want now?* She creeps toward the phone and peeks at the screen. Her eyes go wide, and she scrambles to answer it.

"Hannah!" says the voice greeting my mom. Overhearing their conversation, I recognize who it is and abandon my delicate unloading technique. I shove the rest of the fresh produce into the tiny fridge drawer so I can properly eavesdrop.

"Hi, Carter. How are you?" Mom's voice is cheery and warm. Her freckled nose scrunches as she smiles.

Olivia helped facilitate an interview for my mom with Carter at the public library for an open technician position.

"Did you get it?" I say in an overenunciated whisper.

She shoos me with her hand and turns her back to me. "That's great . . . Of course . . . Yes, I'm getting settled in the new place."

Olivia's been incredibly understanding of everything going on lately, giving me the right amount of space for my mom and I to begin reconnecting while also being on standby when I need to get my mind off everything and play some video games on my new flame-retardant couch. It's been a lot to face, but with my dad too preoccupied with the upcoming Hall of Fame announcement to pay us any mind, hockey is once again my safe retreat.

"I can't wait! See you then." With her phone clutched in her hands like a bouquet of flowers, she turns to me. "I got it." Relief washes over her face and a smile blooms.

"Wooo!" My arms shoot up in the air like I'm celebrating a goal. "Knew you would."

"Sit, sit," she says, making her way around the kitchen. "I'm making you your favorite, bibimbap."

My mom grabs a dish towel and tosses it over her shoulder. With excitement radiating through her body, she dances around the kitchen and begins to gather fresh ingredients.

"You don't have to, Mom. I can grab something at the rink before the game."

She grabs me by the forearms and forces me to sit down at the kitchen island on a barstool that was delivered this morning. "I cook when I'm happy, and I haven't been able to cook in a while."

I'm glad she's insisting because my stomach rumbles in hunger—I haven't eaten anything in like forty-five minutes. It's been years since I've watched my mom cook. When hockey took over every second of my life, slowly cooked, timely pickled, messy-fingered, love-labored food was replaced with chalky protein bars in the car ride to the rink.

I do as I'm told and let her cook, except I don't remain sitting. When she used to cook for me, my nose would be buried deep in a book—or a handheld video game, depending on how lenient my mom was feeling that day. When I moved out and got to my billet parents' house, I realized the only thing I knew how to make for myself was a peanut butter and jelly sandwich. My billet parents taught me the basics, but they couldn't teach me halmeoni's bibimbap recipe.

With the rice cooking, my mom preps the meat before teaching me to julienne a carrot.

"I missed this—you and I together." I get sentimental as I chop.

My mom adjusts my grip, changing the angle at which I cut and in turn making it easier and more efficient. "Let's not cry on the food."

I wonder how much of our pain is the same. How, as our relationship faded, the isolation I felt got worse and along with it my sense of reality weakened. As her delicate hand rests upon mine, I'm reminded that parental love is a gentle touch, soft guidance. She steps back and lets me cut. Eventually, I get the hang of it on my own.

"Will you at least tell me why you didn't ask for help sooner?" I ask.

My mom's focus never wavers from the large skillet heating up on the burner. The meat sizzles like heavy rain on the ocean when it touches the hot oil coating the bottom of the pan.

"It's not your job to worry about me. I didn't want anything—myself included—getting in between you and your big hockey dreams."

With the carrot chopped, I move on to the zucchini, practically breaking a sweat to keep up with my mom's feverish pace.

"That's ridiculous. I've been in the NHL for years now. I thought you hated me."

She turns to me, her face held in a forced stoic stare, and her eyes sunken with sadness. I've missed those intimidating black eyes that could always suck the truth out of me with one glance. She draws a breath. "Pass the shiitake mushrooms," she says.

I do as I'm told. As we cook, the only conversation is instruction, and by the end, I've learned to make my favorite bibimbap. We sit and eat together at the table I helped assemble. The true testament to a good meal is the silence that falls once it's served, and right now it's blissfully quiet, save for the occasional tapping of my chopsticks while I get the hang of using them again. I set them on their rest and lean back, having devoured the best pregame meal I've had in years.

Mom glances over at me between small bites. With her lips pursed, she sighs. "Your father had me convinced that giving you space was best for you and your career."

"He's never known what's best for me or my career." My words come out much snappier than I intend.

"After you were drafted, you stopped coming around as much. When you did come home, you locked yourself in your room. It became apparent that you wanted to create some distance from us." She squeezes her eyes shut. I want to reach out and tell her it's okay, that everything is going to be okay from now on.

"From him," I say, hoping my words offer some comfort.

I've been running from my dad for so long I didn't stop to think who else I was leaving behind.

"I wish I knew then what I know now. Everything is so clear to me now that I'm out of that house, but before . . ." She trails off, shaking her head. "I was stuck and I couldn't see anything."

She plays with her food, prodding at my perfectly cut vegetables, as if the answer to repairing our strained relationship is hiding at the bottom of the rice.

"I'm glad you're here."

"You're not supposed to be the one comforting me, Brody." She reaches across the table and squeezes my hand. She says, "I'm sorry," before letting go. She brings another bite to her mouth. "More gochujang next time," she says, chewing.

I help clear the table and tidy the kitchen, exhausted from the physical work of a move and the emotional labor of beginning to rebuild a relationship. Yet, I'm excited to get to the rink. Sixty minutes of unrelenting game is exactly what I need.

Before I leave, my mom calls out to me. "Don't forget your banana milk." She hands me a cold one and slips me a folded note written on decorative stationery. Inside she's written, *Good luck*, in Korean and English.

Coming hot off my shift, I grab a seat on the bench next to Chef. He hands me a water bottle and I squirt it into my mouth as I scan the crowd. I haven't seen any phantom Erik Parkers since that one game back in December but that doesn't stop me from apprehensively checking the crowd each night. There are a lot of faces in tonight's sold-out home crowd, but none of them are my dad's.

A whistle stops play and the ice crew rush out to shovel the snow off the ice during a TV time-out. Chilly bangs on a drum, summoning the crowd in a ritualistic chant. The significant others and family members are all sitting together in the lower bowl, and I strain my neck to find my mom. Seeing her up in the crowd is as calming as meditation.

"Easy, Lover Boy." Chef elbows me in the arm.

"That's a new one. What happened to BilBro Baggins?" With such frequent nickname changes, I've been answering to anything that sounds remotely close to "Bro" all season long.

"I haven't caught you reading *The Lord of the Rings* in a while. Besides, that was before I caught you making eyes at someone in the crowd." Chef leans over the bench and squirts some water in his mouth before spitting it out on the ice in disgust. "Ugh, is this tap water?" he groans. He shoves the bottle back on the bench's inner shelf.

I give a sympathetic smile to the ice crew member passing by with a shovel, scraping up Chef's nasty spit take. "I'm not making eyes at anyone. Olivia works at Five-Hole Donuts during games."

Chef cocks his neck and leans over the bench, stretching to get a peek at the family and friends section. "Then what are you looking at? Is there a hottie I should be aware of? Come on, hit me with another assist this game." He puffs out his chest.

"I'm making sure my mom's here."

"Oh, forget it." Chef plops his ass back down on the bench. "I don't get involved with my teammates' moms anymore."

"Touch her and die." I give him a playful smack in the shin with my stick.

He laughs. "What are you going to do? Hold me? Hook me? Hit me from behind?"

Coach taps my shoulder as the TV time-out ends. With one leg straddling each side of the boards, I turn to Chef and say, "You'd like that wouldn't you?"

"Not as much as I'd like another goal." He follows me out on the ice for our shift.

We get a lucky bounce and the opposing team's d-man turns over the puck in the neutral zone. Chef is there to pick up the loose rubber. I call out, letting him know I'm open and ready, and he hits me with a tape-to-tape pass inches before the red line. It's onside, and good thing, because I'm wheeling toward the net at an unstoppable speed. I cock my stick back with full focus on my target—until it isn't. I hear his voice in my head yelling at me to shoot. *SHOOT!* My mind takes over the rest. *You're running out of space. Out of time. Out of angle. Shoot and score, you fucking idiot. The Parker legacy is at stake.*

The puck launches off the wrong part of my stick. Catching too much toe, it whips to the right, hitting the post, spiraling up out of play and into the mesh above the glass. The referee blows the play dead. I hang my head. I should have had that.

As I line up around the circle for the draw, I see his face in the crowd. Erik Parker is sitting right behind the net, a few rows off the glass. I close my eyes. I press them tightly shut, trying to squeeze the image of him out of my mind, but when I open, he's still there. He's burned into my retinas. His disapproving scowl is a photographic memory I can't shred.

I drag my glove down my face before taking my place on the circle. He hasn't moved.

No, it can't be.

It's my imagination.

Deep breath, Brody. Breathe.

I give my head a shake and look up again. He's still there, glaring at me from his seat. It's as if my missed shot was a personal attack on him, as if he suffers from my shortcomings more than I do.

I look down at the ice and ready myself to take the face-off. With a tight grip on my stick, I go over the game plan in my head: win the draw back to our defense and head to the net. I need to be ready for the tip, which will hopefully result in a goal. But like an itch I can't ignore, I'm unable to stop myself from looking up at my dad again.

It's real this time—which is more terrifying than the mirages I experienced earlier this season. While I'm locking eyes with my dad, the ref drops the puck, and I miss my cue. I lose the draw and the other team clears the puck. Caught flat-footed and gobsmacked, I don't back-check in time and they score on Jordy. I skate off the ice with my head hung, wondering what horrible things my dad has to say await me after the game.

TWENTY-SEVEN

Brody

We lost. And I lost it for them. After seeing my dad, I couldn't get my head back in the game. I spiraled further and was responsible for another goal on Jordy in the third, one that solidified blowing the lead. As soon as Coach wraps up his postgame scorn, I'm texting my mom, telling her to take a rideshare home. The last thing I need after a game this brutal is a showdown between my divorcing parents in the parking lot.

All I want to do is leave this loss on the ice, but I know my dad is waiting for me after my shower. He's charming his way past security, down to ice level, into the family room, into the ears and hearts of anyone who will listen. He's charismatic until he isn't. There's a pit in my stomach swallowing me whole. No bibimbap, no matter how good, will fill the hollowness I feel when I'm around him.

I round the corner, approaching the open door to the family room, and hear his cackle seep into the hall. Before going in, I put on my best face. The game is over, but the happy family charade is about to begin. My dad's slouched over a chair chatting loudly about the glory days to Andy's parents.

The remaining wives are gathered on the couch sipping wine, while the last of the players pop in and out to pick them up on their way out to the parking lot. Some guys linger around the food, loading up a plate to take home with them. Even though people are leaving, the walls are getting tighter.

When my dad sees me, he rises from his chair. His body tremors as if the anger is pulsing through him so powerfully it causes vibrations.

"Brody!" he calls out cheerfully—a ruse for those in earshot. His face, only visible to me, hardly matches his welcoming tone of voice. "I'm surprised you're not the last one out of the locker room. You sure you don't want to get a postgame workout in?" He stabilizes himself on the back of his empty chair. The drink in his hand spills over the lip of the cup and onto the toe box of his shoe.

"I think it's time to head out." I keep my eyes fixed on him, not wanting to face the reactions of everyone else in the room.

"I just got here. Playoffs start in a month, and this is the first game I've been to all season. I'm going to enjoy it." He empties his cocktail into his mouth. "No matter how badly you played," he adds under his breath.

"Why don't we chat in the hall?"

"I'm not going anywhere," he says firmly.

Reading the room, the remaining people quickly scatter and leave. I dip my head and wish them a good night. It's humiliating to be seen like this. Bearing the weight of his shame is too much for me to carry any longer.

He's followed me to road hotels, intercepting me in the lobby for pregame prep talks, which consist of telling me I'm never going to be a lasting name in hockey if I keep playing soft. My teammates always thought he was supportive. They envied the fact that I had access to someone so knowledgeable and successful in the national league, wishing they too had fathers who took such passionate interest in their success and well-being. Things aren't always as they appear.

Once, after a home-game loss, a teammate overheard my dad telling me he was ashamed I was his son. I tried to convince my teammate that my dad was joking, but he looked at me with such pity that I knew he didn't buy it. I'm not sure I can keep convincing people everything's okay. To be honest, I don't want to pretend anymore. I'm so sick of trying to protect him. It's gotten to the point where I don't care if I go down with him and the Parker name. The only thing left of our "family legacy" is hockey, and I'd much rather have my mom and my dignity.

"I wasn't asking. You need to leave," I say firmly. I don't have the energy to anxiously await his reply. I stand my ground because I'm tired of seeing his face every time I look into the crowd.

He slams his empty cup down on the table next to us and steps up to me. He's doing his best to give me an intimidating glare, but it's the void stare of a broken man. Looking into his eyes is like staring into oil. It's lifeless and cold.

"You score one nice shoot-out goal and think it gives you the right to talk to me like this?" He scoffs. Not waiting for my reply, he adds, "Back in my day, I was the highest paid player in the NHL. I didn't earn it by scoring showy goals in a meaningless competition. I played hard and put hockey above everything." He puffs out his chest, but I know it's hollow.

"And look how that turned out." I shake my head in disgust.

"What did you say to me?" He steps closer, finger pointed at my chest.

A knock at the open door interrupts our heated dispute and we both turn to look.

"Hey, Brody." Olivia is standing in the doorframe. Her hair is tied back in a frayed bun and her cheeks are flushed.

"What are you doing here?" I ask.

Caught off guard by my question, her eyes restlessly shift around the room. "I was bringing down some trash after my shift and I heard your voice," she says.

"Excuse me, but we're talking here," my dad interrupts.

She glares at him and he reciprocates. Her poise is unwavering as she struts over to my side. "Erik Parker? I didn't recognize you. You look a lot different in person than you do on TV," she says, folding her arms across her chest.

Usually, my dad's tone softens in the presence of others, but even Olivia's arrival doesn't slow his verbal hostilities. "Let me guess, you're the famous Olivia," he announces with an unnerved chuckle to himself. "The girl who keeps Brody so busy that he hardly has time for his family. The reason he missed his first All-Star game." He eyes her up and down with judgment so uncalled-for that my fists clench and jaw tightens.

"Enough," I warn him.

This is all so predictable that it's tired. He was the one who encouraged me to meet someone and settle down with them so the Parker legacy could live on for another generation. And yet, here he is poking holes in my life so he can criticize every aspect of it. Nothing is ever good enough for him. I'm not going to let him do that to her. She doesn't deserve that.

His lip snarls like an animal's. "At first, I thought having a girlfriend would knock some sense into you. Show you how important family is, and you'd come around yours more. But now I see she's messing with your game."

"Okay. *She* is right here," Olivia interjects.

My dad isn't some opponent out on the ice who I can silence with a solid check into the boards. I have to use my words, and finding the right ones around him never comes easy to me. Olivia tucks her hand into mine and it's like someone rips the duct tape off my mouth. I find my voice.

"Being with Olivia this season is exactly what I needed to realize what is truly important in life. It's not about living up to the Parker legacy. It's about living for myself. Something my game and this team has greatly benefited from."

Dad throws his arms in the air. He looks foolish, far too old to be acting so childish. "This—" he motions around the room "—is nothing. Your career is fleeting. If you continue to play like you did tonight, you'll never have your jersey hung from the rafters, you'll never get your name etched into the Stanley Cup, and you'll never be inducted into the Hockey Hall of Fame."

"And I'm okay with that." I don't raise my voice. I don't let him work me up. Calmly, I continue, "You had your career, you need to let me have mine."

"Don't forget who you have to thank for that little career of yours."

Erik Parker is relentless on and off the ice. But so am I. "You keep saying that, but you haven't been helpful for my career in years."

"Because you don't listen to me. That's why I had a hundred-assist season when I was your age." He keeps going like we're skating laps around the rink.

His tactics won't work on me anymore. I'm not angry. I'm not scared. I'm done playing this game with him and I'm finally getting off the ice.

Olivia on the other hand still has more to say. "You were playing with Dimitri Pavlova. I could have had a hundred-assist season playing alongside the Russian Assassin. More than half of your assists were secondary. Congratulations for touching the puck momentarily in the neutral zone." Her tone is as cold as ice, and judging by my dad's reddening face, he's hot as hell.

"What do you know about hockey?" It's rhetorical, but knowing Olivia, she's got an answer.

She smiles like a pleasant memory washes over her, like she was hoping he'd ask. "My dad taught me a lot about hockey. I know that Brody plays with enough intensity to intimidate the other team, motivate his, and have every fan in this building on their feet night after night. He's got speed and a great shot. He makes everyone around him better. Unlike you. You were a selfish player, and apparently an even more selfish father. Brody helped unite this team and together they've fought from the bottom to the top of the standings."

I don't think I've ever felt so seen in my life. She gets my game. She gets me.

"Dad, I don't ever want to see you back here," I tell him with game-time intensity. "I'm telling the owner that you're not welcome in this arena or at any of my away games. I don't care about the Parker legacy anymore. You can have it." I step aside, showing him the door.

"Don't be stupid. You need my help. We will sort this all out after the Hall of Fame induction announcement." His nostrils flare.

As a kid, this was the sign that I went too far, that I needed to backtrack with a heartfelt apology or score a hat trick to make it all better. I swallow the lump in my throat. No longer the little kid who needs his dad's acceptance, I stand firm. I'm playing for myself, my team, and Freeze fans—not him.

He scoffs. "Good luck then. You don't have what it takes to win the Stanley Cup, because you're not a winner. You're a Lee—soft and weak like your mom." He gets in one last vile word, and I let him because I know it will be the last he ever utters to me. He storms out of the room, passing me by with enough speed to create a breeze against my face.

Olivia gasps and begins to shout after him, saying, "Dimitri Pavlova is to thank for the first two Cups and your team had to petition for your name to be on the third, so let's humble ourselves a bit!" She turns back to me, her sharp flared face melting into a soft sympathetic pout. "He's gone," she says in a gentler voice. Her hand rests reassuringly on my arm.

"He's gone," I repeat.

Olivia wanders over to the standing beverage fridge, searching through the drinks. "That guy's a real piece of work." She cracks open a can and takes a chug.

Suddenly, I feel lightheaded. A panicked flightiness that only my dad can induce. *Was I out of line? Am I in the wrong? How bad does it have to hurt to count?* I've got scars to prove I've broken bones, but anything my dad's inflicted on me is invisible to any medical exam. I begin to stumble, panically wobbling to find somewhere to sit. I hardly make it to a plush armchair before the tunnel vision forces me to take a seat. Momentary total blackness takes over.

"Brody?"

I can't see her, but I hear Olivia's sweet voice calling out to me. Blinking open my eyes, I find her squatting close by my side. She presses the cold can to my cheek and I sit up straighter.

"You okay?" She strokes her hand through my shaggy hair. It's long enough again that my ends curl around the base of my helmet. The flow is finally back and just in time as the team nears playoffs.

It's been a rough night and an emotional weekend, but in this moment none of that is on my mind. Her brown eyes sparkle with golden flecks. As I look into them, the only thing I feel is gratitude. To have found someone I trust enough to exist around. Through all my imperfections, she still finds me someone worthy of defending. Worthy of holding a cold can of soda to their cheek and making sure they're okay. Some things fall apart so better things can come together. Olivia is that. She's my better thing.

"I love you." It comes out like a stream of consciousness. Like letting go of a helium balloon, I watch it float away because it's no longer mine to hold.

She smiles softly, bowing her head. "You just lost consciousness. You're delirious."

I cup her chin, lifting up her face to get a better view of her marooning cheeks. She's as red as a face-off circle. "Deliriously in love with you," I say.

"And yet, I love you more."

I cackle out in unfiltered joy, and she lunges at me with a kiss hard enough to knock me out again.

TWENTY-EIGHT

Olivia

April is a rough month for me. No matter how prepared I think I am for the emotional warfare that awaits, I always cry enough tears to rival the puddles of melted snow that decorate the city's landscape. The ground thaws and I harden with bitterness. Every anniversary is another painful reminder of the finality of my dad's life—his death, his funeral, boxing up his clothes and donating them to the local Goodwill, shutting off his phone, finishing the last of his favorite cereal that used to always be stocked in the cupboard, canceling the specialty cable TV programs. He didn't die once; he kept dying. Every irreversible action was another small death.

It sounds ridiculous to mourn the NHL package, but much of my most cherished time spent with him was watching the hockey games. Before his headaches were inescapable and back when the ringing would let up long enough to enjoy conversation, we would sit together and watch the Freeze play.

He did it for me. I know now how painful it must have been to sit and watch the game that took so much from him. To see others doing what he was born to do. He would break down plays for me and explain the game in detail in a way only someone who has experienced it would know. And for a fleeting moment, he was happy. At least I like to think he was, because I know those were the happiest moments of my life.

We canceled the NHL package on April 15th, before the next billing cycle took effect. I sobbed into my pillow because it was the only thing available to absorb such excessive tears.

Eventually, the deaths became smaller and further apart. I felt a big one when it was announced that Brody signed with the Freeze. And an even bigger one when he told me he loved me. I want so badly to tell my dad about Brody. I want to tell my dad that I stood up to Erik Parker and told him off, then I want to gush about Brody ad nauseam. *He's nothing like his dad, you'd love him*, I would say. I wish I could talk to my dad right now, but instead I'm trying to put on a happy face as Brody leads me blindfolded from his car to a special surprise date.

"Take off your blindfold," Brody says, letting go of my hand.

I pull up the sleeping mask he uses on the team's plane and blink rapidly, refocusing my eyes. He snuck me into the public library after hours and has a picnic set up on the floor in the same clearing where he delivered his compelling speech on children's novels. His audience is gone, and all that's left is us and a room full of stories. Two beanbag chairs sit in the center of a blanket surrounded by the essentials needed for a perfect date.

He tilts his head toward the space, welcoming me to step into the world he's created for us. Like a kid rushing to secure a swing at recess, I run over and crash into a beanbag. Brody chases after me, falling down onto the other. I sink into the mysterious comforting innards of the bagged chair, letting it mold around my frame as it makes way for me. Much like Brody, it's the perfect place to rest.

Spread out in front of us, Brody has prepared a variety of Korean dishes his mom's been teaching him to make, and for after, some of our favorite snacks. Fairy lights hang from the ceiling like stars. The quietest place in the world just got quieter. Hidden in here, we're only two people in all of existence tonight.

"You're not going to make me write a book report, are you?" I ask jokingly.

Brody gets to work uncorking a bottle of wine, while I ready two glasses. "No, but I have something for you to read."

"*Parker Perfection*?" I joke.

"Absolutely not." Brody laughs. The cork slips from the bottle with a suctioned pop. "It's a social media post. I guess more of an announcement. I'm changing my last name to Lee and I'm going to post it after the last regular season game."

"Wow." A piece of spicy cucumber goes down the wrong pipe and I break into a coughing fit. "That's a big decision." I choke out the words.

"Not for me, but it will be for everyone else. I want you to be the first to read it because you get me. The real me. Not the hockey player everyone thinks they know."

My mind spirals over the words *real me*. I gulp down mouthfuls of wine, hoping to drown out the guilt in my stomach that churns mercilessly.

What about me? Does Brody know the real me? He might not know my real last name or the reason I'm a natural at hockey, but I'm more honest around him than I've ever been with anyone else. I discreetly pinch the flesh of my arm between my fingers, hoping the pain I feel in my heart can be overthrown, but now I've got a heavy heart and a freshly forming bruise.

"Here," Brody says, handing over his phone. He tucks a loose tuft of shaggy hair behind his ear.

In the Notes app, Brody has constructed a short statement.

This season has been transformative. I've evolved not only as a player, but also as a person. As part of my evolution, I am dropping the Parker last name, from my life and my jersey. The next time you see me, call me Brody Lee. I might have gotten a head start in hockey because of my father's legacy, but I've put in the work to outskate its shadow.

It's brief but the sentiment is powerful enough to choke me up. Not wanting to upset Brody, I fight back tears. "Looks like I'll need a Freeze jersey with your new last name on it," I say, handing back his phone.

He smiles softly. "That can be arranged. You looked so good in my last one, you'll look even better wearing my new one."

My smile strains under the weight of my lies.

Brody's homemade bibimbap offers a tasty distraction; with every bite, I remind myself that I am an unworthy recipient of its comfort. We sprawl on our beanbag chairs, ignoring the "quiet" signs hung in every viewpoint while we exchange hearty belly laughs.

Between bites and drinks, we exchange funny stories. Inching closer together both physically and emotionally with every embarrassing childhood confession. He tells me about the time he jumped out on the ice for his rookie lap and skated into the wrong end of the rink. He took a shot on the visitor's net, sending the puck into the back of it. It caused a big commotion and reporters claimed he was being cocky: "Erik Parker's protégé already claiming what is his before the first puck drop." Truth was, he was so nervous he accidentally skated the wrong way. After that mistake, he had no choice but to score in his first ever NHL shift. He was awarded first star of the game and decided to never tell his secret—until tonight.

I tell him that my dad used to drive Tori and me over to Edina for Halloween every year because the hoity-toity neighborhood was known for handing out full-size chocolate bars. If you went late enough and all the chocolate was gone, nice women with freshly highlighted hair would reach into their designer handbags and slip you a dollar or two. I took all my collected chocolate bars and ate only one—saving the others and selling them to friends at school and to parents at hockey games. I bought myself a bike with the money. The freedom those two wheels offered was sweeter than any treat.

We eat and laugh until our bellies hurt and we can't tell which is the culprit. I remain wrapped in his arms as we share a beanbag. I'm close enough to hear the thumps of his heart and ride the rise and fall of his chest, yet I want to be closer. If there was a door I could open and crawl inside, I would. Like a house, I'd walk right in and exclaim, "I'm home." We lie together quietly, surrounded by millions of silent words.

Silence has always been a scary place to sit, until Brody came and sat with me. In the quiet, my mind always finds the darkest corners to rest. Brody is like a ray of light that has shown me there really wasn't anything to be scared of in the first place.

"April is usually filled with bad memories, but tonight you gave me something good I'll remember forever." I stare up at him from the spot I've claimed as mine in the crook of his neck.

A single tear drips from my eye, trickling down my cheek at a snail's pace. Brody tucks his chin and presses his lips to the tear, his kiss absorbing it. For the moment, the stabbing sadness is gone.

He tightens his grip on me, saying, "I love you."

I press my lips to his warm musky neck and taste his skin. "I love you more." My words vibrate against his flesh and the buzz tickles my bottom lip.

Brody tilts my head up, his eyes swallowing me whole. My sadness dissolves in his protective embrace. When he presses his mouth against mine, the only thing on my mind is getting closer to him. His tongue swirls inside my mouth softly, teasing me because I know he's capable of more and I want all of him. His hands tighten in my hair, and mine are fussing with the buttons of his pants. I get them undone and slip my hand down the front of his underwear. He's firm in my hand, and gasps into my mouth when I give his shaft a squeeze and gentle tug.

Brody breaks our kiss, but only to lift his shirt overhead and toss it off to the side. I follow suit, and in the time it takes me to tuck my hair behind my ears, he's reached around and unclasped my bra. I'll never tire of that trick. He watches me slide off my pants like I'm something he's about to devour. Like I'm made for him.

"What?" I ask, lying beside him in my underwear.

"You're beautiful." He runs his fingertips down my sternum. My nipples harden as he traces over them. Goose bumps sprout all over my body. Time stands still with Brody. And I'm grateful it does. I could be here tangled up with him forever and still be left wanting more of him.

He ditches what's left of his clothing but pulls a blanket over us. Kissing Brody feels like being hit by car—I would know. It's a full-body experience, with a dizzying effect powerful enough to disorient. My legs are like spaghetti, flopping open as he moves on top of me. His hard dick presses between my legs and I feel myself swell beneath its weight. I'm impatient when he's this close to my opening. He loves to watch me squirm in anticipation.

The eye contact is so strong I forget how to blink. I almost forget how to speak too but after a gulp I say, "Please. Please, fuck me." My voice breaks and I tremble.

Looking down at me with a heavy gaze, he shakes his head. "I want to go slow this time."

He starts at my mouth and begins to slowly kiss down the length of my body, eventually disappearing beneath the blanket. I press my eyes shut as he savors each kiss along the way. He teases me with pressed lips on the insides of my thighs, slowly inching closer and closer to my center. He kisses my clit and the pleasure shoots through me, causing me to involuntarily shake. He holds me in place, digging his big hands into the flesh of my thighs, as his tongue firmly rubs up and down on my clit. He sucks and kisses and licks until I moan out in pleasure. He slowly makes his way back up, and I take his tongue in my mouth, tasting myself, dazed with pleasure, drunk off his touch.

He presses himself against the slick opening of my pussy, and I take a deep breath. As I exhale, he guides himself inside me. My fingernails dig into his back and I moan out his name. "Brody."

"I love you." His voice is hoarse.

"I love you." We exchange the words like we're exchanging breaths.

Brody is a man of his word. He thrusts in and out of me slowly and with intention. I feel everything. The weight of his body pressed on mine. The heat of his breath on my neck. The friction of his hands running over me and into my hair. I can't get enough of his touch—I can't get enough of him. He watches me the entire time, studying my face to see what I like and what he needs to continue doing to make me orgasm.

"You're so perfect," he says. I feel myself getting closer to the edge with each thrust. "Come with me, baby," he pleads breathily.

With locked eyes, I let myself release. My body convulses beneath him as he continues to thrust in and out of me. He moans in my ear and together we finish.

While he's still inside me, he kisses the cap of my shoulder and across my collarbone, tickling his way up my neck. I regain a bit of composure when he finally pulls out, but I still hold him snug. We pull the blanket higher, tucking ourselves in as we settle into place together. I wish we could hide here forever.

TWENTY-NINE

Olivia

I'm fifteen minutes into my job interview with some tech bro and I've already zoned out twice. He's talking an awful lot about himself for *my* interview, so much so that he's got a sudsy white froth gathering at the corners of his mouth. To avoid bringing attention to it, I keep my eyes fixated on the embroidered company logo stitched over the heart of his Patagonia vest. No matter how deeply I stare, I can't seem to picture myself in fleece.

Dax Newton, principal data scientist at Harvest for the last ten years, where they do software solutions for farming—I think? I don't know. The whole thing is putting me to sleep.

Oh, no, now he's quiet. The glare of his computer screen projects on the lenses of his thin-framed glasses, but behind the screen saver his beady gray eyes are locked on mine, his mouth drawn in a thin line. *He's waiting for me to say something. What did he ask?*

Panicked, I ask, "What type of projects would I work on in this position?"

He pauses before launching into another long-winded spiel

about Python. Relieved, I retreat back into my mind. Recently, I got word that Felix is nearing a full recovery, which means my time in the mascot suit is coming to an end—and with it, the extra paychecks. Which would be fine, if I hadn't spent the entire season neglecting my data research business. While Brody has stolen my heart, I've been bleeding out clients and hemorrhaging my savings. My hopes of moving into my own place are just a fantasy if I don't land another big client.

After a bunch of dead-end emails, Harvest replied, looking to schedule an interview. Except they aren't looking to hire a freelancer; they're trying to fill an open full-time position. A year ago, this was exactly what I always wanted. Today, I'm bored.

Even falling asleep wouldn't be enough disassociation to remove myself from this situation. I'd need to hurl my body out the window to end the misery. I can't picture myself enthusiastically waking up every morning to work in this sterile lifeless office building. Like a lonely fan for the opposing team surrounded by home team spirit, I feel terribly out of place sitting here. It's painfully quiet. There's no energy in this building. No one's offered me a high five. The uniforms suck. What's the point of having a job if you can't yell, "Let's fucking go!" at the top of your lungs. Screw a keyboard, give me a drum.

"We'll be in touch," he says, shaking my hand, and I hope he's lying.

Outside the office building, I search the streets for Brody. He's meeting me and together we're going to watch the Barn Muckers in what will be Tori's first game back from injury. A championship showdown and I'm coaching. Since it appears I'm going to be stuck in her guest room awhile longer, this is the least I can do to get on Tori's good side before I have to tell her this interview was a bust and I'm extending my stay indefinitely.

I spot Brody across the street, wool sweater and all. It's been spring for weeks and yet he's still dressed ready to fight a deep chill. I used to make fun of him for it, but now it's endearing. He's always got a warm hand to put on my bare shoulder—plus, this is Minnesota, after all; snow in April isn't uncommon.

I wave him down enthusiastically.

"Olivia!" someone shouts from behind me. Before I can turn around, they're shouting for me again. "Olivia Hinckley!"

The sound of my last name feels like a fist squeezing my lungs. With Brody in earshot, I turn around to find Dax hailing me down.

"Hi," I reply tightly, hoping there's no need to repeat my full government name—like ever again. Brody's at my side. He's standing politely while I stand guard.

"You!" Dax says. "It didn't hit me until after you left the interview. I was a huge fan of your dad growing up," he gushes.

Right when I was finally free from his long-winded spiels, he finds me again. I thought data scientists were supposed to be quiet introverts. And why does everyone in this goddamn state love hockey so much?

"Thanks." I don't look over at Brody. I keep my answers short, willing this conversation to end.

Dax keeps going. "Killer Kev? That was your dad, right?"

I nod once, holding my lips together and pressing my tongue to the roof of my mouth so I don't vomit.

Dax's eyes dart between Brody and me until it finally clicks. "Oh, my God," he gasps. He's as passionate about the Freeze as he is about farming corn data.

"Most people just call me Brody." Brody does that thing where he ducks his head and averts his eyes like he's trying to go unnoticed in the background. As if that's ever possible for someone so recognizable, so handsome, so noticeable. Either way, it's too late. He's been spotted.

I get it. This is my interview, and Brody wants to be respectful of that and not overstep by taking anything away from me. Which is why he needs a push—because I'm going to need him to take that step. This is my out.

I give Brody a firm backhanded smack to the chest. "Just Brody? Please, this guy is so humble. It's *the* Brody!" I say, hamming it up.

Brody stiffens, thrown for a loop by my charisma. I give him a shove forward, wedging him between me and Dax.

Brody takes Dax's hand and makes Dax's whole year by giving it a shake, then taking a couple selfies together. It gives me the opportunity to hang back while whatever's left of this uncomfortable conversation drags on. Time moves slowest when all you want is a whistle and yet . . .

"Look, I don't want to string you along," Dax says to me. He puts his phone away but can't get rid of the smile on his face and giddiness in his voice as easily. "The job's more than likely going to our CFO's idiot son who was kicked out of his fraternity for a beer butt-chugging incident. But I've got contacts in the industry who are always looking to hire out for various projects. I'll pass along your contact info."

"I'd like that." I remain polite and professional, despite having just dodged two bullets. "The freelance work, not the butt chugging," I add.

Dax leaves too enamored with Brody to give my dad another thought. He got his selfie and I got away.

"That was weird," Brody says once he's gone.

"Not really." I shrug it off, hoping he does the same. "Having a well-connected parent really opens up a lot of employment doors."

"I'm well aware of nepotism," Brody says. "I meant what he said about your dad. What was that last name he used? Hinkle?" Brody uses his deep-thinking face, which I usually find incredibly sexy. I've never seen someone so terrifying. Good thing all that loud pump-up techno music has left him hard of hearing.

"I'm not sure. Those tech bros drink a lot of coffee and smoke even more weed. It's a delicate upper to downer balance. They're like kids on a seesaw and he's clearly off-kilter." I use my hand to shade my eyes, checking up at Brody to see if he buys it. He laughs and we move on, walking on the sidewalk under intermittent shade from business awnings.

"You hardly talk about it," he says, grabbing my hand.

"Substance abuse in the tech industry?"

"Your dad."

I knew what he meant. "It's sad."

I drop his hand, wiping off my clamminess against the thigh of my pant leg. I fiddle with the strap of my handbag. It's way too hot for wool today. The type of spring day where you get overzealous—drunk off the hot sun—and jump into a lake only for your lips to turn blue five minutes later. The type of sunny day when enjoyed in the spring gives you hope, but when faced in the fall, lets you know winter's coming.

"What about the good memories?"

I could tell Brody that my dad used to take us to the Minnesota State Fair every summer and we'd see who could eat the most deep-fried Oreos. How when I was seven, I scaled up the giant cherry spoon at the Sculpture Garden, and despite his debilitating fear of heights, my dad climbed up after me. Or my personal favorite, the time he lost Tori and me in the Mall of

America amusement park for hours and had to bribe us with ice cream so we wouldn't tell Mom.

Instead, I tell Brody, "You would have liked him, and he would have really liked you."

I wish coaching my sister's hockey team paid the bills because I'd be earning my salary tonight. The team is already up 3–0 thanks to a few line changes and the new face-offs I've implemented. Not to mention the *League of Their Own*–inspired pregame pep talk I delivered before warm-ups was moving to say the least—someone cried. I might not be able to make a living standing back here, but I'm earning my keep tonight.

Minnesota rinks are famously cold, but I've been pacing back and forth on this bench long enough to warm myself up. The team is hot and has been applying pressure all game. Skates carve into the firm ice, pucks snap between tape-to-tape passes, and fog seeps out of the mouth of every winded player as they miraculously back-check.

The turnout tonight in the fan section is incredible. A beer league record attendance. Ivy and four other girlfriends make up the passionate cheering section. I'm the exact amount of delusional to believe it's because of my incredible coaching and not the fact that Minnesota's biggest hockey star is in attendance. I mean, it's got to be at least 50 percent because of me.

We're on the penalty kill and there's a commotion at our end of the rink. Like any good coach, I start shouting. "Muck! Don't be scared to get in there and muck!" Several players on the bench turn, giving me a look; some are surprised, while others start laughing. "Not my fault you guys can't stay out of the box." The ref whistles the play dead. "Aaaand, I just heard myself." Hockey is so sapphic.

I send out the next line. While both teams line up for the

draw, I spot Brody in the crowd. Standing right behind the glass in the same spot my dad used to watch me play. His dorky thumbs-up makes me blush.

He's been so much lighter since cutting off his dad. Now when someone calls Brody's name in a crowded room, he doesn't jump. On the ice, he skates with a newfound freedom. Having fun is the most underrated skill in professional sports because the better you get the harder it is to hold on to.

The thing plaguing both of us is finally gone, so why aren't I having fun? If Brody and I can finally live happily-ever-after, then why do I still feel so terrible? Like the big horrible unspoken thing between us isn't Erik and it hasn't been for a while.

Cutting corners in youth hockey drills. Lying to my high school secretary about unexcused absences. Crying in my professor's office using whatever excuses stick for an extension. Have I always been horrible? I was a kid trying to survive. Young shenanigans; my stories are endless. They were funny. It's who I am. Let's all laugh about it, and then heavily sigh before the silence. I'll make you feel better about yourself by proxy. Isn't that why my dad's old teammates were still checking in on him toward the end?

Brody's already seen the worst in a person who was supposed to love him, and yet there he is at the end of the rink smiling over at me through the plexiglass like I'm not capable of worse, like I haven't thought about it. I want to wrap him up and shield him from any pain, but I'd be shielding myself because I've been playing for both teams.

I'm getting too old to be living this carelessly. I'm loving too hard to be this reckless. I want a do-over, but my dad taught me that you can spend years locked up in the dark waiting for one of those. They never come. Even in death, my dad remains locked up in the dark. Tucked away in the back of my mind and out of harm's way. I want to tell Brody all about him—all of it. I don't want his legacy to die while my lie lives.

After the playoffs, I remind myself. The timing is wrong right now, but I'll sort everything out once the playoffs end. The Chilly gig will expire, I'll tell Brody about my dad, and even confess that I might have tried to Icy Hot his balls into playing poorly. We'll laugh about it while riding a float in the Stanley Cup parade. We'll skate off into the sunset together.

We have to because I can't survive another loss.

THIRTY

Olivia

Today was supposed to be my day off, but at the last minute there was a Chilly appearance request, one we couldn't turn down—whatever that means. Who could possibly *need* Chilly on a Sunday afternoon?

I should be meeting up with Brody right now to attend a team get-together before the dinner-and-movie date we've had planned for weeks. The Uncrustables and juice boxes Quinn packed will have to suffice.

Of course, I tried to get out of this appearance. I faked food poisoning, texting Quinn an hour ago that I was violently spewing out of both ends. She told me to chug some Pepto-Bismol, strap on a diaper, and suck it up.

I'm told in 2015 Chilly came down with a terrible bout of food poisoning from a pregame street meat vendor outside the rink but still pulled through the overtime shoot-out win. The strength and stamina cemented Chilly in the mascot community as somewhat of a legend. She calls it Chilly's "flu game." To which I reply, Gross.

I slam another Uncrustable and Quinn says, "For someone

complaining of a tummyache, you sure are housing those sandwiches."

"Don't shame me," I say through a mouthful. "I should be at a party right now eating expensive charcuterie."

"And I should be at my bungee fitness class, but I have to spray your butt with aerosol deodorant and make sure you don't walk into any doorframes. Getting called in on your day off sucks, I know how you feel."

Quinn rolls up the tinted windows of the team's sprinter van and I roll my eyes. It's officially time to go incognito mode. Which is ironic because pictures of Chilly are plastered all over the outside of the obnoxious green-and-gold vehicle. It's as subtle as a puck to the face; I feel like I'm driving around in the Mystery Machine.

I eye my costume sliding around in the open back as we take a sharp turn, self-loathing coursing through my veins while Quinn sings loudly to Chappell Roan. Not even the OG Midwestern princess can settle my stomach into a melancholy clap-along car ride karaoke duet. I might not have food poisoning, but my tummy churns every time I see that mascot suit. I'm in the home stretch of this mascot gig. The Freeze advanced to the playoff conference semifinals and Felix will soon be cleared to come back to work. For me, the end is in sight.

Quinn takes a right turn so violently that we ride the curb. Disoriented by the turbulence, my head shakes like a paint can being mixed. Quinn's erratic driving is enough to make me vomit, but there's no use in that—she'd still make me put on the suit and give a show. Her driving slows as we coast down a quiet cul-de-sac lined with perfectly manicured storied houses like the ones I would visit on Halloween as a kid. For a second, I feel a rush of déjà vu, but it passes by the time Quinn pulls up to a house I recognize. We're at Andy's.

I almost snap my head off my neck turning to Quinn. "You didn't say the appearance was for a player!"

She turns down the music. "It's not. It's for their son's birthday party."

"Who's all going to be here?" I try to calculate the possibility of Andy's teammates showing up to the kid's birthday party in my head, but all I can think about is my dad and the five Freeze players who crashed my hockey practice on my seventh birthday. I feel sick.

"Ten little kids." Quinn jerks the van into Park. "Should be an easy afternoon compared to the school visit last week with five hundred high schoolers. You won't have to perform any viral dances for social media this time." Quinn shakes her head, laughing.

Unbeknownst to me, part of the trending dance I performed was a reference to marijuana use, and the video went viral. "Chilly does the 'kush kick'" plastered all over the internet. A meeting was held. I don't mention that the virality of the video landed my fifteen-second clip on a popular late-night talk show and earned us tens of thousands of new followers. Instead, I stare out the window at the familiar towering house and panic silently.

I hop out of the passenger door, something that still causes Quinn to gasp. She would prefer I crawl through the van into the back, but I need to stretch my legs and get one last drag of fresh air before I retreat to my furry alter ego for a couple of hours.

As I twist my spine, releasing a crack in my lower back, I see Brody's sports car turn onto the street. Panicked, I superman-jump through the open sliding side door. My ungraceful landing into a pile of water bottles knocks the wind out of me and I lie in agony momentarily. Quinn looks back, checking to see what caused such a dramatic reaction. She turns to me and then again cocks her head up the road toward his approaching car until it hits her.

Confusion is quickly consumed with a flash of rage until the disappointment sets into her posture. It's a roller coaster of emotions and I'm ashamed to have taken her along for the ride.

"Let me guess, Andy's wife makes a beautiful charcuterie spread?" she asks rhetorically. Before I can babble out an excuse about not knowing the party connection, she says, "You said you were ending things with Brody after All-Star Weekend."

"No, I said I would come clean about my intentions and family tree after All-Star Weekend." I slowly prop myself up into a sitting position, nestled in the mess of mascot necessities: baby wipes, aerosol deodorant, and butt powder (swamp ass is the one true universal mascot weakness).

"Well, how did he take it?"

"I didn't tell him." My voice strains getting the words out. Quinn steps into the van, slamming the door shut behind her. I tense up. "I came close a couple of weeks ago. He found some green fur on my shirt. I thought about telling him everything, but instead I told him it was from a green fox taxidermy Ivy was working on."

"There's no such thing as a green fox."

"I know, he's so gullible," I say fondly. "Which is why I'm waiting until the season ends."

"As your coworker, I must say, I appreciate your dedication to protecting the true identity of Chilly. I'm not sure I've ever seen a 'scot go to such lengths to not only sabotage themselves, but also somehow manage to deliver an incredible mascot experience every time they put on the suit." Quinn's hand is a firm comfort on my shoulder.

"Wow, thank you."

"I'm not done." She drops her embrace as I go rigid under her touch. "But as your friend, what are you doing? You're going to ruin this season for us, and I won't take pleasure in saying 'I told you so' when you do."

Quinn crawls out of the van. She turns back with an arm on the open sliding door. "Now get dressed. You've got five minutes, Chilly."

"Quinn, wait!"

She slams the door in my face. As I sit in the back of the van alone, I'm thankful she went easy on me because I know I deserve so much worse.

Inside, the party is chaotic—far more than the last time I was here. Quinn leads me through the lobby while I pretend to not know my way around the house. We pause in the kitchen, where a large group of players and their significant others gather around platters of food. Quinn pauses to talk to Vera, Andy's wife, when I hear a familiar deep belly laugh to my right.

It's Brody. I freeze in place, listening to the conversation beside me without turning to look. I begin to break out in nervous perspiration.

Someone asks, "Where's Olivia? I thought she was coming today."

Quinn looks back like someone shot a spitball at the back of her head in class, but represses the urge to do something impulsive and pivots back to Vera, who is explaining the party's itinerary.

"She got called into work last-minute. There's a Disney on Ice matinee at the rink."

The conversation pivots to playoff hockey. The Tampa Storm also recently clinched a spot in their conference semifinals. The looming possibility of a Tampa Storm and Minnesota

Freeze Stanley Cup Final clearly has everyone on edge. Brody reins everyone in, reminding them that first they must beat the Dallas Stampeders.

There's no more time to eavesdrop as Quinn pulls me into the backyard. "Chilly, it's time for a ball hockey game with Liam and his friends out back." I make a few overexaggerated hand gestures as I nod my head so hard I feel dizzy.

Andy's backyard is as impressive as his house. The type of backyard where all the neighborhood kids congregate from dawn till dusk. There's a beautiful pool on one side of the yard surrounded by patio furniture and giant umbrellas for shade. A golden number seven balloon sways in the breeze. The other side is landscaped with a miniature rink equipped with boards, nets, and all. I assume it makes an epic outdoor rink in the winter.

As sweat burns my eyes, I desperately wish to be sitting in the shade sipping sangria with the other significant others. I stare at them longingly as Quinn shoves a stick into my paws.

"Chilly is so excited to play with everyone!" Quinn's camp-counselor voice shakes me back to reality and I turn my attention to the job at hand. "Does everyone know the rules?" she asks.

"My dad plays in the NHL," says the snot-nosed kid in the back.

"My dad plays in the NHL too. He's not as good, but Mom says we have to love him regardless," another speaks up.

"My dad sleeps on the couch."

"Alright," Quinn interrupts. "I'll drop the ball."

Initially, I drag my feet, getting in position for the face-off. But as the game plays on, I can't help but have a little fun. I throw gentle yet devastating hip checks to seven-year-olds left, right, and center, getting them off the ball and passing it in the slot. I'm stealing hats and tossing them over the boards. I'm picking up the birthday boy and throwing him over my shoulder as I carry him for a victory lap around the rink after scoring a goal.

It's in this moment that I love the game again. It's not when I'm in the stands pumping up fans and running around taking pictures. It's when I'm at schools playing ball hockey or on skates at hockey clinics making appearances, or even this private event where I get to set up a kid with the perfect pass to score her first of the game. Hockey hasn't taken anything from these kids yet, and the joy is evident as their arms shoot up in the air with pride. I'm going to miss this part of the job once my assignment comes to an end.

As my team dominates, Brody approaches with a stick in hand and a mischievous smile spreading across his face. "Hey, Chilly! Mind if I join?" He taps his stick on the hot pavement.

I snatch the stick out of his hands and toss it across the yard and into the pool like a javelin. Brody is stunned, the children laugh, and Quinn gives me *that* look. The game continues, until Brody's by my side with a wet stick like a dog retrieving a fetch. He steals the ball from me, and I contemplate tossing him in the pool next.

Brody is in the game with a vengeance; I almost stop to wonder if he has a thing against cats. He took note of every hit I laid and every stolen ball I took from these kids and is getting payback. Despite his undeniable skill and strength, I will not let him beat me. I mean I won't let him beat Liam, the birthday boy.

The score is tied, and the ball is on my stick. As I run up the rink, waiting for Liam to get close enough to the net to set him up, Brody is at my side. He's battling to get the puck off my stick. Like a scratchy tag on the back of my collar, he's quickly becoming a lingering irritation. He playfully gives me a shove, but I still get the pass off. Liam scores.

As we celebrate, I don't notice one of the kids bent down tying his shoelace. With both my arms extended toward the sky—vigorously pumping in celebration—I go tumbling over the child and freefall to the ground.

I belly flop on the pavement and the force of the impact sends my mascot head popping off like a cork shooting out of a bottle of champagne. My chin hits the pavement with enough power to chip my tooth, and before I can cover my face with my paws, everyone is shrieking.

The kids scream in terror as they point and gawk. You would have thought their family dog was picked up by a hawk and carried off out of sight. They all gasp, refilling their lungs before exhaling another loud petrified wail. *Am I that hideous?* I run my tongue over my top teeth and feel the jagged edge, but there's no time to search for the missing chunk.

"Chilly's a girl!" one kid screams.

"Its skin is so sweaty," another says.

"Kill it!" a kid shrieks, and I realize I've hit a new low in life—even for me.

Then I see him—Brody. Mouth agape like a child and stunned silent. He drops his stick and stumbles backward. This is my rock bottom. My bottom lip quivers as I search for my head. I need to hide before all these kids see me crying.

"Olivia?" I've never heard Brody say my name with such disgust. He stares at me, searching for verbal confirmation as if the entire reveal is so unbelievable that seeing my face isn't enough, he needs to hear me confirm it out loud.

Everyone is silent and it's so much worse than the screams

of ten petrified children. Quinn is at my side covering my face with a team-branded sweater. "I can't believe you didn't fasten the head covering properly. Everyone's traumatized," she says.

"Don't be dramatic."

"Hammer is crying." She drags me out of the backyard rink in what will surely be my last time in the Chilly suit.

THIRTY-ONE

Brody

Olivia's cheeks are an endearing rosy pink, flushed from exertion and embarrassment. I had to chase her down, and now that I've caught up with her, she is still withdrawn from me as she sits half-dressed like a cat centaur in the open van.

When she bailed on our plans at the last minute, she said she was called into work. This doesn't look like a donut emergency.

"Here, I found your tooth." I hand over the chicklet that landed at my foot. "You're going to want to put that in milk and get to a dentist ASAP."

"Thanks, but that's a Tic Tac." She tosses it in her mouth.

I look at the photo of Chilly on the side of the van, and then over to her. Comparing the two, it looks like a school poster for the before and after effects of drug use. Rough day for the cat.

"What's going on? Did the mascot guy call in sick today and you volunteered or something?" I ask.

Her hair is slick with sweat against her scalp. She sits there, despondent, staring into the distance. "I'm Chilly," she says robotically.

"This is a first, but I don't have a sweater or scarf to give you, sorry."

She looks up at me, flinching at my smile. Her glassy eyes are on the verge of tears. "No. *I am* Chilly. I'm the mascot guy." She delivers it like an epic plot twist, and I never saw it coming. "Mascot woman, technically. It's actually a bit misogynistic of you to assume they're all men. The majority are incredible former collegiate athletes," she says more conversationally.

I start to say sorry for being presumptuous but realize I don't know what I'm apologizing for. "Why didn't you tell me? This whole time I thought you worked at Five-Hole Donuts."

Olivia leans back on her arms, her legs dangling out from the side of the sprinter van as she settles into a comfortable position. "Lying about being the mascot was part of the job but lying about all the other stuff wasn't."

"What other stuff?"

"My last name isn't O'Chairlock."

I bring my hand to my mouth. "Wait a minute, are you even half Irish?"

She shakes her head somberly. I press the pads of my fingertips into my temples, willing my head to stop spinning.

"I'm lightheaded. I need to sit down," I say.

She shimmies to the side, making room for me to plop down next to her on the edge of the van. We sit facing opposite Andy's house—thankfully, because I'm sure they're all peeping at us from the window. *How am I going to explain this one to the boys?*

"My last name is Hinckley. My dad, Kevin Hinckley, played for the Freeze. It's how I wound up with this job." She picks at her bushy green fur, balling up the threads between her finger and her thumb and flicking them into the wind.

"Why couldn't you tell me that?"

She turns to me with a quivering bottom lip. "Because my dad's career ended after a dirty hit from behind delivered by a very famous Erik Parker."

"Ah." Words don't form, just an indistinguishable sound coming from my dropped jaw. It's the sound of someone landing on their ass after the rug is pulled out from beneath their feet.

My stomach knots. I knew Olivia and I clicked right away; our bond was effortless. Growing up as children of professional athletes means we have unique shared experiences. Having complicated feelings toward Erik Parker and my family's hockey legacy makes us members of an even more exclusive club. It's why she was never starstruck around my dad, why she never asked me for his autograph, and why she didn't invite herself to Parker family Christmas. I reach for her hand, weaving my fingers between hers until they perfectly interlock.

I don't know Kevin Hinckley. My dad never mentioned him or the hit, but if there's one thing I can relate to, it's being disappointed in Erik Parker. Olivia never had to hide this secret from me. She never had to lie about who she was.

"Don't feel bad for me. Not yet." She pulls her hand out of our unbreakable connection. "I tried to sabotage you earlier this season. I hated the idea of the Parker legacy bleeding into the Freeze's history and the idea of your dad in the Hall of Fame. I convinced you to cut your hair. I tried to ruin your game by swapping your sticks, oversharpening your skates, and putting Icy Hot on your jock. Then I tried to make your dad look stupid at the library, and when he didn't show up, I was willing to let you take the fall instead."

I jump up, slowly stumbling back. The truth hits me like a wave—hard upon impact and then an all-consuming rush swallowing me whole. I faintly hear her firing off a hundred "sorrys" a minute, but I'm submerged in water. My movements slow, my vision clouds, and my hearing is muffled.

Her complicated feelings toward my father are justified, but to hate me by association . . . That makes her just like everyone else. She assumed I was like him. No, she assumed I was *worse* than him.

"This whole thing has been a lie." I say the words out loud as I realize them in real time.

She stands up, the bottom half of her costume pooling around her ankles. Underneath, she's wearing a tight black bodysuit. She looks like a villain, and she's been acting every bit the part.

"No. Not all of it. I have real feelings for you," she pleads.

"Maybe now you do, but the only feeling you had for me a few months ago was hatred."

She tries to take a couple steps toward me, but stumbles over her costume. "I mean, sure, in the beginning I had ulterior motives, but so did you. You didn't seem to mind how genuine our connection was when you were using me to avoid your dad." She peels her legs out of the costume, slowly freeing herself from the visibility of her lies one limb at a time.

"Those two things are not the same. You knew I was telling my dad about us to keep him away. I didn't know about any of this." I motion to the pile of fur on the ground. It lies there lifeless like roadkill.

This is too much to process on the side of the road. If I stay here, I'm going to say something I regret. My dad would have already caused a scene, which is exactly why I storm off toward my car. With each step, I try to feel angry at the situation, but the betrayal is too heartbreaking to be mad.

Things have been so good for me lately. Without the constant pressure of living up to the perfect Parker family standard, I'm enjoying playing hockey—and more importantly, life is fun. My mom and I have never been closer. I have a standing volunteer slot at her library where I help her host a children's book club. The Freeze are in the Stanley Cup semifinal, and we have a fighting chance to come out on top this year.

When I close my eyes to picture the next month, I see myself lifting the Stanley Cup over my head. Every time I visualize it, Olivia's there. She's rushing onto the ice at the end of the game to jump into my arms and celebrate with me. I can't believe she tried to ruin me intentionally and secretively. It's somehow worse than what my dad was doing. At least he was honest in his attempts to destroy me emotionally. He disguised it as parental advice or good PR, but Olivia disguised it as love.

I tug on my car's door handle, but Olivia pulls me back. Her hand is momentarily on my wrist until it drops back to her side like a returning pendulum. Standing in front of me, she shakes with remorse. I so badly want to wrap her in my arms and take away all her pain, but disappointment prevents me from giving in to what feels natural.

"I can't believe you were responsible for the Icy Hot jock," I say, shaking my head. My balls were on fire that night. So was I, but that's not the point. "I thought Hammer and Jordy were initiating me to the team with a prank. I retaliated by filling their trucks with Ping-Pong balls. Do you know how many Ping-Pong balls it takes to fill two F-150s?"

She wipes the tears streaming down her face with her palms, dragging her hands across her face aggressively as she slowly crumbles into a hard cry. "A lot," she whimpers.

"Yes. A lot of Ping-Pong balls." I open my car door and turn to leave but realize I have more questions. "And where are my missing sticks?"

"I sold them on eBay." Her chest shakes as she lets out more tears.

"eBay?"

She stops sobbing to say, "I donated the money to charity." She peeks up at me through her hands. "Stop AAPI Hate," she adds. With her forced smile and chipped front tooth, she looks like Lloyd Christmas.

"Okay. Well. Thank you." I guess even at her worst she isn't a complete monster. I cling to my car's door as it anchors me in place.

"I promise I was going to tell you everything during All-Star Weekend, but then your dad showed up and my sister was in the car accident. I kept coming up with excuses and talking myself out of it. Things were so perfect with us, and I didn't want to ruin the season or throw you off your game." Her explanations ring hollow.

"Isn't that exactly what you wanted to do?" The longer we talk, the angrier I get. I'm so mad I could scream, but instead, I go mute.

"No, not like this. I love you so much, Brody. I was completely wrong about you, and I learned very quickly what type of person you really are. You're selfless, and thoughtful, and introspective, and goofy, and kind. Maybe a bit gullible, but you know what's important to you and, dammit, you go after it. You're nothing like I thought you were." She reaches out for me.

"And neither are you." My voice breaks and I have to bite down on my lip to distract myself from my growing urge to cry. "The next few weeks are really important to the team. I've never come this close to winning and I can't have anything or anyone jeopardizing that. I need space. I need to focus on my game."

I get into my car and slam the door before she gets any closer, before I have to hear any more.

THIRTY-TWO

Olivia

Everyone hates me but not as much as I hate myself. I haven't heard from Brody since he let me off easy with a slammed car door in my face. Quinn has no reason to hang out with me now that Felix is back in the Chilly mascot suit. Tori has been not so subtly dropping hints about me moving out. Everywhere I go, I'm in the way.

I can feel myself shrinking as the days drag on, melting in place on the lumpy queen mattress like a fallen ice-cream cone. Only no one is mourning my demise. If I withdraw enough, I could disappear altogether. Then those I love will be safe from me.

As I wither away, everyone's lives move on. Including Brody's. The team's playing their first game of the Stanley Cup Final tonight against the Tampa Storm. Locked inside my sister's spare room, I hide from the consequence, but mostly from myself.

The only times I've left this bed in the past two weeks have been to go to the bathroom, grab the mobile food orders I couldn't stomach from the front door, and the one-time trip to the emergency dentist's office. Getting my front tooth repaired ate into a chunk of my savings, but at least it doesn't hurt to bite into my food anymore. The repair certainly wasn't done for cosmetic reasons, seeing as I don't plan on smiling ever again.

The door opens and my sister's outline fills the frame. The glow from my tablet—previously my sole light source—is now overpowered by the bright natural light bleeding into the room from the open door. My most depressing playlist blasts through my noise-canceling headphones. I pull the covers up to my nose, hoping for protection, hoping she leaves me alone.

Instead of grabbing something off a shelf and leaving, Tori lingers in the doorframe. I don't bother lifting my head off the pillow. From where I lie, I squint and shield my eyes, trying to get a look at her. Her mouth is moving, but all I hear are Bon Iver's tragic folk cries. I slide my headphones down around my neck. "What?" I call out with a hostile hiss.

My eyes adjust to the light in time to watch hers roll with frustration, as they have been every time we talk.

"Have you talked to Brody yet?" she asks.

"He made it pretty clear that he wants nothing to do with me," I reply dryly. If I give way to the sadness, I'll never get it bottled up again.

Tori musters up some phony enthusiasm and pivots. "On the bright side, that means more time to grow your freelance business."

I prefer her thinly veiled disappointment. This passive-aggressive motivation thing is patronizing.

"Oh, yeah, business is thriving," I reply, deadpan.

She glances over at my open tablet. The screen reads, *Your Results: Moderate Depression*. A heavy sigh is her segue into the parental lecture she's been dying to give me. "You can't lock yourself in the apartment forever doing free online quizzes trying to figure out what's clinically wrong with your psyche."

I quickly stuff the tablet under my pillow. "Actually, I can. And I'll have you know, it's a recurring personality trait."

Tori leans against the doorframe with enough forced casualness to raise suspicion. Her eyes don't roll; instead they soften. "Look, I don't want to add any additional pressure to your already stacked plate, but you've gotta get your own place. Ivy can hardly keep up with the demand for her drag queen rats. She needs her space back."

There it is, the other tiny yet fabulous drag queen rat shoe drops.

Four of my joints crack loudly as I shoot up into a sitting position so I can better display my animated outrage. "Are you kidding me? I just learned that I'm moderately depressed, and now you lay an eviction notice on me? I'm totally doing the is-my-sister-a-narcissist quiz next." I know I'm out of line, but I already feel so horrible. In the moment, it's hard to care if I make things worse.

"You have until the end of the month, but for your own sake, you shouldn't procrastinate," Tori says calmly. Her regular look of annoyance is replaced with something much more triggering—pity.

I have no choice but to turn up the sarcasm. I've dug myself into a hole and the only thing I'm good at is digging deeper. "Oh, how generous," I say, clutching my heart. I quickly drop the facade. "Maybe if I had your cold heart, none of this would have ever affected me."

Her face hardens. "You think you're the only one who was affected by Dad's death?"

"Sure seems that way."

"That's because some of us haven't been using it as an excuse for the last seven years. You're stuck in the past and it's the reason you have no future."

I want to shout back at her, *Of course I'm stuck in the past, that's where Dad is!*

Before I can find a response, Tori says, "And I want my sweatpants back. You've been wearing them for days."

As she turns to leave, I shout, "Farting in them too!" She slams the door on her way out and I toss a pillow in frustration. It silently crashes into the back of the door.

I've never felt so alone. How can my body house so much grief and not burst at the seams. How am I not exploding?

I roll over and turn on the lamp beside the bed. On the nightstand, propped up into a fierce stance, is a taxidermied rat. "What are you looking at Trixie Rat-tel?" I say, before slamming my head onto my lone remaining pillow. In a time like this, there's one place left for me to go—and I worry I've even worn out that welcome.

I walk up to a familiar doorstep, surrounded by the smell of freshly cut grass and a quietness so still that it can only be found after a forty-five-minute drive out of the city. It's scary how many years can pass and yet some things stay preserved, frozen in time like a photograph. This house remains as familiar as my drive through the reserve. I feel as stuck in place as the welcome mat on the front porch. There's still a red stain from the rhubarb pie my dad dropped Christmas 2011. If the stain hasn't moved on, why should I?

I knock, second-guessing myself as soon as my knuckles make contact. I look over my shoulder and contemplate how fast I'd have to run to hide in the neighbor's bushes—a prank I successfully pulled off with two good knees. Before I have a chance to play ding-dong ditch, the door swings open.

"Nimkiikwe," Nookomis says, standing in the doorway as if I were the last person she expected to see. The use of my

Anishinaabe name makes me realize how much I've missed her, and I almost fall into her arms sobbing. With much reluctance, I stand guarded in place on the welcome mat with my arms wrapped around my torso, willing myself not to cry.

She's a spitting image of my father and me. Looking into her soft sunken eyes, decorated with an impressive amount of squiggly laugh lines, is like looking into the future. I hope someday I'm as lucky to have lived a life with a smile that never quits, surrounded by people who keep me laughing. A breeze catches her long flowy brown hair. The face-framing gray highlights have spread since I've last seen her. Intricate beaded earrings dangle from her ears like vibrant flowers on a spring tree.

Her face contorts as if she's about to offer sympathy, but instead she steps aside and grants me hospitality. "Come in. Get the game loaded and I'll get started on the bannock."

Inside is preserved like a museum. The same couch Tori and I grew up jumping on before being scolded not to. The same coffee table Nimishoomis built with Dad that summer I got stitches from flipping a canoe. The same throw blankets Nookomis knit while watching Dad's hockey games as a way to keep her nerves at bay. A lot of stuff inside here was built by Nimishoomis or crafted by Nookomis—beadwork, ribbon work, wood carvings, moccasins. I'm surrounded by all of it. They aren't just things, they're memories that tell the story of my family. Everyone knows my dad had a heavy slap shot, but only the people around here know how skilled he was with caribou hide.

I go straight to the living room TV console. Like I did as a child, I open the cupboard and press Power on the vintage video-game console. It powers up like an aircraft. Nookomis takes her controller and her spot on the rocking chair. I anchor myself to the area rug just far enough from the TV screen to not be scolded by an adult on the dangers of retina damage.

We sit in silence playing *The Legend of Zelda: Four Swords*. The iconic background symphony music plays as the clicking of our buttons applaud—but eventually Nookomis is doing most of the work while I keep falling into holes.

I grew up in this house just as much if not more than I did in my own family home. This is where my dad was raised. Where we spent family holidays. Where we played pond hockey on the frozen lake out back. Where I lost my first tooth chewing into moose meat. It's where we all gathered to feast after the fourth day of my dad's funeral and it's where I eventually stopped visiting.

"It's been a while. How are things?" Nookomis says between clicks. It's been a handful of years, but her video-game skills and elder senses are as sharp as ever.

"Good."

"Good?"

"Yeah. I'm good." I'm attacked by a rope and die. I drop the controller on the floor beside me.

She pauses the game to say, "You don't show up at my doorstep unannounced for the first time in years because things are good."

I turn to her. She sits patiently on her intricately handcrafted wooden rocking chair that I'll someday be handing down to my grandchildren. Swaying like she's been waiting for me all these years and is willing to continue the wait however long I need her to. I wish I were as indestructible as that oak chair. I tuck my knees to my chest and wrap my arms around my legs. I self-hug and let myself feel the weight of everything I've done with no internet quiz to distract me.

"I've made a mess of everything. For as long as I can remember, I've been blaming everyone else for anything that goes wrong in my life, and now I've got no one left. There's nothing to distract me from the fact that all I want is my dad back." I choke up, holding my breath as I try to hold myself together for Nookomis's sake.

A timer chimes from across the house. The corners of her lips creep into a soft smile as she scoots out of her chair. "Come on, there's nothing bannock can't fix," she says, making her way into the kitchen.

It smells better than I remember, and tastes even better than it smells. Between bites smeared with homemade jam and sips of warm tea, I relax into my chair, feeling full in a way I haven't in years. Over two servings and a cup of tea I tell her everything—including the part where I punched that guy in the face at the bar on New Year's Eve, to which she replies, "Damn right you did."

"I used to make this for your dad when he was upset. It's the best cure for a bad hockey game or big loss," she says proudly.

With a full mouth, I reply, "I'm not sure there's enough bannock in the world to make me stop missing him."

She sits next to me, sipping her second cup of steaming tea. "You know, the second greatest thing your father ever did with his life was have daughters."

I laugh half-heartedly because I already know the punch line to one of my dad's favorite jokes, and I deliver it the same way Dad did. "And the greatest thing he ever did was teach them to play hockey." We laugh together, until the happy memory sours into the realization that he's no longer here to tell it. Even my nostalgia is spoiled with grief.

"Hockey gave this family a lot, but we sacrificed for it. You might never stop being angry at what happened to him, but your dad wouldn't want that anger to consume your ability to feel anything else."

"But letting go of the anger feels like I'm letting go of him."

"Oh, Nimkiikwe. It's okay to miss him. I miss him too."

"Tori doesn't. Mom doesn't." I speak candidly, drunk off the comfort of Nookomis's home-cooked food.

"Yes, they do. We all do. But we all grieve differently."

"Then I must suck at it."

She drops her mug. "Follow me," she says, once again leading me around the house, like she does in *Zelda*. Always taking me right where I need to be to secure the key and unlock another level. "I want to show you something."

We stop in front of her bedroom window, the large rectangular one that overlooks the backyard garden and lake. It's the one she would open to yell out to us to get off the pond and come inside for dinner.

"If the rez dogs are getting into your garden again, it's because you always feed them."

She ignores me, just as she does Nimishoomis's continuous cautionary tale of feeding stray rez dogs.

"See that?" She points to the hummingbird feeder hanging from the windowsill.

"Nenookaasi." Speaking my native tongue is like finding a favorite hoodie you thought you lost forever: It still fits just as I remember and its comfort is instant.

The hummingbird's wings flap at an unquantifiable pace. They move with such vigor, but its body remains still. It's like my restless mind these past few days as it's been trapped in my stagnant body.

"Yes. He's been coming here for seven years. Every spring, he arrives to drink from my feeders." A proud smile engulfs her face as she watches the bird dance through the air.

I didn't know she took up bird-watching. Does she want me to ask what she's feeding her birds or something? "There's no way that's the same one," I tell her.

"Shhh," she hisses. Instead of calling me out for what she would normally dub elder abuse, she lets my joke go and is careful not to spook the hummingbird away.

She stares out the window at the hummingbird with such polite attention and warm welcome that I worry she's going to open up the screen and invite it in for bannock and tea, and like she's a Disney princess, it will become her loyal and comedic sidekick.

She glances at me out of the corner of her eye. "It's your father's way of saying hi to me. It's my sign that he's still alive in my heart and watching over me. I talk to him every day."

"Hopefully not around the neighbors or they might have you placed in a home."

This time, she groans loudly and gives me a playful pinch on the fleshy part of my arm. "You got that attitude from your father." We both laugh. She wraps her soft arm around me. Her thin skin is delicate like lace around my shoulder. "Open your heart and he will speak to you too." In her comforting embrace, we watch the hummingbird buzz off toward the garden and disappear out of sight.

"I have to run into town. How about you come along for the ride?" she suggests.

Nookomis pulls into the town's local rink, which I'm surprised to find is still standing after all these years. It's the type of rink that makes you realize why arenas are nicknamed barns, and it's where my dad grew up playing hockey.

"I'm not sure you should be playing hockey with your hip replacement," I joke, getting more comfortable around Nookomis. We used to joke like this all the time, with my dad and I ganging up on her. We were always the ones to dare try her, and she was quick enough to never let us get away with it.

"And you shouldn't be playing *Zelda* with those slow thumbs," she says. "I'm here to pick up my bingo winnings. Betty thinks she can dodge me at council and not pay up. Fat chance." She slams the car door, and with her handbag tucked under her arm, she marches inside.

While Nookomis handles her business, I slink around the rink. The old baby-blue linoleum floors have been redone, but the original wood beam ceilings remain. As soon as I leave the lobby and step foot in the stands, the rink's chill hits my bones like a shiver. I sit in the cold and watch the bare ice, waiting for my sign. In the quiet, I wait for my dad's voice to bellow through the crackly old PA system and tell me how to make everything better. A play-by-play announcement of how I can right all my wrongs would be clutch at a moment like this. Unfortunately, all I hear is the low hum of whatever fifty-year-old cooling machine is on its last life struggling to keep the ice frozen.

If he's got nothing to say to me, then there's no point in sitting around freezing my ass off. I head back into the lobby, cold and discouraged. All alone, I linger past the relics of our local hockey heroes. Hung in the display cases are old photographs and tarnished trophies. I easily find my dad's photos—his personality was as big as he was, even as a kid. I immediately spot the dusty silver trophies with his name on them because he used to point them out to us, bragging that he was once a "big deal around here." For a building that feels haunted with his spirit, it doesn't have much to say to me.

As I turn to leave and go wait in the car, I see a poster tacked to a corkboard hanging over the water fountain. *JOB*

OPPORTUNITY reads the sign in big bold letters. Below is a description. The local college is looking for an assistant coach for the Ice Dogs, the women's hockey team. I burst out into laughter. It's uncontrollable, like a coughing fit. This might not be some beautiful metaphor like a bird that defies gravity, but it's as literal as he could get. My dad really said, *You want a sign, well here it is, you dumbass.*

I take down the contact info because I can't think of anything else I want more than to get back into the game. "Miigwech, Dad," I whisper to myself.

THIRTY-THREE

Brody

My heart pounds in my ears. A combination of nerves, adrenaline, and fatigue have me panting like a dog in the sun after a long walk. My shift is running long, but we're stuck in the defensive zone with no whistle in sight. The Tampa Storm cycle the puck around the net, waiting for a shot to open up, and we're trying our best to not give them one. Game's tied up late in the third with a goal apiece. Any closer to the edge of your seat and you'd be on the ground.

There's a scramble in front of our net. A bouncing puck squeezes past our defense, but not our goalie. Hammer covers up the loose puck and the ref whistles the play dead. Right when I think my legs are going to give out from under me, the Tampa Storm call a time-out.

As we skate to our respective benches for a strategic time-out, an announcement plays on the jumbotron. Before I even reach the bench, Coach Carol has his clipboard out and is going over face-offs with the team. I don't need to watch him draw *X*'s on a whiteboard to know where to go. The play is simple: Don't get scored on. Instead of listening, I stare up at the jumbotron watching the highlight reel of my dad's best moves. The Storm's play-by-play announcer provides the voice-over.

"Congratulations to legendary Tampa Storm forward Erik Parker on his induction into the Hockey Hall of Fame," the voice bellows, tauntingly so.

I pay no mind to this announcement, just as I've paid no mind to my dad's retired jersey number hanging in the rafters. It's not at all surprising. I got a tip last week from my agent, Lamar, that a formal announcement from the Hall of Fame was soon to come.

As much as my dad hated my name change and the controversial press it attracted, he was always going to get the Hall of Fame call. When you're hockey royalty, there isn't much people aren't willing to forgive. The old boys club never revokes a membership. His jersey, the Hall of Fame, and his pathetic attempts to repair his image are just noise. When you play in front of thousands of fans every other night, you have to learn how to block out the madness. Filtering it through the lens of motivation and turning it into fuel to carry on.

I'm sure the Storm thought by playing this announcement at this very moment, they could throw me off my game. Maybe they wanted to show me what I was missing, what I threw away when I turned down their contract offer and signed with the Freeze. The video ends and I feel anything but regret. Instead, my legs are fresh, my pulse is rested, and my body is buzzing to get back on the ice and finish this game.

We win the draw but struggle to clear the puck out of our end. The Storm's bulkiest defenseman is fed the puck. I follow his windup, anticipating where the release is headed, and drop a knee. Despite my better judgment, I'm laying my body on the line to block a shot from this season's NHL All-Star Game's hardest slap shot winner. I cover my teeth with one hand and dangle the other between my legs to cover more space. It's game 4 of the Stanley Cup Final and we're down in the series three games to none. We're looking to make a historic comeback, and it starts tonight. Anything for the boys, everything for the Cup.

I hold my breath as he releases his windup. No time to second-guess myself now. I brace for the biggest bruise of my life—or worse, a broken hand. His stick slaps loudly on the release, except there's no puck hurtling my way. Instead, his twig snaps at the shaft, near the blade, and the puck skips like a stone into open ice. As if time stands still, we all take a second to realize what happened.

I explode out of my crouched position and in a couple powerful strides am the first to the puck. It's mine and so is this winning goal. My legs, which seconds ago burned with such sharp pain they shook, are now weightless beneath me. My lungs, which felt stretched to their capacity, are now breathing deep steady breaths synchronized with my strides as I blow past a flat-footed Storm defenseman. My mind, which was focused on protecting Hammer and keeping pucks out of our net at any cost, has now flipped a switch. From a defensive mindset to an offensive hunger, I shift as quickly as I find my opening into the offensive zone.

This isn't a puck on my stick. It's a pulse in a must-win game.

The crowd—which was just on their feet to celebrate my dad's induction announcement—goes silent, watching in horror as I come barreling down center ice. The sound of my blades carving into ice has replaced the loud cheers that once boomed when the Storm had possession of the puck. The puck taps on the blade of my stick steady like a metronome as I carry it into the offensive zone. Six ounces isn't much, but in the palm of my hand, it's lethal. I toe-drag past the last Storm defender with my vision locked on their goalie, Eli Gauthier.

Gauthier is out at the top of his crease, challenging me as I enter his territory. He's been stellar all game: no rebounds, always in position, and vision through any screen we put in front of him. Those things won't help him now.

I take the puck for a walk, skating it way wide through the face-off circle. With Gauthier at the top of his crease, I charge in on him, faking a slap shot. Gauthier drops to his knees, flinching in anticipation. Just like I practiced, I pretend to pull the shot to my backhand and he slides across the ice toward the middle of the crease where I skate, leading him with me. However, Gauthier is ignorant to the fact that I've left the puck behind. My fake-out shot has just enough heat on it to slowly slide through his five-hole opening. The momentum carries the puck across the goal line.

It's a Goal Horn. I pull off the impossible move for a second time this season. The boys come crashing into me as we celebrate in the corner to the sound of seventeen thousand boos raining over us. We live to see another game.

There's no sense of relief. Every remaining game is going to be an uphill battle harder than the one fought before it. For a moment, I look forward to getting off the ice and texting my person—Olivia. She'll commiserate over my bad pass in the second but remind me that I ultimately came through when my team needed me the most. As soon as I picture her sweet face, I remember that we're not speaking.

In all the pain, I've been seeking understanding. I thought I felt betrayed, but as the days have dragged on, it feels a lot like loss.

As soon as I got home that afternoon after the party, I researched and learned about her dad, Kevin Hinckley. It's a devastating loss. I've tried to empathize with her, put myself in her shoes, but I can't imagine losing a father worthy of vengeance. What does a dad worthy of carrying such inner turmoil look like? Does he always know what to get you on your birthday? Did he give the best shoulder rides growing up? Is he funny? Is he kind? I bet he doesn't micromanage your career. I bet he doesn't show up the day of your skills competition to tell you he and Mom are divorcing. Whoever said you can't miss what you never had is full of shit because I wish I had a dad worthy of such grief.

In remembering everything I clung to while hoping my dad would be the father I needed, I'm able to better understand why Olivia did what she did. If she could love me—half Erik Parker coursing through my DNA—then her feelings for me were real. And what's more, I'm not the monster he is. I push the emotional pain out of my mind by focusing on the physical aches—my hips, my shoulders, my back. It all stings as we inch closer to the end. It's going to be a long, lonely flight home.

Back on home ice, tired and aching after practice, I linger in the locker room. It's a thin line between focused and consumed and I've got a skate on each side. The guys give me space; not giving too much pushback when I turn down their offer to grab lunch. There's something more important than carbo-loading on the docket today.

Alone, I wander down the hall, moving unsuspectingly around the vast underground maze known as ice level. I stop outside the door with my hand wrapped around a cold metal doorknob. Before I can knock, Derek Thomas sees me through the sidelite. He waves me into his office.

"Come on in, Brody," he says. Unphased by my impromptu visit, he sets his work aside.

I grab a seat across from him and brace myself on the arms of the cushy office chair. "I need your help with something," I say.

He rubs his thumb and pointer finger in small circles over his eyelids as he sighs deeply. "Please don't put me in the middle of this. A few seasons ago, I caught one of the rookies messing with the coach's daughter. Let's just say only one of them is still with the team. I have no interest in any hockey romance."

"What rookie?" I scoot my chair closer before realizing I'm getting off track. "Never mind. That's not why I'm here. I want to do something for CTE research. The Players' Association says you've been trying to get something off the ground for years."

Ever since I read the words *died from CTE complications* in Kevin Hinckley's Wikipedia page, I haven't gotten them out of my mind. Of course, I know the acronym, every hockey player does. Just like every hockey player thinks they won't be the one to suffer from it. At twentysomething, you're invincible, fast and strong like a superhero, so focused on your next game that you don't stop to think about life after hockey. There is only hockey.

Lately, I've been asking myself, how did everyone fail Kevin Hinckley? And how am I failing the next generation of guys, enabling them to suffer in silence?

Derek smiles, relaxing into his chair. His gaze drifts across the room to the picture hanging on his wall. It's one of him and Kevin Hinckley as Minnesota Freeze teammates. "Now that's something I have a lot of interest in," he says with a cracked voice. "I've been trying to form a coalition. There's plenty of interest from retired players like myself, but we need current guys to move the needle."

"What are you thinking?"

"The CBA comes due for renewal this summer. The PA needs to push for more CTE preventative measures and lifetime health care."

The Collective Bargaining Agreement is the legally binding contract negotiations between the NHL and the Players' Association. We've got some leverage on the league this year and could use it to make the game a safer sport. Fewer concussions mean fewer players having to retire early due to head injury. A healthy player is a happy player.

"I'm the Freeze's player rep. I've been in some of those meetings," I say eagerly. I only wish I had thought of this sooner. So much of my energy was consumed trying to live up to the expectations my dad had for my career that I never thought what legacy *I* wanted to leave behind.

"That's why you're the perfect guy to help me with this," Derek says. "Players respect the hell out of you. Plus, you've got everyone's attention right now with the way you've been playing. A guy like you starts talking and everyone is going to listen."

"If we get enough current and past players on board, the league will listen too." The wheels turn in my mind as I think of everyone I can get involved.

Derek slides over to his computer, his hands typing feverishly over the keyboard. "Looks like I've got some emails to send."

"Let me know how I can help." Both my knees crack as I push myself out of the chair.

Without looking up from his computer screen, Derek says, "You just keep playing the way you are. I'll have more for you to do once the season ends."

My lower back throbs as I make my way to the door. *Just a few more games*, I tell my herniated disc.

"Oh, and Brody," Derek calls out to me. When I turn back to see what he needs, I find him looking directly at me. "Kevin would have loved a teammate like you," he says.

I leave before he can see the tear trickle down my cheek.

THIRTY-FOUR

Olivia

I startle at the sound of Tori's keys clanging like a trip bell. I know she's right outside the apartment's front door. While she fumbles with her carabiner, I panic. She and Ivy are back early from book club, and I'm not done setting up my surprise. I lunge for the front door, my foot blocking it from swinging open.

"Hey, what's going on?" Tori pushes harder.

"Just a minute." I bear down and force the door shut.

"No way," Tori says, but it's too late, I've already relocked the dead bolt. "No more schemes. No more elaborate plans. I'm coming in," she adds.

"I have to feed my ant farm before sundown or they get indigestion," Ivy complains.

I can't fend both of them off. "Fine but give me a minute." While Tori unlocks the door, I race back to the kitchen.

Tori stomps in like I've just slammed the door on her last nerve.

"Surprise!" I shimmy my hands toward the kitchen table where a brown bag of take-out dinner is half unpacked. The decorations are pathetic; I only had enough time to blow up three balloons. One end of my congratulations sign comes unstuck from the wall during the big reveal.

"Oh, no, whose demise are we celebrating now?" Tori asks apprehensively.

I tuck my hands behind my back. "I got a job and wanted to do something nice for both of you."

Tori's body relaxes. "Oh!" she says, eyeing up the take-out bag from her favorite Mexican spot.

Ivy gasps. "Success is the best revenge. Well, success and tire slashing," she says, trailing off. "Is it the fancy tech firm? Or some other powerful corporation with questionable ethical business standards? I bet the benefits are amazing."

"Neither." I reach down into my bag, digging past the streamers and balloons that never made it on the walls, and pull out my Ice Dogs hoodie. The confusion on Tori's face as I hold up the sweatshirt quickly fades when I show her the other side. Assistant Coach is stitched across the back.

"Coach Hinckley." Tori looks proud of me. So proud that for a minute I see a glimpse of our dad in her face. "Dad would have loved this," Tori says.

"Trust me, he does."

For the first time in months, I hold my head high. This morning, I met my own gaze in the bathroom mirror and sat inside myself comfortably as I stared back at my reflection. My dad and I have the same eyes; it was my perspective on the game that needed to change.

Not even the news of Erik Parker's induction into the Hockey Hall of Fame could spoil my week. Turns out the thing I feared most wasn't the Parker legacy, but my dad's fading into oblivion. I won't let that happen; instead of lashing out, I'm reaching in. My dad is with me every time I step on the ice to coach his teachings. This is our legacy.

At my job interview, the Ice Dogs' head coach and I hit it off so well that she hired me on the spot. They've got me running a recruitment camp for prospective freshmen this week. I'm getting back in the game, and this time it's for all the right reasons.

Must be a bad day for seasonal allergies because both Tori's and my eyes are watering. I drag my sleeves across my cheeks and finish unloading the rest of dinner on the table.

"The job doesn't come with stock options, but I'll get to apply my analytics background to the power play. They're even helping me find an apartment through the school's housing connections," I explain.

Tori almost drops an armful of plates and utensils. "A job *and* an apartment?" Her eyes light up. She calls back to Ivy, "Ivy, grab the good Diet Pepsi."

"But your resolution," Ivy warns.

"She got an apartment too," Tori shouts back.

Ivy lets out a celebratory shout from the kitchen and returns with three cans. Together at the table, we dig into our enchiladas while I tell them all about my new coaching position. Over churros, I show them pictures of potential apartments I'll be touring next week. They hang on my every word with enough genuine enthusiasm to reassure me I've made the right career change.

Tori and I both reach for the last churro, but I get to it first. "I'm sorry I haven't been the best roommate lately." I hand it over to her.

She accepts the peace offering. "It's okay."

Leave it to the eldest daughter to downplay my entire downfall so I don't feel guilty about how I treated everyone. This time I don't let her let it go so easily.

"I mean it. I'm sorry. You don't have a cold heart. You might be a bit patronizing at times, and you dress like a UPS delivery driver, and you make this weird clicking noise in the back of your throat when you drink fluids, and you always—"

"Okay." She raises her hand to cut me off. "I got it." She bites into the churro and a bit of cinnamon sugar falls on her chin.

"But you definitely don't have a cold heart," I say with a smirk. "You're always there for me, and I appreciate that."

"Aw. Classic sisterhood moment, am I right?" Ivy jumps in. "I mean, I don't technically have any siblings per se, but I have a cousin who is a couple years older than me. We've had our own squabbles too, like the time she swapped my shampoo with Nair, and I blew up her car." Ivy tosses her head back and cracks up with laughter.

"Okay, now the borax on your workbench is a bit alarming." I give her the side-eye from across the table.

"That reminds me," Ivy says. "I've been working on something special for you." She excuses herself and I mentally prepare for what she's about to gift me.

She returns with a taxidermized green cat. It's a miniature Chilly, tiny Freeze jersey and all. She practically shoves it into my arms. I don't know where to hold the figure; it all seems so offensive. When I accidentally touch a claw in the exchange I make a noise—ironically—similar to that of a dying cat.

"Wow. You really didn't have to do this. Letting me stay in your room was more than enough." I bare my teeth and hope it comes across as a smile.

"But I felt so bad that our time living together was coming to an end. When I'm emotional, I create my most thought-provoking work." Ivy reaches out and pats the cat on its head. A puff of glitter shakes off and dances to the ground around my feet.

"And I thought I was emotional," I remark.

A look of worry contorts Ivy's face. Have I offended her? Or is this the moment she realizes the absurdity of the gift? Suddenly, a look of realization. "She's missing her drum. She needs her drum. Be right back." Ivy darts out of sight.

I quickly drop the cat on the table like it's burning my palms. "I don't want this," I hiss. I shake my head, unable to look away from the cursed animal.

Tori leans across the table and in a low stern voice says, "Listen to me when I say this: That thing isn't spending another night hiding under our bed. Take it and I'll forgive you for everything. I'll even forget about you clogging the shower drain last week with your hair and the five-hundred-dollar plumber bill to fix it."

I groan, staring the cat in its beady little green eyes. "Deal."

My whistle signals the end of practice and the relief on everyone's faces proves that I'm pushing them as hard as I was instructed. A few girls hang around, helping me gather up pucks. I take mental note of who's putting in the extra effort. There's a dull sting in my knee, reminding me I'm alive. My toes are cold, my body is hot, and I'm right where I should be.

With the bag of wet pucks slung over my shoulder, I step off the ice to let the Zamboni flood it before our next session.

"Coach Hinckley." One of the recruits gets my attention. "Someone is looking for you," she tells me.

Quinn steps out from behind my player. She makes her way up the tunnel to me. Her face is so indifferent it stings. I swallow the lump of spit that settled on the back of my tongue. It tastes like the black coffee I had for breakfast. My leg jitters under my weight, also a lingering effect from this morning's brew.

I'm on the road to bettering myself, which means I need to

make things right with the people I selfishly took down with me. It was an honor to work with someone as dedicated and passionate as Quinn, and I don't want our friendship to end on the same note as my time with the Freeze. I should have properly strapped down my head covering. I should have listened to Quinn.

"Coach Hinckley, huh?" Quinn says. "I'm shocked you gave them your real last name."

"I'm trying this new thing where I'm honest with people."

"Wonder who gave you that good advice," Quinn mumbles under her breath.

Quinn and I sit on the bench and together we watch the Zamboni slowly lap around the ice.

"How have you been?"

Quinn coldly replies, "Busy." She checks her watch. "And I don't have much time before I have to head back into the Cities."

I figured. The team is hosting a game 6 watch party at the rink later tonight and, win or lose, both Quinn and Chilly will need to bring their A game for the fans.

"It means a lot that you came."

"You said it was important."

Sometimes actions speak louder than words, and with a bond like Quinn's and mine, you don't always get to speak to each other.

I begin doing a slew of overexaggerated hand gestures to her. The first resembles crab claws—this one means "we need to talk." She looks surprised. They're the official mascot handbook hand signals I was supposed to learn before the season started. The next signal, I point my finger to the ground three times. This one means "something is malfunctioning." She nods in agreement. Lastly, I hold my open palm out and trace a circle on the palm with my other finger. This one means "lead me."

"A little late for all that, don't you think? You were supposed to learn those back in October."

She's right. It's not enough. "Rule number eighty-five," I say with pleading eyes.

"You know rule number eighty-five? That's really far back in the handbook." She looks impressed, amused even.

"It states the bond between a mascot and mascot handler is sacred."

If you would have told me about rule number eighty-five at the start of the season, I would have laughed and been concerned I was being indoctrinated into some weird cult—which I'm still not entirely sure didn't happen. Yet, our bond *is* sacred. Like two middle schoolers who cut their palms and pressed the bloody wounds together at a sleepover summer camp. Except the camp was All-Star Weekend and the palm was her mouth on Chilly's toothy opening pretending to give me mouth-to-mouth resuscitation when I fainted briefly during the obstacle course. I can still hear the roar of the fans as I slowly regained consciousness.

She breaks, her mouth curving into a smile. "It is sacred, isn't it? I mean, I held up your furry torso while you peed. More than once."

"Sorry isn't enough, but I'm hoping this helps." I reach into my gym bag and pull out the taxidermized Chilly—touching it for what I hope is the last time. I hand it over like I'm discarding a curse.

She gasps, as if the wind was knocked out of her. Her eyes widen. There's a pit in my stomach. Have I miscalculated my friend and made things worse? She begins to cry, sobbing into her hands. Big loud violent sobs.

She hates it—and me. It's obviously terrifying her as it stands there like a haunted ventriloquist doll waiting until we're all asleep so it can go on a murder spree.

Quinn lets out a long exhale. "This is the most beautiful and thoughtful gift I have ever received." She takes my hands in hers. They're moist with sweat. "It's an Ivy creation, isn't it? A personal commission?" She grabs the cat and begins inspecting her new art far more closely and personally than I ever ventured.

"Yeah. It's a one of a kind piece of art for a one of a kind friend."

The Zamboni driver rounds the corner and almost crashes into the boards at the sight of it.

"I guess if Brody can forgive you for lying, then I can forgive you for not fastening your head covering properly," Quinn says, petting her new art piece. She carries on, rambling about where she's going to display the cat, but once I hear Brody's name, I'm stuck. What would make her say that? Did he say something about me?

"Brody and I haven't spoken since that afternoon at the party," I say. "I can't disrupt the Minnesota Freeze comeback magic that's happening right now. They actually have a shot at winning the—"

"Shut up!" Quinn violently interrupts me before I have the chance to finish my sentence and utter the words no superstitious sports fan wants to hear: Stanley Cup. "What is wrong with you? Don't say it out loud." She plugs taxidermized Chilly's ears with her fingers.

I laugh her off. "You're too superstitious," I say, already settling back into our familiar back-and-forth banter.

"And you're clueless. You really haven't heard about the new initiative Brody is spearheading, have you?"

My chest tightens. My body practically lunges forward, needing to know more. I sit on my hands in an attempt to restrain my eagerness. "No, I've been avoiding anything Brody-related because it makes me cry." I try to sound indifferent, but Quinn can't be fooled.

"Well, get some tissues ready because word around the office is he and Derek Thomas have formed a coalition of current and past NHL players with the goal of getting the NHL to instill more CTE preventative measures and getting lifetime health care added to the CBA this summer when it comes due for renewal. They've got like a hundred signatures from current and former players already," she says.

"Why would he do that?" I don't let my mind go there—the needy place where you'll find my heart. The place where Brody and I are curled up together under the library's string lights with our bellies full and sore from laughing.

"Isn't it obvious?"

"To . . . make new friends?" It's awkward realizing that Brody might still be in love with me. It's like being wrapped up in one of his overzealous wool sweaters—my nose starts to bead with sweat. Quinn's shoulders sink in a disappointed slump.

Brody is the last on my long list of wrongs to right. I'm not sure redemption is in the cards for us. Before speeding off that afternoon, he told me he needed space. I have no idea what he's been up to these past few weeks. I figured in our time apart he'd realize that what I'd done was unforgivable and he wouldn't want to see me again anyway.

When my dad played hockey, there were no spotters, there was no concussion protocol, and you would rarely see a game without a fight. Since then, the game's changed, but there's still more the league can do. I would hate to see other families go through what mine did. I can't believe Brody is leading this change—even after I lied to him.

I look up at Quinn with watery determined eyes. "I need your help. I need to win him back."

She perks right up. "Are you asking for my help orchestrating a grand romantic gesture to get the guy?"

I nod while rejection anxiety already jitters my teeth. Is his coalition an act of love or pity? Knowing the truth can't be any worse than sinking deeper into this state of unknown.

"I have the perfect glitter for such an occasion." She digs through her purse.

"No glitter."

With a pot of green-and-gold glitter already in her palm, she looks up. "Not even a little glitter?"

"Maybe a little."

THIRTY-FIVE

Brody

I get to the rink early. I'm dialed in for the big game. The only thing that should be on my mind is how we're going to beat the Tampa Storm tonight, but while I should be focusing on my pregame routine and how we're going to get through their solid defense, it's hard to keep the thought of Olivia from sneaking in.

She was there when I was alone playing video games before my pregame nap this afternoon. Again when I walked past the players' lounge and spotted a game of Catan on the table. Even now when a drop of banana milk lands on my lapel. *One more game.*

Months ago, I had far worse fears weighing on my mind. Knowing the value of a family legacy no longer balances on my shoulders, I walk confidently into the locker room ready to kick ass tonight. As I slide my phone on the top shelf of my locker, I notice an envelope sticking out of one of my gloves. Apprehensively, I pull it out; hockey players can't resist a good prank, even if we're getting ready for the most important game of our lives. The card is addressed to me in a distinct penmanship I recognize immediately—I'd recognize that loopy *Y* anywhere. My hands go numb as I claw the envelope. It's no prank. It's a letter from Olivia.

While the room begins to fill with anxious teammates, I step out into the hall with the letter tucked inside my suit jacket. The air cools as I approach the ice. It's quiet now, as employees dart around with a nervous excitement getting everything ready for the last puck drop of the NHL season. In a few hours, this place will be so loud I won't be able to hear a ref's whistle. I take a second to breathe it all in. The air is as crisp as the flooded ice is glossy.

My first Stanley Cup Final—the coveted game 7. I should feel paralyzed with fear, anxiety stricken with severe doubt. Instead, I'm weirdly calm, like this is all happening exactly as it's supposed to. Before, I would have been too scared of my dad to enjoy this moment. Worried I'd look up into the crowd and find him shouting at me. Worried about the horrible things he'd have to say to me after the game if we lost, and worried what retaliation would occur if we won. Now that I'm free from his criticism, I know that, win or lose, I will be okay. Win or lose, I am still me: a person who belongs to himself and not a family legacy.

I slide my finger along the envelope's seal and pull out a neatly folded piece of paper. Under the bright rink lights, I read silently.

I miss you. The type of missing that leaves you halved. It's the same type of hollowness that got me into this mess in the first place. Except now I know that the void isn't something I can fill with anger or even revenge. Loving you temporarily mended my brokenness, but I can't love you properly until I take accountability for the hurt I've been ignoring—the hurt I tried to pawn off onto you. I've been working on it. I've grown since you've last seen me. You might notice—I hope you do.

I'm sorry. For all the lies but mostly for misjudging your character. You're nothing like your father and that became apparent the day I met you and your instinct was to offer kindness. This used to piss me off. I wanted so desperately for you to be him, or worse, because it would justify what I was doing. But I kept falling deeper and deeper in love until I couldn't see a way out.

We might be the only two people who could ever fully understand each other. When I say I love you, know I mean all of it.

Get what's yours tonight. I'll be watching, cheering you on without a doubt in my mind that Brody Lee is a man who has been through far worse than a challenging game and lived to smile his perfectly cocky grin.

Look for me after the game if you still feel the same way about us.

She signs it Olivia Hinckley above a smudge of green-and-gold glitter in the shape of a heart.

I tuck the note back into the inner pocket of my suit jacket and head back into the locker room ready to win the Stanley Cup.

It's not until the Tampa Storm call a time-out with two minutes left in the third period that I let myself feel the excitement of the moment. It creeps in—the thought of lifting the Cup tonight—only for a second before I push it to the back of my mind. It's not over yet. This is the type of game you have to take second by second.

The scoreboard looming over center ice says we're up three

to two. My hands shake as I squirt water into my mouth—nothing will satisfy me until we win. I throw my leg over the boards and hop on the ice, ready to take the draw. This is about to be the longest two minutes of my life—and I've been lit on literal fire before.

As soon as the Storm get possession of the puck, Gauthier is skating off for the extra attacker. Six of their best versus five of ours. The goal is to box them out, get possession of the puck, and kill off as much time as possible. Every single player on the ice is ready to play the best defensive hockey of their life to run out the time remaining on the clock. If we're really lucky, we get it out of our zone for a line change, but if not, we're prepared to play the game out. Right here, right now.

Our defense gets possession and chips it into the neutral zone. This buys us a bit of time while they get onside. The Storm quickly get set up and are back in our zone before any of us have a chance to get off the ice for a line change. I knew stepping on this ice there was a possibility I would play until the clock ran out. Since this is what I've trained for my entire life, I welcome the challenge, bearing down on my stick.

As the clock continues to tick, I can practically taste the champagne. Despite the extra-long shift—grinding in front of the net—I feel surprisingly refreshed. We're using our bodies and whatever gas we have left in the tank to ward off the six skaters and prevent a clear shot on Hammer. We're fueled by the adrenaline of being seconds away from the sweetest victory any of us have ever tasted.

There are so many bodies in front of our net that it feels like a too-many-men penalty. The puck is momentarily lost in a scramble in front of Hammer, until it pops out near Chef's stick. I check the scoreboard's illuminated red countdown. Ten seconds remain. I take off skating, getting myself in position for a cross ice long pass. I call out to him, "Chef, I'm open!" He looks. Snap. It's tape-to-tape and I'm barreling down the ice toward an empty net.

The old Brody would have let his nerves get the best of him. I would be second-guessing myself, wondering what my dad would do if I shot wide. Then searching for him in the crowd after I fumbled the puck, hanging my head in shame when the other team stole possession and scored to win the game. Hiding from my phone and whatever damage control my dad suggested for repairing the Parker legacy's image.

Finally, there's no doubt for me to silence. I wind up, releasing an absolute bomb into the empty net. It's a cocky shot, and normally one that would end with a fist in your face, but this is the Stanley Cup Final and I don't care. Consider it payback for the dirty hits Storm players have handed out this series. Our fans deserve a grand finale finish.

The puck flies into the netting and the final buzzer sounds. Game over. The rest is a blur.

I throw my stick and gloves into the air, and they fall like the confetti that's soon to come. I launch my body into the glass where fans are screaming and banging on the opposite side. Fists pound against the plexiglass like a drumbeat vibrating the entire rink. I fly down center ice, skating faster than I was during regulation as I join the rest of my teammates dogpiling on top of Hammer.

Players always say this moment is indescribable. I always thought they said that because they didn't have the vocabulary. I never thought I'd be left without the right words, but that's exactly what this moment is. It's the unknown.

Everything I've ever done in my life led me here. This is exactly what I've been fighting for every time I've stepped on the ice. I know how to play hockey. I've done it my whole life.

But this moment is a first: My first time winning the Stanley Cup. It takes me a second to get used to it.

I let the moment marinate for a few beats. The crowd lingers. Still cheering, they press themselves as close to ice level as the barrier allows. They're wheeling out the Cup now. It doesn't take a whole lot of reflection for me to realize that I like this feeling, but is it indescribable? Nah, I'd say it's as fucking fantastic as you could imagine.

The Cup is weightless over my head as I take it for a spin around the ice. After I hand it off to Chef, a reporter shoves her mic in my face, asking me how I feel, as if I'm in the right headspace to string together something coherent and safe for live television. I feel a lively "fuck yeah" on the tip of my tongue but swallow it for later.

Instead, I give her the sound bite she wants. I bend down, taking the mic into my hands, and say directly into the camera, "We're Minnesota nice until the puck drops." I let out a primal "Woo!" followed by a spirited "Fuck yeah!" I can't help myself. She wrangles the mic out of my grip, and I skate on my way.

Family members begin making their way onto the ice. Players are reunited with significant others who pelt them with kisses. Andy's kids jump into his arms and try to catch the last of the tiny shards of green-and-gold confetti falling from the roof. I look for Olivia in the mob of excited wives, girlfriends, and partners rushing the ice, but she's not there. Of course not. She probably meant we would talk much later after the game—like tomorrow. She doesn't have a pass for ice level. She would have to pull a lot of strings to get down here. I try to rationalize it, but I still wish she were with me.

Right when I think I won't get a reunion, Olivia appears at the bench. She stands in the middle of the open bench door, looking up and down the rink until she spots me. Our eyes meet. I smile, even bigger than I did when the clock ran out. Her bottom lip trembles as she smiles back. Her wide eyes glisten under the bright lights. In the middle of a chaotic rink, everything is silent. The moment is still, as if she's the only person in all of existence, and in this moment, to me, she is.

I lift my bare hands, fanning them in front of me like they're on fire. Her smile swells into a laugh. I blow out the left hand. Then I blow out the right hand. She mirrors the same back to me. Finally, ready to hoist the real prize in my arms, I wave her over. It's all happening in slow motion like a highlight reel playback.

She takes off from the bench, running across the ice toward me. Too impatient to wait, I skate to her. She steps with grace and strength on the snowy ice and as we reach each other, she jumps into my arms right where she belongs. Her hands link around the back of my neck and mine squeeze her waist.

I kiss her as if it's our last. And she kisses me back with such passion that I know it won't be. I could hold her here forever, until the last fan begrudgingly leaves the stadium, until the last speck of confetti is picked up, until they lock the doors and turn off the lights, but she wiggles herself down.

"How's it feel?" she asks. Her feet are back on the ice, but she's still pressed against me.

My hands linger around her waist. "Kissing you is better than I remembered."

She gives me a playful shove as she kisses her teeth. "You know what I mean."

And I do. It all feels good right now. The love and victory are blurred together. It's hard to know if it would be as sweet without her. I'm glad I didn't have to find out. Win or lose, she's the person I want to see after the game.

"It feels like the type of thing I want to celebrate with my girlfriend." I tuck her under my arm. I eye her up and down, looking for a VIP ice-level authorization pass, but there's nothing hanging around her neck. "How did you get down here?"

"Same way I got that letter in your locker," she says, gloating. "I know some very powerful people around here."

She looks off toward the bench where Chilly is entertaining the crowd. Quinn stands nearby, pretending like we didn't catch her peering over at us. We wave. She gives us a very sporty thumbs-up before quickly turning back to Chilly where she intervenes as a drunk fan attempts to pour beer down the cat's open mouth.

"You know, when I first saw that letter, I was worried you were tampering with my things again." I pause, hoping it's not too soon to joke about her swapping my sticks. There's a brief moment of strained silence before we both laugh.

"That's not my style anymore," she says as her cheeks flush. "If I have any suggestions for you, I'll tell them right to your face. Like I can't believe you took a slap shot into an empty net."

I grimace, thinking of the flurry of angry posts about me on social media right now. I bet the Storm fans are having a field day with that one. Luckily, I'll be somewhere for the next couple weeks where they can't reach me—celebrating this win. "Yeah, that was really stupid of me."

She shakes her head. "It was very Minnesota Freeze fan favorite of you."

Olivia points to the crowd of fans gathered by Chilly. We listen closely. "Victor!" one loud person shouts. "Lee!" the crowd chants back. This goes on for a few rounds before it dies down and they are chanting something about a big Hammer.

Slowly, the team starts to head back to the locker room

where our champagne shower awaits. “What do you say we get out of here and go celebrate?”

She cocks her head over at me and says, “You’re not taking me to another Catan tournament, are you?”

“I hope so. That would be two championships in one night,” I say. “This couple can’t lose!” I pump my arms and the nearby crowd gets rowdy.

Together, hand in hand, we head off the ice to celebrate tonight’s many victories.

EPILOGUE

Olivia

Two years later . . .

Brody was right. And that's not something I typically care to admit so freely. The ocean is incredible, and this beach has become our favorite spot. Don't get me wrong—we love Minnesota and its ten thousand lakes. But this beachfront home is our very own paradise getaway.

Two years ago, after the Stanley Cup parade, parties, and award ceremonies, we took a trip back to California together. After a few too many peanut butter desserts, we drove up to Malibu where we fell in love with the view and waves. We left that trip with an active offer on this house.

Since then, we've made so many memories here. The time Brody confidently bet me ten dollars that he could do a round-off back handspring. He did one—with so much momentum that he put his ass through the drywall. His cheeks are forever immortalized in our living room wall. Or the time we had all his teammates out here for bye week and Hammer and Jordy attempted to craft an air mattress raft while filming a *Titanic* re-creation "for science" (TikTok) and needed to be rescued by coast guard officers. Those idiots made national news. Or my personal fav, the bat incident—don't ask. And yes, it involved a series of four shots over the following two weeks and several bad Dracula impressions.

Every time we come out to Malibu, we leave with a story better than the last. I think it's the lack of ice rinks nearby that forces us both to take a break from the game. This is our last trip of the offseason—our last break—and we're soaking up every sun-filled minute of it before Minnesota Freeze training camp starts next week.

Brody and Uncle Derek's coalition aimed to make hockey safer was successful in implementing more preventative measures to combat the threat of CTE into the current NHL CBA. It also includes new affordable and potentially free health care options for qualified retired players. It's not a perfect solution but eliminating dirty hits to the head makes it easier to watch him play.

Seeing Brody do something for others inspired me to start giving back to my community. Together, we run a free summer camp on the rez at my dad's old rink. I love any excuse to be in that barn because it's where I get the most signs from my dad. Nookomis was right; I needed to open my eyes and heart to him, because now I can't get my dad to shut up.

Between all the summer ice and training, I'm trying to enjoy as much time with Brody as possible before my schedule picks up. The college hockey season isn't nearly as grueling as the PWHL's season; Assistant Coach of the Minnesota Whitecaps has a nice ring to it, and a hefty load of pressure too. Luckily, it's the type of pressure I've learned to thrive under.

My dad always said hockey was in my blood. When my playing career faced the same fate as my father's, I thought I did something wrong. This must be what he meant. It's in my blood, but mostly in my mind. I've been able to apply my analytics-focused college education in combination with my hockey knowledge to be a real asset on the bench. Disruption, I'm learning, has been something the game of hockey needed greatly.

As the Whitecaps' newest hire, I've spent all day completing orientations and online training seminars. I finally pull myself away from my computer to shower and get dressed for tonight. Brody has a celebratory dinner planned. I tried to remind him that we already went out in Minnesota with all my friends and family to celebrate last month when the coaching position was first announced. Still, he insisted we do something special together, and when he gets these romantic ideas in his head, I've learned it's best to go with it and enjoy the effort rather than give in to the feeling that I'm not worthy of it.

My stomach rumbles loudly as I indecisively flip through summer dresses. I get one last night in a breezy milkmaid dress before it's nothing but matching team tracksuits. There's just enough time left to add a touch of makeup before heading into the living room.

When I step out of the room, I expect to find Brody waiting for me slouched on the couch deep in the middle of some epic video-game battle. Except I find the room empty. In fact, the whole house is empty.

I call out his name, but there's no answer. As I snoop around for any sign of him, I spot a card on the kitchen island. Inside, the note says, *I know you've been hard at work all day, but you've got one last assignment. Follow the trail of notes to your surprise.*

I look around and find the next note taped to the back door. It says, *Yours is the first face I search for in any crowd.*

Out on the back deck, I find another. It says, *I love keeping your cold toes warm at night.*

By the third note, which says, *A life without you is an endless losing streak*, I've clued in to the fact that Brody's celebratory dinner tonight isn't for my new position. A trail of notes leads me out toward the beach. With my hand to my mouth, I silently sob my way to him.

A fat teardrop falls onto the next note in hand, which says, *Your dad is so proud of you. And so am I.* A couple more notes lead me through the soft sand. *Your laugh is the best sound in the world* and *You're my family* lead me toward the beach's shoreline where Brody is waiting for me. Having read my last note, I run to him with a fist full of love letters.

The sun is setting, and the orange and yellow hues are ablaze on the lively ocean. It's a beautiful backdrop, but it's the sight of Brody that takes my breath away.

"Hey," he says nervously as I approach.

Knowing what comes next and not wanting to ruin any part of his romantic plan, I come to a halt, ready to listen. "Hi," I say, winded from the excitement. I tuck my hair behind my ears. The breeze from the ocean slaps my red-hot cheeks but isn't enough to cool the flush of nervousness rising inside me.

He grabs my hand. "Before I met you, I struggled to find myself outside of being a hockey player. I lost myself trying to fit in, trying to be everything everyone expected of me. With you, it's always been easy. You see the real me and more importantly, you understand me. There's no better testament to the strength of our connection than the fact that we could have been enemies, but it's obvious that we were always destined to be lovers. You're effortlessly cool and funny and inspiring. There's so much strength in your sensitivity. You're the best teammate I could ask for. The person I want to spend all my lazy mornings, chaotic afternoons, and late nights with. I can't picture any tomorrow without you. We both overcame a lot in life to finally get to the good part. You're my good part, and I'm never letting go."

He drags his knuckle under his tearful waterline. I'm too shocked to move. He reaches into his pocket. With a tiny velvet box in hand, he drops onto a knee and flips open the top. "Will you marry me?" he asks, looking up at me.

The ring is staggering. A simple gold band with a beautiful oval-cut diamond. It's all so overwhelming. I'm sobbing trying to get my mouth and tongue to coordinate. "Yes!" I shout.

He slips the ring onto my finger. Once he's back on his feet, I jump into his arms and we embrace, kissing each other as the waves crash into rocks behind us.

I hold up my hand, mesmerized by my dream ring. "The ring is perfect. How did you know?"

"Because I know you."

Cheers and clapping erupt from behind us, and when I spin to see who's there, my eyes tear up again as all our closest friends and family watch from the sideline. He flew them in to celebrate. I scan the beach. Taking in the moment, I notice the photographer to our left. He thought of everything. It's perfect.

As we approach our friends and family, the blur of faces becomes recognizable. I search for Dad's face in the crowd—even though I know he's gone, I'll always look because there are pieces of him hidden in each one of us. My sister's statuesque height, my mom's wedding ring strung around her neck, Nookomis's warm eyes, and Nimishoomis's hearty laugh.

I let myself feel the rush of sadness that threatens to spoil the moment. It moves through me like the wind. It dishevels my hair, hurts my eyes, and chills my skin. I wish he were here and yet I know he is.

I look up at Brody. He squeezes my hand. Tender and intuitive—like my dad. Someday Brody and I will teach our future children to play hockey, but until then, this is the greatest thing we've ever done. With tears in my eyes, I squeeze back. "I love you."

"I love you more," he says.

★★★★★

ACKNOWLEDGMENTS

It takes a village, and I am beyond thankful for mine. My agent, Deidre Knight, for always having my back. My editor, Lynn Raposo, for pushing me to be my best. Everyone at MIRA and HarperCollins Canada, for championing my work. You all make me better than I could ever be on my own.

To my husband, JT, and children, Lily and Booker, words wouldn't make sense without you. Nothing would.

Last but not least, I'd like to thank my Mémère. Thank you, merci, meegwetch, and maarsii. She is no longer with us physically, but her spirit is deeply woven into the fabric of my being.

So much of what I know about being Indigenous is tied to loving hockey. The intro to *Hockey Night in Canada* would summon my family together like a dinner bell. Racked with nerves, we'd gather around the TV to watch the Toronto Maple Leafs, placing team-branded trinkets on or around the screen when the team needed a boost of good luck. I'm not sure how much good it did the Buds, but it always brought us closer together as a family. Loving hockey is deeper than a fandom—it's a tradition passed down from generation to generation.

There's no one way to be Indigenous, but there are sacred

traditions. Warm bannock slathered in melted margarine, boat rides on ancestral waters, beaded gifts handed over with tender finger pads, and gatherings as a family with food and love at the table's center, but it's on the ice where I've always felt the most connected.

Hockey's in my blood; it's in our blood. Never let anyone tell you differently.